Alice
in Bed

Alice
in Bed

A NOVEL BY

Cathleen
Schine

Alfred A. Knopf · New York · 1983

THIS IS A BORZOI BOOK
PUBLISHED BY ALFRED A. KNOPF, INC.

Published in the United States by Alfred A. Knopf, Inc., New York,
and simultaneously in Canada by Random House of Canada Limited, Toronto.
Distributed by Random House, Inc., New York.

Library of Congress Cataloging in Publication Data
Schine, Cathleen.
Alice in bed.
I. Title.
PS3569.C497A8   1983   813'.54   82-48721
ISBN 0-394-52982-0

Manufactured in the United States of America
First Edition

To my mother

Others merely live, I vegetate.

—CYRIL CONNOLLY,
The Unquiet Grave

I

For four weeks she had been living in her parents' big bed—
a king-size bed, extra long because her father was tall and had
big feet. She stared at the ceiling and remembered lying on the
bed as a child, groaning with impatience as her mother put on
lipstick or talked on the phone. Every morning, before it was
really light, she had trailed her father around the bed, stepping
in the enormous talcum-powder prints he left on the carpet.
She followed him to the closet where he kept his big shoes, to
the bathroom where she listened to the buzzing of his electric
razor, to the dresser out of which came the shirt cardboards he
gave her to draw on. "Pack up your troubles in your old kit
ba-a-a-g," they sang with the radio.

"Am I delirious?" Alice asked.
"Feverish," said her mother, dipping the washcloth into a
paper cup filled with lavender water.
"I thought I might be delirious." A delirium would at least
seem romantic. "You're sure I'm not delirious?"
Her mother said she didn't think so and wiped Alice's forehead with a washcloth. The lavender water smelled prim, like
a biddy's drawer of nighties.

"Drink lots of fluids!" her mother reminded her a minute
later, handing her one of the soggy paper cups from the bedside
table.

Alice put the cup to her lips. I have suffered brain damage,
she thought listlessly. This water tastes funny. It tastes like . . .

"Oh, Mom! This is *lavender* water. Ugh, it's disgusting."

"I've poisoned you! Oh, my God, I've poisoned you!" her
mother cried, kissing Alice's hands.

The pain came in hot waves, like acute embarrassment. It
started in her hips and flowed in almost rhythmic bursts to her
knees and feet, then to her whole body. She moaned loudly and
wanted to stamp her feet in rage, but sometimes she couldn't
move them at all.

The night, the wet summer heat, and the strange pain would
all hover and then slowly intensify at once. I must be delirious,
she told herself. The nights were the worst, and her mother
would stroke her forehead. A walker, somehow shabby in spite
of being brand-new, stood by the bed; it was shabby the way
only aluminum can be shabby. When she looked at it, she knew
she was not delirious. The bathroom loomed six feet away.

Dear Katie,
My mother told me you finally went into the bin. Is it
awful? I know I haven't spoken to you since the day you
threw the plate at me, but I have thought about you.
Anyway, since that day—and you know all I said was
"Hello," I don't know what you were so mad about—
I seem to have gotten sick too.

About two weeks after I saw you, after I'd gone back
to Sarah Lawrence, I was babysitting and I stood up to
get the little brat a glass of water, and I fell down! I
just fell down. Pain, pain, and more pain in my legs.

The kid's father helped me home, even though it was only across the street. I literally crawled—like a cockroach—into the bathroom, into bed, to the phone the next morning when it rang. Luckily it was a friend of my mother's who wanted to know if I wanted a ride to Westport. She came and got me and helped me down to her car and drove me out, and I stayed there for a month, in bed.

The doctors had no idea what was wrong. First they thought it was an infection and they stuck a needle in my hips to see if they could draw pus out. They tried it twice: No pus. Then they put me in this rinky-dink traction. It looked like a late-night TV-commercial contraption— "It slices! It dices! It mashes! It whips!" They hooked me up in my own bed. Actually, my parents' bed—my room is really damp. One of the walls is crumbling too (bad drainage, I think). Anyway, my poor parents alternated sleeping in the guest room and on the floor next to me. It was very odd because they had separated about three weeks before. My father therefore thinks the whole thing is psychological. He feels very guilty. Of course, he feels guilty anyway for dumping my mother. But I'm *glad* they finally got a separation. They've been fighting for ten years, so what's the big deal? But I can't say that to them. At least not to my father—he's so solemn.

So I slept for a month in the soggy bed. It was so humid there. And I sweated a lot because I had a fever. I used to get mildew on my shoes in the closet, so I thought I might see some green moss growing on my legs, but it didn't. I probably have some kind of arthritis —that's what they tell you when they can't find pus and they really don't know—so the damp probably made it even worse.

The bathroom was four steps from the bed—I know

because I counted—and I had to use a walker to get there. Sometimes I put heating pads on my hips and knees, and then, since they didn't work, I put ice packs on, and then, since they didn't work, I put the heating pads back on. It helped to pass the time, and improve hand-eye coordination.

My father snored on the floor and jumped up yelling, "Whah? Who?" every time I made a sound, and every time I moaned, my mother flew in from the other end of the house. I don't know how they heard me.

I'll have to take incompletes in all my courses, and I was supposed to go to Florence with Cindy this summer, but that's obviously off. She felt guilty, too, because she's still going, so she came and spent a weekend. She tried to entertain me by dancing around wearing only ice bags and singing Carmen Miranda songs. She was moderately successful.

I had a fever—about 102—the whole time, so the doctors decided I better go into the hospital. The ambulance looked like a station wagon. Very painful journey on stretcher to station wagon. Felt like groceries when stashed in the back. Screamed a lot.

Everyone thinks I'm a hysteric. Except my parents, of course. I guess no one can really imagine being so sensitive to pain. It does sound excessive—I mean, the cracks in the floor between the linoleum tiles hurt me as the stretcher rolls over them.

So here I am in the hospital. In New York because the doctor is supposed to be good. There were cigarette butts in the corner of the room and they still don't know what's wrong with me. They won't give me any drugs because I'm a teenager.

I'll write again when I have some more cheerful news. Will you write to me? I know this is a very self-centered

letter, and centered around a not tremendously interesting self at the moment—I mostly cry, scream, and try not
to pee since it hurts to walk to the bathroom—but it is
a letter nevertheless.

Love,
Alice

Curtains hung around one of the beds like sheets drying in
an alley. One woman stared at her suspiciously from inside an
oxygen tent. Another sat up in bed, suddenly shy, arranging
Kleenexes and glasses on her bedside table as if she were tidying
up for an unexpected guest.

Alice was afraid someone would vomit or die. She tried to
smile politely. What if they snored, or coughed all night? She
felt intrusive. She hated them.

"Isn't the view magnificent?" the lady next to her asked,
pointing down to the street. It was clogged with traffic. Faint
honks occasionally drifted up. "I've just had surgery. Well, I
never was robust." She sighed. She began describing her dead
husband—pink skin, sparkling blue eyes, white hair—and then
began to sob.

"Oh," she suddenly cried out, "my friends have tried to fix
me up with a few dirty old goats in Florida. . . ." Her accent,
which had been full-blown genteel, like a posturing homosexual, suddenly assumed a leering quality and Alice wondered
with horror what this frail old lady might go on to recount. But
"none of them measured up to my darling," she declared loyally in her former tone.

"That's good," Alice said respectfully.

The woman on the other side had fallen asleep. The lady in
the oxygen tent was obscured by the reflection of the setting
sun, but Alice was sure she continued to stare at her with un-
compromising suspicion.

Alice rang for a nurse. When a great big woman stomped

up to her bed, Alice asked for her shot. She waited in the dark until she realized it had been a long time since the nurse had left and then rang again.

"Okay, okay," said the same big nurse. She handed Alice a little pill.

"Shot," Alice said, groaning and writhing. "My doctor prescribed shots."

"Shot? You can't have no shot. You asked for a pill. You don't get no shot."

"Shot. I get a shot, I want a shot."

"Do you see a needle here? I don't have a shot, I have a pill. And that's what you're getting."

"Shot."

"Don't you tell me," said the nurse. All Alice could see in the gloom was her beefy hands. Hands holding a small paper packet and a paper cup. "I opened the paper this pill is served in. What do I do with it if you don't take it?" demanded the nurse.

"I'll take it later. Just get me the shot now. I haven't had one all day. I'm allowed to get one every four hours."

"We will have to *throw it away*," declared the outraged nurse, dropping the white pellet in the wastebasket. It made a tiny ping, and the nurse left. She brought back the shot, which she administered with vigor.

The woman with the dead husband vomited all night. It seemed to Alice that she dramatized the incidents a little, making loud retching noises long before and after the actual event.

Then the woman in the oxygen tent died, discovered by the male nurse when he came to take the five-o'clock temperatures. Stone cold. Alice wondered if they would really carry the corpse out feet first, but the aides pulled the curtains around her bed and she couldn't see.

She moved to a private room the next morning.

"Lie down," said Dr. Witherspoons that afternoon. Alice was sitting, dangling her legs off the bed as her doctor in Connecticut had told her to. This in preparation for the long journey behind the walker to the bathroom to brush her teeth. A little numb from the pain, she had been delaying.

"Lie down," Dr. Witherspoons repeated. He was tall and tan and looked as if he'd be cold to the touch. He took care of famous football teams and was famous himself. "Lie down this minute."

"But my doctor at home . . ."

"Lie down." Dr. Witherspoons lived in Westport, and Alice's neighbors knew him. They had told her that he changed his name from Wittstein, drove a Mercedes, and had a horrible wife. "Your bones are inflamed. They must be kept still. I don't *ever* want to see you sitting up again."

"Okay, okay," she said as he turned and walked out.

"The stroke in nine-fifteen wet her bed," Alice heard a voice in the hall announce. "And I could not help but notice that Mrs. Pulman is sprawled across the floor."

"Huh!" answered an indifferent voice.

"Oy gevalt," slurred a third scrawny voice. "Oy gevalt, Johnson."

"Huh!" grunted the indifferent voice. "I ain't Johnson. You ain't Johnson. You Mrs. Pulman. Nobody here named Johnson. And why can't you keep still? Fussin' and kickin' and we have to truss you up with sheets and you slip right out, skinny as you are. . . ."

"Oy gevalt, Johnson," answered Mrs. Pulman. "Oy gevalt, Johnson."

Alice's door opened and hefty Miss Darty came in carrying a bedpan.

"There's only one of you?" cried Alice as the nurse walked

toward her. "You know I need two. Please don't try it yourself. It hurts this way. Please . . ."

Miss Darty was silent, but her breath was sharp, her nostrils flared, her hands poised like a movie strangler's.

"Don't touch me!" Alice cried as the nurse approached. "Don't come any closer . . . Owwwwwwww . . ." The bedpan was pushed under her as Miss Darty held her up with one arm.

"You'll be sorry," said Alice as her left leg leaped up in an emphatic spasm. "I hate you," she said as her right leg jerked in silly arches that threatened to overturn the bedpan.

Miss Darty gave a sudden cry. "Oh! It's going to overflow!"

"Good!"

Miss Darty ran off to get another pan and pushed in the empty as she pulled out the full.

"Disgusting, inconsiderate, imagine voiding only once a day. And with all those IVs!" she muttered and walked out of the room, leaving her charge whimpering, fists pushed into her hips, trying to hold down the spasms that were rocking the bed and turning her face pale.

It still took her a few minutes each morning to recognize the touch of all the equipment. Unfamiliar, ludicrous, and slightly sinister, it surrounded her, touching her in uncustomary ways: the matted sheepskin beneath her, the sheepskin booties attached to strings attached to weights that she couldn't see, the tight white elastic socks with no toes, the cold plastic tube dripping antibiotics into her arm. Sometimes the traction clanked.

She held up a hand. Her nails were as long as a mandarin's. The life of leisure, how ironic. If only I could reach that itchy sore on my coccyx, she thought. A month ago I didn't know where my coccyx was.

A pretty Filipino nurse had given her a manicure and

painted the shapely nails a bluish purple that her friends found unwholesome. Hands, she apostrophized silently, you look lovely. Pale and delicate, decadent and dangerous. Old people look at their hands like this, she thought. And ugly people with pretty hands.

She pulled the large red plastic mirror out of the drawer next to her bed. Her complexion was grayish, pale, and circles as dark as caves surrounded her eyes. She let her lids droop and tried to look vampy. Her lips looked a little blue, but at least they weren't chapped. There were hollows beneath her cheekbones, which she rather liked, and a small spray of pimples across her forehead. She watched two tears swell over her eyelids to slide dramatically down her pallid cheeks. Pain pounded through her body. I know I don't deserve this, she thought.

She put her watch on. She put her watch on every day. Remnants of her old routine clung to her new life. Others had dropped away. She had stopped brushing her teeth, but still used deodorant.

When she thought about it, she felt eccentric and frightened. She reached for her toothbrush and began to brush vigorously, then to floss. She put the watch in a drawer and referred instead to the clock radio by her bed. It was eight o'clock.

"Now that wasn't so bad, was it?" said Miss Darty at eight-thirty. Miss Darty was a large but sallow woman who wore tiny, delicate rings on her huge fingers. She spoke cheerfully, but it was forced, the way people talk to senile relatives who ask how long-dead uncles are doing in college. "That wasn't so bad. I don't know what you were screaming about. Just a little washcloth. And now we're going to do something about those bedsores."

"But I don't have any bedsores."

"And we don't want you to get any, do we? I'm going to

turn you over on your side—first on your left side for twenty minutes, then on your right side for twenty minutes. What's wrong *now? What* is all this screaming?"

"I *can't* lie on my side. I'll die. Leave me alone. Why can't you people leave me alone?"

"You have to lay on your side."

"*Lie* on my side and I won't. Go away. Call the resident. Call the doctor . . ."

"The *doctor* ordered this," Miss Darty retorted. "Dr. Witherspoons."

"Then fucking Dr. Witherspoons can fucking turn me over. If you touch me, I'll sue. I swear I'll scream bloody murder and I'll sue you and everybody else in this dump for malpractice." But the determined Miss Darty approached the bed with grim disinterest born of habit, a bored bulldozer crunching protest under her thick, fat treads, looming, inescapable, on the left side of the bed. Alice reached for the phone, tugging slightly on the IV as she did so, and held the receiver between them.

"I'm calling Daddy!" she said.

She was sobbing and her voice sounded squeaky and unconvincing. But Miss Darty, rolling her eyes and tapping a white-shod foot, let her make the call. When Alice got through, she sobbed, gulping air. "Daddy, this horrible nurse is trying to make me turn on my side. You know I can't turn on my side —it pushes right on the joint. What are they trying to do to me? . . . Dr. Witherspoons . . . She won't call him. . . . Okay . . . Here . . ." She handed the receiver to Miss Darty, who took it with a small sigh, held it to her ear, put her great yellow hand on her large white hip, and listened.

Miss Darty's complexion, generally an unhealthy lemon color, became red. Her mouth, a firm, stony feature, began to quiver. Miss Darty, a smug, crisp accessory to her pressed white uniform and funny cap, began to gasp and sputter.

"Well!" She slammed down the phone and stalked out of the room.

"Miss Darty!" Alice called. But Miss Darty did not turn.

Alice waited for reprisals. Uh oh, she thought, as Dr. Witherspoons walked in.

Why are all orthopedic surgeons so thin? she wondered. Had Dr. Witherspoons been an acquaintance or a relative, she might have been tempted to stick things—candy or pencils—in his ears and nose to provoke some reaction. What a stiff, she thought, avoiding his cold blue eyes. As it was, she thought along the lines of grenades. One in each nostril, one in each ear, grenades in the pocket of his white coat, grenades in his pants cuffs, anal grenades, oral grenades . . .

"I have given orders for you to be turned on each side for twenty minutes at a time three times a day. Is that understood?"

"No," Alice blurted out.

"No matter how many nurses you bully . . ."

"They bully *me!* I just wanted to see you because . . ."

"No matter how many nurses you bully, you will be turned on your side. Twenty minutes on your left side and twenty minutes on your right side. Three times a day. I will not have a patient with bedsores."

"But, doctor, I can't. You know I can't. All that festering bone pushed together—it hurts! You've seen the x-rays. You take enough of them. It's all raw and it hurts! It *hurts!*"

"I'm sorry," said Dr. Witherspoons, who didn't look very sorry. "But that's the way it is. Twenty minutes a side. Three times. Every day."

"But it hurts!" Alice had begun screaming. "Pain is not good." Dr. Witherspoons shrugged at this observation. "Can you at least give me something? Something to ease the pain? At least a little? Please give me something," she begged as Dr. Witherspoons moved closer to the bed. "Please, you've got to give me something first."

Dr. Witherspoons looked a little bored. "That's just about enough," he said, an exasperated parent slamming on the brakes and ordering the raucous five-year-old to walk home. "You're hysterical."

"I may be hysterical, but I'm right!"

Dr. Witherspoons left the foot of the bed, went to her side, and flipped her over. The tidy little room spun. I'm fucking fainting, she thought.

Alice blacked out for only a few minutes, and woke up to a blurred nausea, a desperate pain snuggling around her with the oppressive intimacy of a hateful boyfriend.

She told herself it was bad luck to say she wanted to die. She wanted the pain to stop. She didn't want to die. She just felt like she wanted to die.

Why is that doctor wearing black? she wondered, looking up through a haze of drugs. And who does he remind me of? He was thin and bald, with high cheekbones in a gaunt face the color of paper and a wafer-thin and beaklike nose. What kind of doctors wear black?

"Alice Brody," he said gravely.

Dante! she thought. She had a postcard of Dante's death mask over her desk at school. He looks like Dante's death mask with spectacles.

"Alice Brody," he said, "my name is Reverend Householder."

"Ah." Not a doctor. A priest. Am I dying? Alice wondered. Has he come to sprinkle water over me? She was so tired. Maybe she was dying. In the half light she couldn't be sure if it was early morning, early evening, or just an ugly gray day. The venetian blinds were closed, and uninspired bands of weak light floated through the cracks. The room was soft and remote. Dr. Dante was so tall she could hardly see his face. He was so thin she could hardly make him out. Where had he gone? Why had Dr. Dante gone? Was he an immunologist? Or a rheumatologist? Or just another orthopedic surgeon?

"Alice Brody," he said severely, and she opened her eyes.

It's that priest, she thought. I'm dying. Her sheets were damp with fever although the room was cold. His lips are almost as blue as mine.

"You are a member of the Park Hill Temple?" he asked.

"Huh?"

"You are . . ."

She nodded, the thought of the awful modern structure waking her a little.

"Yes," said the Reverend Householder, clasping his long fingers together, as if to illustrate the alliance.

How does he know? Maybe this is an investigation. And his fingernails are as blue as mine too.

"Yes," said the Reverend Householder, his fingers wriggling through each other like worms through wood. "And let us pray."

"Huh? Well, okay, but . . ."

His hands spread over her, palms down, close to her face. His voice spread over her like his hands. He spoke in the confidential tones clergy seem always able to adopt with the perfect strangers they must minister to. I hope he's not trying to convert me, Alice thought.

"Amen," said the Reverend Householder.

"Bye," said Alice, relieved he had given her no pamphlets.

But the Reverend Householder came back, often. He carried a list of names and put a check next to hers each time he turned to make his dark exit. This man is not comforting, Alice thought, although she knew now his appearance didn't mean she was dying. This man wears black and marks off names on a clipboard and looks like Dante's death mask and talks about shadows and valleys. His face was white as paper, but his brow was dark with great worries, and she wondered if he was carrying germs from one patient on the clipboard to the next.

"Let us pray," he would say, inclining his bald head with its ascetic profile.

Let us not. But after all he was only trying to help, to be kind. Some kind of ecumenical priest, probably. And Alice determined to be polite to him even though he frowned and read to her from the Bible.

" 'My flesh is clothed with worms and clods of dust; my skin is broken, and become loathsome,' " he read. Alice would smile politely and nod her head.

"Amen," the Reverend Householder would say with a somber dignity in his hushed voice.

"Bye bye," Alice would sigh with relief when he made his way slowly to the door.

" 'Tremble!' " the Reverend Householder would cry, lifting his nose toward the ceiling. " 'Tremble, ye women that are at ease; strip you, and make you bare. . . .' " And then there would be more about sowing and loins and servants.

" 'And I will destroy thy mother,' " he said one day, slowly retracting his hands, which had hung like low clouds over her eyes. "Amen." He put his two long hands together with satisfaction.

"Ah, Alice," he said, aiming the Dante nose at the ceiling again, and then lowering it toward her. "Ah, Alice, I hope you recover from these trials soon, my child. And then I look forward to seeing you in church."

"Church?" she said. "Me? In church?"

"Why, yes, Alice. The Park Hill Methodist Temple."

"Church? Methodist Temple? Who ever heard of a Methodist Temple? The Park Hill Temple is Jewish. I mean, it's reform, but it's not *Methodist*. It's in Westport, Connecticut, but it's not *Methodist!*"

The Reverend Householder was quite red. "Oh!" he said. "Oh!"

She had never imagined the Reverend Householder capable of scampering, but now he suddenly seemed to, in the direction of the door.

"Well, God bless you, anyway!" he called, which she thought was rather gracious under the circumstances.

She rang for a shot. It was eleven and she wanted to try to sleep. Her legs pounded.

"It's too early," said the voice from the speaker on the wall. "You had one at eight."

"Eight A.M. I had one at eight *A.M.*"

"You had one at eight. It's on your chart."

"In the morning. Eight in the morning!"

They argued over the spitting, screechy box until Alice was reduced to screaming "Morning" over and over and banging a spoon on the bed railing until someone double-checked.

Orderlies in white came every day with stretchers.

"X-ray!" they would say, starting toward her, to lift her onto the stretcher.

"Aaaaahhhhh! Back! Call a nurse!"

"Oh, God," she would hear the nurses muttering in the hall. "All right, we'll be there in a minute."

The two giggly nurses wore different pastel pants-suit uniforms each day and chattered about never getting a date, and they would stand on one side of her. Facing them across the stretcher and the bed stood the orderly and the massive Miss Darty. Alice would close her eyes and hold her breath, and the four would poke their hands and arms under her knees, hips, waist, shoulders, and whatever else they could manage, and would push from one side and pull from the other until she was shifted from the bed to the stretcher. Then the orderly would propel her—moaning, legs jerking—down the hall as if she were a skirt rack.

"Watch your back, watch your back," he would shout jauntily at old men in robes pushing IV poles. "Comin' through!"

When her grandmother had died, Alice saw her, stretched out on a white enamel table, in the mortuary, and she had thought how uncomfortable her grandmother would have been had she still been alive. I was right, she thought as she was unceremoniously unloaded onto the cold, iron-hard x-ray table.

But she often passed out from the shift to the table and one day asked if she could stay on the stretcher. The x-rays would be slightly poorer in quality, she was told, but she screamed so loudly, so persistently, and so obscenely that they finally relaxed their standards and relented.

While she lay flat, the picture taking was uneventful. The spasms from the stretcher transfer and ride had usually subsided by then, and she simply held her breath when so instructed. They told her not to move, but she never moved if she could help it anyway.

After a week they introduced a new kind of x-ray. Her legs, which barely bent at all, were pushed until her knees were as close to her chest as possible. An aide held them there, straining against them, while strange geometric pieces of foam rubber were placed around her hips, knees, and legs. The aide let go, and Alice realized she was wedged into the horrible position by the innocent-looking triangles, circles, and squares. The pain was so intense that she felt nothing but a kind of huge, spilling heat.

"Make them use a lead apron when they x-ray you," said her cousin Sam, who was in medical school. "To protect your ovaries."

"How can you take pictures of hips *without* exposing ovaries, Sam?"

He was silent for a minute. The phone made long-distance crackling noises.

"Well, I didn't mean to worry you," he said. "How's the food?"

The humming orderly pushed her stretcher through the halls. The cracks between the linoleum squares seemed as ragged and deep as potholes. Alice moaned with every spin of the wheels.

"Whooooaaaaa," she whimpered.

"Me and Mrs. Jo-o-o-nes," sang the orderly softly. "We got a tha-a-a-ang goin' on. . . ."

"Welcome!" cried a thin technician whose ears stuck out. The result of exposure to radiation? And he has no hair!

"Welcome, welcome. Take your seats for the show. That's right, stay still. And don't breathe. Action! Breathe . . . don't breathe . . . breathe!" He pulled the heavy drawers out from under her and carried them into a dark room emitting sinister rumbles. When he returned, two floppy x-rays were in his hand. He put them on a lighted screen.

"Dy-no-mite!" he said.

The space between the left femur and left socket and the space between the right femur and right socket were gone. There was no thin gray-black line between the ghostly masses of bone. It was one white, lumpy-looking clump. No wonder I can't move, she thought. I'm stuck.

"Whoooaaaaa," she moaned. "Whooooooaaaaaaaaa . . ."

The orderly, singing, "Let's get it on . . ." wheeled her back to her room as she sobbed and muttered, "Shit, shit, shit."

Sometimes she pretended the waves of pain were real waves. Not crashing waves, but the small waves of her childhood, the waves that lapped rhythmically at the mossy rocks of the jetty while she sat and watched faraway white sails and noisy sea gulls and, once in a while, a bobbing duck. The sun skipped across the water like a stone, but not three times or four times or even five or six times, but hundreds of times, all the way to Long Island. Sometimes she could see Long Island, long and flat and curved, across the sound. Sometimes she could see only the three tall smokestacks of Port Jefferson. There were tiny yellow bugs in the pools that formed on the jetty. Fleshy children she had never met rode in cars with blue-and-orange New York license plates. If she sat on the sand at the edge of the water, she could see minnows. Her father put tiny opaque glasses over his eyes and her mother sat under a green-and-yellow umbrella and drew pictures on Alice's back with Sea & Ski. Alice licked dripping popsicles until they fell from their sticks, and then she watched as the sand crawled around the sides and the orange ice melted into sticky streams.

When it got too hot, they would go home and she would sit in the grass and catch pink worms and cut them in half with a butter knife to see if the pieces really would wriggle away in two separate directions, unharmed. But now she couldn't remember if they had. Perhaps both halves had shriveled and died.

She would follow the gardener around and he would tell her stories of the old days, before she was born, when her house was an onion farm. One day she saw two woodpeckers hopping on a branch in the dignified ritual of a mating dance. Another day she watched loud fat sparrows evict a family of stiff-tailed wrens from the little house that swung on a wire in front of her bedroom. The hole was so small that the male sparrow got momentarily stuck on his way into his new domain.

Alice would play in the woods or sit by the road throwing pebbles at passing cars until someone made her stop, and then they would go back to the beach and eat cold fried chicken in the cool gray dusk. And she would jump over the little waves as they touched shore.

Ah, Westport. Alice's eyes were closed. Westport? Could

that ever have been Westport? Now it was full of tennis courts and teenagers. Dogs get hit by cars in Westport. English teachers raise your consciousness.

Her English teacher had been the very relevant Mr. Marcus. "This encounter session will make Greek tragedy meaningful." He made them hold hands and call each other nasty names. Westport had a progressive high school, and the English Department, which offered classes in Media Methodology and the I Ching, was the envy of the state school system. Students were encouraged to experiment, to go on independent study, to get involved. On the day of the student strike, Mr. Marcus let his class congregate on the lawn and paint signs. He discreetly left, not wanting to compromise them, and they painted "Remember Kent State" in red letters that dripped like blood on the cardboard.

"*Gusto malo!*" Alice remembered her Latin teacher sniffing when she saw the lurid sign. "The *vox* of *conscientia* is an admirable thing, *discipuli,*" she added, "but if you don't come to *my* class, I'll have to mark it as an *absentia* unexcused. *Vale!*" she had called cheerfully as she continued on her way.

Then an officious girl in overalls led them in the singing of "Kumbaya." She was a natural leader of the group. Her mother ran a little shop downtown called Third World Paraphernalia. It sold UNICEF calendars and sponsored a silent peace vigil at which no one was allowed to chew gum.

"My arm," Alice said into the speaker in the wall. "The arm with the IV is all swollen and it hurts."

"All right," squawked the box. "Just a minute."

Alice waited, watching the clock radio, which played a worrying modern piece. She hated it but somehow couldn't turn it off. When ten minutes had passed, she rang again. The buzzer, a white plastic case with a button, was pinned to the tight bottom sheet with a safety pin. When she pushed the button a red light went on over her head as if she were having an idea in a cartoon —an angry idea.

"Be right there," said the box.

"Look," Alice said when Mrs. Trawling, the floor's night nurse, came in looking very stern. "It's all red and swollen tonight, and it hurts. It hurts a lot."

"It's supposed to hurt," said Mrs. Trawling. "It's supposed to be red and swollen."

"Oh," Alice said.

She turned off the ominous music and tried to fall asleep. She slept fitfully, the pounding arm waking her up. At ten to five, the arm throbbed and seemed to pump pain. She couldn't fall asleep. She waited twenty minutes, wondering what to do. Then she pressed the button and the red light beamed over her head in the dark.

"My arm is killing me," she said when Mrs. Trawling came in. "Can you pull the IV? Maybe it's been in too long. It's been in a week. It's never felt like this before."

"It's too late." Mrs. Trawling shined her flashlight in Alice's eyes. "There's no one here."

"You're here," Alice pointed out.

"I am not trained to pull out IVs," she said. "And no one else is here."

"How can there be no one here? What kind of hospital is this?"

Mrs. Trawling was already on her way out.

"I'm going to do it myself," Alice yelled after her. She stared at her arm, which in the dark room did not look red but was oversized and bulky. I've watched them pull IVs, she thought. You just pull, literally pull. She put her hand on the tube. The needle in her arm was hidden under the adhesive tape, now frayed and dingy. She tugged lightly, a trial, and felt the needle shifting in her vein. Oh, God, she said to herself, suddenly queasy. She put both arms at her sides, closed her

eyes, and conjugated Latin verbs. But she had forgotten everything but the present tense of the first and second conjugations.
She felt stupid and switched to declining *hic, haec, hoc,* over and
over, imagining sheep in time with the words. The pain in her
arm had become a regular throb. *Hic,* and a giant woolly sheep
would waddle by. *Haec,* another sheep would stare stupidly and
follow the first. *Hoc,* another. *Huius,* sheep. *Huius,* sheep.
Huius, sheep. It was all very boring.

At eight the morning nurse came in.

"Oh!" she cried, seeing Alice's hideous swollen arm. She
reached over and ripped the IV out. "Phlebitis!" she said in
horror. "How did this ever happen?"

She knew it was Monday because the day before she had
been spared a visit from Dr. Witherspoons. The soft-boiled eggs
were waiting in their sanitary shells. She reached over and
touched one; it was still hot.

"Good morning," said a tall, dignified black nurse she had
never seen before. "My name is Stephanie Carter."

The private-duty nurse. After the phlebitis, her parents had
decided to order one up. Stephanie Carter looked very strict.
Her hair was pulled tight into a knot on top of her head, and
she sat very erect.

"I didn't want to wake you up," Stephanie Carter said.

"You didn't?" Alice asked. Everyone else always did.

"Would you like those eggs?"

"You're not going to make me eat them?"

Stephanie Carter raised one eyebrow and looked at Alice
curiously. She spoke the affected educated black English that
can sound so beautiful. Throughout the day she asked Alice if
she wanted things. A bath? Not really, Alice answered, testing
her. And Stephanie Carter said okay, maybe tomorrow. Did she
want lunch? Well, okay. Did she want to turn?

"I have to," Alice sighed. "They check."

"I know," said Stephanie Carter. "They told me."

"I hate to turn. Hurts. But, um, we've sort of devised this system. Sounds crazy, I know, but . . ." Alice was almost too embarrassed to go on. This considerate, sensible woman would think she was a baby, a spoiled brat, a hysteric. "I wait twenty minutes after the Talwin injection, when it's most effective, and then you have to put this pillow here, and this long one doubled up under here . . ." She could see Stephanie Carter struggling to hide her impatience. She thinks I'm a nut, Alice thought unhappily. They all think I'm a nut.

Then her mother rattled in carrying two briefcases, a small pocketbook stuffed inside a large pocketbook, and a shopping bag. The bags followed her in, swooping like a long skirt, as she flopped into her chair.

"Medea," she said.

No, Alice was about to say, Stephanie Carter.

"Medea," her mother repeated. "I have a new student named Medea." She let her bags drop to the floor and pushed her sunglasses up on her head. "Oh, there they are, I've been looking all over for them," she said when she found another pair of glasses already perched there. "Can you imagine naming a child Medea? I mean, why not Medusa or . . .

"Mom, this is Stephanie Carter, the private-duty nurse." They shook hands. Stephanie Carter looked at her watch.

"Time to turn," she said. Alice's mother began folding and stacking pillows. Stephanie Carter looked skeptical, but said nothing. Together they turned her onto her right side. She faced the door. When she was little she had spent hours trying to think of two things at exactly the same time. She tried to think of something besides the pain. When the twenty minutes were over, she slept.

She woke up yelling. Her legs danced stupidly under the smooth white sheet.

"I'm sorry, my darling, so sorry. . . ." Dr. Davis stood, pale, his hands on the aluminum rail. She stared blankly at him, then grimaced as her left leg gave a particularly violent jerk.

"Oh dear, oh dear," he said, rubbing his little hands together. "I bumped into your bed. Poor little thing. Look what I've done. *Merde.*" She started to cry "no" as he put his hand softly on her leg, but he had already found the muscle throwing it around. He pressed it with his palm. His fingers lay lightly on the sheet above her thighs. The spasm passed. Dr. Davis's hand stayed on her leg.

Dr. Davis was an eye surgeon she had gone to see at sixteen, when her eyes began to cross for reasons she never entirely understood. Embarrassed and wearing sunglasses, she had scowled in his waiting room. But Dr. Davis had been kind in a charming, flirtatious way, telling her she was beautiful and gently kissing her forehead goodbye. He fixed the cross-eyes, and she had written him an overwrought poem and visited him whenever she was in the neighborhood, sometimes thinking of excuses to pass by his office, hoping he would seduce her. But he gave her candy he kept for child patients instead.

"I'm so sorry," he said. "I didn't mean to wake you up. And certainly not like that. Will you forgive me?"

She looked at his hand on her leg. He had such clean nails. She put her hand on his.

"Sure."

For the first few days, Stephanie Carter sat quietly and somewhat primly. She didn't wheedle and whine when Alice asked for a shot, she just got it. She moved and worked and helped with a kind of aloof compassion that for Alice was a tremendous relief after the mincing antagonism of staff nurses who always wanted to know "if we couldn't wait just a little longer, dear? We don't want to become too dependent, do we?"

Stephanie sat tall and straight and talked about school. She was studying at NYU. At the moment she was taking Latin. As the days went by, she began to talk about her husband. He too was going to school, engineering school, and she was supporting him. A few more days went by and Stephanie admitted her husband was supposed to be going to school to study engineering, but it was not at all clear that he actually was. She was working two jobs—she also worked the late shift at a cancer hospital—and he didn't work at all. She talked about patients at the cancer hospital. Most of them were terminal. When a patient reached a certain plateau of hopelessness and pain, she said, the doctors would discreetly give an overdose of painkiller. There really was a death rattle, she said. Patients often woke up knowing they would die that day. Most died late at night.

When a week had gone by, Stephanie's careful posture and speech had relaxed to the extent that her feet were often propped up on the other chair and her voice took on street cadences and slang. Their talk became gossip, their gossip intimate. Alice told Stephanie she was in love with Dr. Davis. Stephanie told Alice she was in love with a doctor at the cancer hospital.

They had no clocks in the eleventh century. She stared at the clock radio which said 11:15 wishing she were in the eleventh century. In the eleventh century she would already have died. She would long ago have died of this disease, whatever it was, that instead saw her stretched out on a bed, high in the air, her feet encased in woolly booties, her arms wired with dripping tubes, her face turned to the clock that never seemed to move.

When most people entered the room, they stood sheepishly, their hands folded, looking down at the tan linoleum floor, like Jews in church. They spoke uncertainly, hushed, and handed over their presents quickly—the Picasso posters, the fresh plump raspberries, the mysteries, fashion magazines, and tape cassettes. Visitors thrust flowers at her like timid boys offering corsages. She remembered shifting her feet and having nothing to say at the bedsides of ailing relatives. But this is *me,* she wanted to call out to her friends, not a shriveled great aunt.

Throughout the hemming and hawing of visiting friends and cousins, her mother sat in a white chair by the window. She read her incomprehensible journals of psychology, in preparation for her doctoral orals, and worked on needlepoints that she never finished. Her latest was a tiger reclining in a field of red poppies. It was strategically tiny, but the tiger was soon put aside, forgotten, abandoned for a pair of lips whose teeth spelled out THANK YOU.

Her mother had begun to come in at nine every morning and now stayed until nine or ten at night. The nurses had at first pointedly informed her of visiting hours. By now they were used to her and asked her to help with the bedpan.

She had given up teaching her classes and had taken an apartment a block from the hospital. Her friends began to call her at the hospital to arrange lunch dates in the hospital cafeteria, to visit her in her daughter's room. "What a day," they would sigh, sinking into the second armchair her mother had brought in, before discussing their divorces and their classes.

A big man with a big mustache sat in the visitor's chair. Middle-aged, weary-eyed, he stared at her and sighed. A long, heavy sound. Alice stirred, and the man sighed again and hung his head. Gravity worked visibly in his corner of the room: his head drooped, his arms hung down, even his mustache seemed a burden.

She was not asleep. The slight movements that followed his full sighs were spasms of irritation. He had to leave soon, she thought. How could anyone, even her father, sit and stare at someone who was obviously pretending to be asleep? She kept her eyes carefully closed. He sat staring at his knees, his hands hanging between them, his head hanging down. He sighed again.

"Why do you lie there like a lox when your father comes to see you?" her mother asked later when he'd slunk out the door.

"Because his eyes are red and wet. He makes me sick."

"My poor darling," said Dr. Davis. "My poor brave girl." He pulled the chair close to her bed and leaned forward as if to deliver the evening news. He looked a little like a television anchor man. He had handsome regular features and distinguished gray hair. But his eyes would suddenly go all sultry, his lips would purse slightly, and he would quote Shakespeare, or wink, or ask to try on your high-heeled shoes. He was a small, silly man.

"I brought you some violets. Voluptuous and prim. Just like . . ." She thought he was going to say "you."

"Just like . . . me!" he purred, and laid the elegant little posy on her chest. Just like a corpse, she thought.

"This hospital sucks," she said. "Can you get me out?"

"All hospitals suck, little one," he said, pleased to show he was young enough at heart to use a contemporary vulgarity. "This sucks a shade more than others, but you can't be moved. If you could be moved, I should move you," he said dreamily. His eyes took on their cloudy, sultry look. "How I should move you," he sighed, and put his delicate surgeon's hand on her cheek.

He stroked her forehead softly and whispered things. She was so young, it was so unfair, she was so patient, so brave, so beautiful, so young, so young. . . .

He cooed and cooed, lulling her into a soft, sexy stupor, making her want to crawl into his lap.

She stared up at the sky. It was so hot, the sun so bright, that the sky glared back white.

"Can I go back in now?" she asked over her shoulder. But the nurse who had wheeled her out was back inside.

She lay there, alone on her stretcher, awash in white sheets. The sun roof was empty except for her. She was sweating. Getting outside, they had told her, would be good for her.

"Hey!" she yelled. "Can I go back in now?"

For the first few weeks she tried to read. It seemed like the perfect opportunity. So much free time. She started *The Magic Mountain* but got trapped in the first hundred pages, reading them over and over, forgetting where she had left off, where the characters had left off. The drugs made her groggy and she had trouble with her eyes. She read two exciting Raymond Chandler novels and only later realized that she had read the same one twice. She gave up, left *The Magic Mountain* near her bed so her friends would think her morbid, and watched television. The only shows that interested her were soap operas set in hospitals.

Dr. Davis began visiting every day, before seeing his patients. He brought her more flowers. Daffodils, tulips, irises, more violets, a bunch of daisies that occasioned a little speech about simplicity, a rose, and more violets. He brought her Godiva chocolates, Kroger chocolates, Greenberg's chocolate cakes, and Bazooka bubble gum. He brought her Edith Wharton novels and sent her funny postcards of cats dressed up as

people. He kissed her forehead very softly and very slowly at
the end of each visit.

What an absurd man, she thought. When he was late, she
snapped at the nurses and sulked at the ceiling.

"Hello, my little friend," Dr. Davis warbled. He was so
small—no taller than five feet five, she guessed—and so elegantly dressed that he reminded her of a foot used to model
Italian shoes—shapely, a perfect size 6 1/2.

He pulled a bulging bunch of green grapes from a bag and
held them over her mouth. She pulled one off the stem with her
lips and saw him watching her. When he bent over her for the
routine goodbye kiss, she trembled and he stared for a moment,
then kissed her on the lips.

"Such lovely lips," he murmured. She wondered with horror if she had brushed her teeth that morning.

He kissed her, with his mouth open like a fish's. He murmured lines of what sounded like poetry, but she had no idea
whose. He kissed her again, gently pulling her hospital gown
up to her neck, where it stayed in an unromantic pile. He kissed
her and whispered. Had a younger man talked to her like this,
she would have squirmed with embarrassment. "My darling
. . . lovely breasts . . . like rosebuds . . ."

He stood upright. His pants bulged like a teenage boy's at
a dance. Behind the aluminum bar, the bulge was eye level and
she put out her hand and slowly unzipped his pants, watching
her own hand, watching the zipper part. She almost forgot he
was there in his button-down shirt and knit tie. His tender
words sounded vague and inappropriate. She felt a little cruel
—the secret, guilty thrill of squashing an ugly bug. She pulled
the fly of his gray flannel pants apart and looked at the white

jockey shorts, trying not to leer. She felt powerful for the first time since getting sick.

Dr. Davis watched her unzip his pants. He glanced at the door.

She pulled his penis out of its white underpants. The door did not open. The penis stood at exactly the level of the lower aluminum bar across the bed. It accidentally brushed the aluminum bar.

"Cold!" cried Dr. Davis. The door still did not open.

The penis was pulled under the aluminum bar. It was pulled over the aluminum bar. But it still didn't reach her mouth and still the door did not open.

"Lower the bed," she ordered. But it was already as low as it could go. "Then lower the bar."

The door stayed closed for half an hour more. It stayed closed until he, slightly flushed and clearing his throat, pushed it open to leave.

"Your temp is up," said Miss Darty, who had come in a few minutes later and pushed the thermometer into her mouth. "Your pulse is up. And your blood pressure is up."

"I'm okay," she said, and turned her face to the windows and fell asleep.

They devised an intricate lock and alarm system. If the bathroom door was left wide open, the edge stood inches from the door to the room, which opened inward. They discovered, one day when the door was accidentally left ajar, that when anyone tried to come in the doorknobs would lock, rattling loudly and barring the way. Stephanie, who seemed to have divined most of what was going on, would eat Jell-O in the cafeteria or pace outside the closed door.

He would sit, lightly, on the edge of the bed.

"Did you know the color of a woman's nipples and clitoris

is the same?" he asked. "If the nipples are dark, the clitoris is dark. Yours are a very pretty pink. Has anyone ever told you that? Have they?"

"Not recently," she said, thinking that, similarly, her lips and fingernails were the same shade of blue. "Did you learn that in medical school?"

"I adore you," he said. "Did you know that?"

She adored him too, she knew, even if he did wear black bikini underpants sometimes. She kissed his hand and put it on her cheek. It felt cool.

"You have a fever," he said, stroking her cheek with his thumb.

"And have had for two months," she said. "Two months." His daughter had gotten married the week before.

"I brought slides to show you," he said. He pulled a yellow box and hand viewer out of the L. L. Bean fishing bag he carried instead of a briefcase—"It's easier, on my bike"—and handed them to her. She pushed the plastic button to see the first slide.

"I don't think this is your daughter's wedding," she said. A tiny baby lay on an operating table. It was black and crisp and swollen with burns. The white bones of one foot peered out from raw flesh. One eye seemed to be missing, the other swollen shut.

"Oh, dear," he said when he looked at it. "Wrong box."

The first hard-on she had ever seen belonged to her first boyfriend, Jeffrey. Her bedroom on the ground floor was far from her parents'. It had its own door to the outside, through which Jeff had quietly slipped, according to plan, early one morning. They necked and undressed in the single bed. It had been a canopy bed when she was little, but she had recently dismantled it.

"An erection!" she said, pointing to the swollen crotch of Jeffrey's underpants.

"That's not an erection," Jeff said. "An erection is when you, you know, when there's sperm."

"That's ejaculation," she said, suddenly nervous and uncertain.

"Are you sure?"

"Well, that's what the words mean—erect, ejaculate."

"Yeah," he said dubiously. "Yeah."

They looked at each other, a little puzzled.

"Oh, who cares," Jeff said, and saw it was time to go.

"Why was Jeff Klein running across the lawn at six o'clock this morning?" her father asked her at breakfast.

"Oh . . ." she said. Oh, God, she thought. "Oh, he was on his way to, um, baseball practice and I gave him breakfast."

"I see," said her father. He looked down at his bacon, which, she noticed, he had uncharacteristically not complained about as being "too pully."

He didn't look her in the eye for a week.

He has that same shifty, hurt look, she thought now, watching her father pace the small hospital room. He moved unhappily from large foot to large foot.

"We have something to tell you," he finally said. His mustache looked as weighty as a problem. There were dark circles under his eyes and heavy bags. That's where I get them from, she thought. Thanks, Dad.

"We have something to tell you both," her father said. Her brother, Willie, sat in a chair with his long adolescent legs out, his face screwed up in distaste.

You are finally getting a divorce, she thought. About time.

"Your mother and I have decided to get a divorce." Her father coughed slightly, cleared his throat, and twisted his neck inside his collar. "We have decided it would be better this way.

For both of us. For *all* of us," he added quickly. "I hope you children understand." He coughed.

The children stared back at him, Willie from the chair, Alice from the bed, unwilling to ease his discomfort by speaking. His neck twisted in agony in his broadcloth collar.

"So that's that," her mother piped up. Her mother had red hair. She was overweight, well dressed, and her name was Brenda. She had a hearty optimism that often expressed itself in invitations to eat during difficult moments when no one was hungry.

"Does anyone want dinner?" she now asked. "I could bring up veal parmigian' from the Italian restaurant on the corner."

Her children squirmed a little and politely declined. Her husband said that he really had to get back, and he approached Alice, who glared at him and tried not to let her lip curl in a snarl. Her mother didn't want this divorce, Alice was sure.

"Goodbye," her father said, looking desperate and beaten.

That hangdog look won't work on me. Not really, she thought, as she softened a little in spite of herself. "Goodbye, Daddy," she said, kissing him.

He coughed as he walked sluggishly through the door, en route to the Yale Club, his new home address.

Her brother looked as if he were going to cry, but just scuffed the heel of his sneaker across the linoleum again and again.

Her father decided to move to Vancouver at the end of the month.

"As far away as he can go and still be on the same continent," her mother said. "And he's in a different country." She shook her head. "Oh, well. He's always wanted to live in the woods."

Her father's family owned a lumber company. There had once been lumber mills in Vermont and Maine, but they were gradually sold off until only a single mill in British Columbia, outside of Vancouver, remained. The mills had always been her father's favorite part of the business, which otherwise consisted of a lumberyard, warehouses, a large hardware store that sold inferior goods to the poor, and a dock where cement ships unloaded. Her father had never been comfortable as a businessman, thinking somewhere deep down that he should have been something more genteel—a poet, perhaps, or at least a judge. His affectations were many and detailed. He once ordered a set of bagpipes, but the red tartan bag arrived with a leak that he never repaired. He had an elaborate sauna built in the garage around a stove he brought back from a vacation in Norway. He played the concertina on his sailboat, which had a wood, not fiber-glass, hull. He waxed his mustache. He found peace at the Yale Club.

The mill in the Rockies was a compromise. It was his business, but trees were pretty, lumber smelled so fresh, and he was treated as the company town's seignorial lord by the colorful lumberjacks. His move to the mountains was no surprise to anyone. Similarly, when her parents had told her in the spring that they were separating, Alice shrugged and said, "Well, I can't say I'm surprised." Her parents had fought every day of the last ten years. Her father complained that the spaghetti was not *al dente* and her mother asked why he would never take a walk with her. They fought bitterly about the Vietnam War, about Nixon, about whether the toilet seat should be left up or down.

They fought primarily at the dinner table. Alice remembered watching her mother light the candles and pour the wine.

With pink cheeks and an excited smile, her mother would survey the table, basking in her fantasies.

"We could be in the South of France," she would say, suddenly touching a ripe pear in the fruit bowl. "Or the *North* of France."

The children would draw their fingers quickly through the candle flame.

"Have some delicious bread," their mother would say. Then she would ask Alice's father how he liked his dinner. Maisie, their housekeeper, had been the cook for a rich Jewish family in the South. There would be light, fluffy matzoh balls, noodle pudding, and brisket one night; fried chicken and steaming-hot cornbread the next. Alice's father would sit behind the plates piled high with food and mutter glumly, "Not bad." And Alice's mother's face would fall.

It happened every night, an inevitable prelude to an inevitable argument, like boxers shaking hands and coming out swinging. As soon as Alice sat down, she would wait for her mother's eager question, which she would follow by mouthing the word "delicious," hoping it would somehow find itself spoken by her father. Her father would say, "Not bad." And the fight would begin. Every night Alice watched her doom-ridden father chip sullenly away at her mother's rosy world, while her mother tried unsuccessfully, with infuriating persistence, to elicit some cheer from him.

When she herself snapped at her mother, her father would always side with Alice, even when she was wrong, dead wrong. Alice would watch with horror as her father yelled, "Why *should* she make her bed? We have a maid." She believed that selfishness was a privilege of youth and indulged in it often, but it was certainly nothing to be defended. The unasked-for alliance with her father shamed her, and she soon tried never to argue with her mother, terrified her father would leap to her unworthy side.

She had once idolized her father, running to the bathroom window each morning to catch a glimpse of him as he drove off to work. She remembered sitting happily in the dark on the floor of his closet, holding one of his shoes. Sometimes at night she would hear him munching Rolaids and her heart would fill with admiration and love.

When had he stopped looking her in the eye? She remembered when he had begun belittling her passions and pursuits. The day she bought her first 45 Beatles record. She remembered the cover, the four skinny Beatles in their high-heeled boots. "I Wanna Hold Your Hand." She had written "Alice and Paul; Alice and Ringo; Alice and George; Alice and John" all over it.

"Fruits," her father had said. "Fairies. A fad. How can you fall for this? How can you be so foolish?"

It was pretty much what all her friends' fathers said to all her friends. But her father seemed hurt by her little 45. Angry. He sulked for days. It seemed to Alice that he began to sulk about everything. When she refused to sing "America" with the rest of the family at the seder one year, he put his face in his hands and swore.

"Why do you want to hurt me?" he asked. "Why?"

"It's not a protest against *you,* Daddy," she said. "It's a protest against the war."

He got up from the table shouting, "Shut up, damn you," and walked out of the room, slamming the door left open for Elijah.

Soon everything about her became an affront—her bangs, her friends, her sneakers. Her father, who had always believed everything she said, even when she feigned a stomachache to stay home from school, began to doubt her. He called her friends' houses to see if she was really where she said she would be. When she began to read *The Idiot*—she had picked it off the library shelf thinking it must be a comic novel about a stupid person—he said, "You'll never understand a word of it," and flipped through until he found a word she didn't know. It was "aphorism." "See?" he said. "You don't even understand the words. How do you expect to understand the book?"

"You're supposed to *encourage* me," she screamed.

The only time he seemed pleased or agreed with her, the only time she was not foolish, was when she fought with her mother.

Her mother sat beside her, dabbing Alice's forehead with a washcloth. There were pencils sticking out of her red hair.

"I hate Daddy," Alice said.

"He's leaving me, not you, dear," said her mother.

No, Alice thought. He's leaving me too. And Willie. We are a sinking ship. And he is a rat. With an ugly tail.

"You wouldn't even speak to him when he was here," her mother added.

"I don't like him. He's depressing. He came here to feel sorry for himself."

"Then you should be glad he's off in the woods."

"He belongs *here.*"

"So you can snub him."

"Well, yes," said Alice. "I'm in the *hospital.*" It wasn't right. She was lying in the hospital with a mysterious disease. He shouldn't move at a time like this, even if she *was* impolite. Her seventeen-year-old brother was home in the big suburban house, tall, sad, living entirely on his own. Maisie came in daily to cook and clean for him, but at night he rattled around, watching TV, feeding the dog, wondering vaguely what had happened to his family and his life.

She had been crying for the past hour. She called her mother "Mommy" and would not let go of her hand.

"I'm scared," she said. "I think I'd rather be dead." She knew she was lying. That's not the sort of thing you say to your mother, she thought, and she felt a wave of guilt. Don't say that to your poor mother. But she couldn't stop herself.

"Dead," she said. After all, she would almost rather be dead. But still . . . "I'm sorry. I didn't mean that. But I don't know how much longer I can stand this." Too melodramatic, that. She looked at her mother's face, kind and strained.

"Well, I guess I can stand it," she said quickly. "I mean I've stood it so far."

Her mother said, "I'm going to call Simchas Fresser."

Oh, God. A weird hypnotist. Had it come to this? He would probably chant or eat a live chicken.

"He's written a book on pain, you know."

"How to inflict it?"

Alice had met Simchas Fresser once, in a tiny East Side deli, while she was having lunch with her mother. He had come in, filling the place like a pinball machine, with all his bells ringing, his flippers swinging, lights flashing, and silver balls flying in all directions.

"Well!" he had said as if it meant something. He was Israeli, a Sabra, in fact. But he objected to Israel's climate and high taxes, and had come to New York a few years before. He'd worn a white sheepskin coat that almost reached the floor, had a black beard that spread out like a fan, black eyebrows that wiggled, sometimes comically, sometimes ominously, over beady brown eyes. When he had taken off his sheepskin hat, his hair rose off his head like a wedge of cake. He was tall, but behaved arrogantly, like a short man with a complex about his height. He was fantastically loud, and his voice was theatrical, his accent foreign and heavy, but not ludicrous.

"Brody!" he had said to her mother. "What are you doing here? And what's this? Another Brody? Oh, my God. And at lunch. Ah, well. Brody—the elder—listen . . ." And they had immediately begun to talk shop. As Simchas extolled the money-making virtues of hypnosis clinics, Alice daydreamed. Obviously having an affair with my mother, she had thought. That's why she chose this little deli for lunch. A rendezvous!

What a nut this guy is. She looked at him as he donned the white sheepskin hat and coat to leave. His beady eyes sparkled for a moment. Then he picked up his check. He's pretty funny-looking, Alice thought, but he has a nice nose.

Simchas blasted into the hospital room. Alice and her father stared at him. Alice's mother smiled.

"Brodys!" he bellowed.

Some bedside manner, she thought. He threw his coat dramatically across the room to a chair.

"Is this the patient? How patient are you? I haven't seen you in a long time. You were very tall. Now you are very long." He sat down on the window sill. "God, what a day. My patients are crazy. Okay, Longo, what can I do for you?" He took off his jacket. He smelled of cologne. Pleasant cologne.

"Now I want you to roll your eyes up. Back into your head. Try it."

She rolled her eyes, the room flickered, and she felt as if the rest of her body would follow her eyes in a backward somersault.

"Marvelous!" he cried, whacking the foot of the bed with his hand for emphasis. Her legs shot up in spasmodic jumps. Her father cleared his throat miserably.

"Please don't do that," she said when the legs had stopped.

"What?" he said, looking up from a tiny tape recorder he had pulled out of his briefcase. "Oh. Sorry."

"You are hypnotizable," he said. "If your eyes roll up, you can usually be hypnotized. If they don't, you probably can't be. It's how we tell. Don't know why, but that's how we tell."

What a phony baloney, she thought. "Mom," she said desperately, hoping she would send Simchas home. But her mother ignored her.

"Okay, Longo, now lie down . . ."

"But I am lying down."

"Right. Now put your arms at your side." He told her hypnosis was just a deep form of relaxation. There would be no swinging watches, no commands. At the count of one, she rolled her eyes up and held them like that. At two, she took a deep breath and held it. At three, she let her eyes close normally and slowly exhaled.

"You are going into a trance now."

I am not.

"I want you to relax. You are wrapped in a blanket. A soft, warm blanket. Relax. Ree-laax."

She listened to his voice, which had become soothing, deep, and musical.

"You feel a tingling—just a slight tingling. It has started in your toes. Now it is moving up your calves. A pleasant feeling . . ."

She did feel a pleasant vibrant tingling. As he talked about it moving up her body, into her thighs, her stomach, her chest, her arms, hands, neck, head, and forehead, she felt it all over.

"Your right arm is going to rise off the bed now, as if a balloon were tied to it, lifting it gently."

Her fingers twitched. Her hands lifted slowly off the hospital sheets, pulling the rest of her arm with it. It felt light.

"Good. Now let it down slowly."

He told her she was in a field. The sun was shining, but it was cool. She was under a tree, on soft grass. Birds were singing. A cool breeze was blowing. Everything smelled lush and delicious. She knew, of course, that she was not really there, he said. But she was pretending she was there under the bluest of skies. She felt her pain, of course, but it didn't hurt. The pain was there but it didn't hurt. It was just pain, the same pain, but it didn't hurt.

When they reversed the eye-rolling procedure and she "woke up" she began to cry. She forgot her parents were there, seeing only pale Dr. Fresser, his black beard draped over his shirt like a napkin.

"Thank you," she whimpered at the rather startled Dr. Fresser. She had forgotten what it felt like to be comfortable. Now she felt calm and relaxed and cried with relief.

"Here's a tape of it," Simchas Fresser said. "Listen to it whenever you like. Of course, you mustn't reproduce it for sale."

Alice laughed. Simchas Fresser didn't.

She was a shut-in, but unlike the aunt in *Swann's Way*—even Alice had read just that far—she couldn't see much of interest to her on the street. She couldn't even see the street. So she tried to follow the comings and goings of her neighbors on the hall.

Directly across from her room, a cultivated and prosperous-looking man spent as little time as possible in his room. He paced the halls in a dark red silk robe that looked like a Victorian sofa. She saw him when she was wheeled to x-ray each day.

"Good morning," he would say jauntily. He would, she was sure, have tipped his hat if he had had one. A youngish blonde girlfriend visited him every evening and brought expensive-looking bottles of wine to drink with his dried, pasty hospital dinners.

"Lawrence, darling," she would call musically. "I'm here."

In the room next to Alice's, a man yowled for three weeks without stopping and was then replaced—Alice never discovered why, or why he yowled—by a comfy lady in a chenille robe who, when Alice rolled past, clung to her IV pole as if she were afraid of toppling over in the stretcher's wake. She looked bewildered, and as she never seemed to speak, the only sound Alice associated with her was the rhythmic scuffing of her bedroom slippers along the floor.

Next to the shuffling lady was Mrs. Pulman, the senile lady

who sat on the floor and held out her arms pitifully, crying, "Oy gevalt, Johnson," whenever Alice was wheeled by.

From the rest of the rooms, terrible noises and worse smells drifted out, but the occupants never did. Alice suspected they had lost all their limbs to gangrene, which would explain both the odors and the absence of activity, but the floor nurses insisted they were just old.

She told herself it was like reading a science-fiction story. You simply accept a weird premise, and the rest follows. Except I hate science-fiction stories, she thought. But after a while she accepted absolutely the premise of her hospital bed, and the doctors and nurses and visitors who intermittently appeared at its side were a matter of course. Gradually the premise grew to include the room. When Alice first came to the hospital, she asked her mother to give all plants and flowers and posters away. They made everything seem so permanent. They made it seem as if she *wanted* to be there. I won't be co-opted, she told herself, and refused to let the room look comfortable or lived in.

But things began to pile up. Cards, books, boxes of candy. A tiny refrigerator was brought in and stocked with Coke and juice. Posters were hung while she was asleep. And the room was settled irresistibly, like a prairie, until it was lined with green plants and urinals sprouting flowers from friends.

"The flowers that bloom in the spring!" her father had sung before he went to Canada, skipping around the room, pretending to throw money around. The private room, its venetian blinds, windows that wouldn't open, and air conditioning that wouldn't go off were costing him $217 a day. Alice had round-the-clock private-duty nurses. At $70 a nurse a day, that was

$210 a day. In addition to Stephanie, who was so tired from working two shifts that she spent much of her time curled up in a chair, wrapped in a blanket, sleeping, there was Holly, the cheery Filipino nurse, and Mrs. Orion, a practical nurse who was part Cherokee, part black.

Mrs. Orion came at midnight each night. She hung up her sweater, looked around her, and went to get Alice's Jell-O from the floor refrigerator. She then began moving plants. The nightly transfer of the plants from the room to the hall was methodical and plodding, one plant at a time. Alice would watch quietly as Mrs. Orion moved what had by now become a thicket of ferns and begonias. Mrs. Orion was convinced the plants used up all the oxygen at night. Without oxygen, Mrs. Orion explained, she would fall asleep on duty. So the nightly exodus of plants was painstakingly effected. Mrs. Orion would turn out the light, settle into the white armchair, and immediately fall asleep. Alice thought she was probably worn-out from moving all the plants.

"Well, that's finally done," Mrs. Orion said one night, wiping her hands together, satisfied that the greenery in plastic pots now innocently sucked their oxygen from the public supply.

Mrs. Orion settled into her armchair. Alice rewound the tape of Dr. Fresser hypnotizing her. She pushed the play button and turned down the volume. Simchas Fresser spoke, but Alice still could not fall asleep. Mrs. Orion, however, had almost immediately commenced her irregular, irritating snore.

Alice wanted a sleeping pill, but it seemed cruel and unnecessarily ironic to wake someone up to get a sleeping pill. She closed her eyes. Mrs. Orion snored steadily.

This is ridiculous, Alice thought. "Mrs. Orion!" she called. Mrs. Orion snored.

Alice called her again, then coughed loudly. She tapped a pen on the aluminum bed bar. She flicked the lights on and off. "Goddamnit, Mrs. Orion!"

Alice finally rang for the nurses' station.

"Where's your private nurse?" asked the voice from the wall.

"I think she's in a trance."

The first time Simchas Fresser had come, Alice felt a wave of benevolence after her initial tears, and said to Simchas, "I could kiss you."

"Why don't you?" her mother asked.

Simchas bent his wild black beard and sharp little eyes toward her, and she'd given him a kiss on the cheek.

Uh oh, she had thought. Something is going to happen. A man who had an affair with my mother. Disgusting.

"Svengali is here," the nurses would chuckle when they heard his voice barreling along before him. He would wade in, complaining loudly, his arms in the air, as if he were talking to her over a wild surf.

"Relax," his amplified voice coaxed at night when she played the tape.

She would roll her eyes, her right arm would drift into the air, she would feel the pain, and it would not hurt.

"You feel a pleasant tingling in your thighs," his deep voice would tell her.

The tape recorder lay next to her on the bed.

The aides lowered Alice into a steel tub filled with hot water. The whirlpool motor growled and water pulsed heavily around her legs. She looked at her feet, the toes floating up above the waterline. Sweat formed on her upper lip.

The therapist moved Alice's arms around in gentle circles she claimed were exercises. "It's a shame you haven't had any therapy on your legs in all this time. It's been almost two months. We might've been able to get a little movement."

"I could move when I got in here," Alice said. "Dr. Wither-spoons told me not to. He told me to lie down."

"Well, the doctor knows best," the therapist said. Anyway, there was no question of moving her legs at this point. What had once been joints, amazing balls and sockets, machines, it seemed to Alice, more clever than the pulley or the lever, or even the wheel, were now as fixed as table legs. And not as good as table legs. Table legs hold up tables. Her legs lay white and thin on a silicone mattress that protected her from bedsores. Her hips were great solid clumps.

She floated leaden in the tub for half an hour. When she was lifted out, her feet looked rubbery. Piles of skin, like shredded Chinese chicken, were left behind in the steaming tub.

"What's wrong with me?" she asked the doctors every few days.

"That's what we're trying to find out."

"What do all the x-rays show?"

"Nothing," they would answer.

"Then why do you take them?"

"To keep an eye on things."

"But my ovaries," she would begin, and the doctors would shake their heads and tell her not to watch so many self-help shows on TV.

She waited for her shot. Her life was divided into the six-hour units between shots, overlapped by the nurses' eight-hour shifts. A nurse would pull aside the sheet and blanket, raise the wrinkled hospital gown, and pat her hip with an alcohol-drenched ball. Her hips no longer curved like a girl's, but were concave and bruised yellow and purple from the needles.

The nurse would jab her with the needle, plunge in the

contents, and then withdraw it. Alice always watched. Her skin was so toughened that it seemed someone else's body was being poked. Stephanie told her that in nursing school she had learned to give shots by practicing on an orange.

The drugs eased the pain for an hour, sometimes two. Then she would wait for the next one, staring at the clock, staring at the brownstone renovation across the street. An enormous picture window was being installed on the second and third floors, which had, since Alice had begun watching, become one floor with a high ceiling. She wondered how much the brownstone had cost, how much the renovation was costing, and how much they would be able to sell it for. She wondered why anyone would want such high ceilings and, moreover, why anyone would want a picture window facing a hospital. She hoped she wouldn't be there long enough to watch them decorate.

Sometimes Stephanie would give her her shot fifteen minutes early. She would turn Alice on her side and take out a brown bottle of brown liquid for bedsores, which had occurred in spite of the turning and silicone mattress and sheepskin mat. She would unwrap an extra-long Q-Tip and dip it into the medicine. When she rubbed it on the bedsores, it felt cold and stung slightly and was refreshing.

"More," Alice would beg when Stephanie stopped. "Please more."

"I really *should* use plain cotton," Stephanie sometimes said. "This stick probably irritates, probably does more harm than good."

"Oh, come on, Steph. Just once more, Stephanie, please." And Stephanie would lightly scratch the itchy sores with her cotton-ended stick for five, sometimes ten minutes. Alice would smile ecstatically, forgetting the pain. How luxurious.

She had dreamt only four times in the two months she'd been in the hospital. In the first dream she was in St. Thomas with her aunt and two cheerful young German men wearing tight European bathing suits. She floated and played in the clear, remarkably warm blue water. When she woke up, she had wet her bed. She was speechless for hours afterward, degraded in a fundamental way she could explain to neither her mother nor the nurses, who assured her it happened all the time.

In her second dream she had forgotten to feed her horse—a fat gray pony who occasionally won ribbons in horse shows and lived in a barn Alice's father had built at great expense in the field behind their house. Alice had sold her pony three years ago, when she was sixteen and smoked pot in the barn instead of grooming the unexercised and increasingly fat pony, or even mucking out the stall. But in her dream she had not sold him. She had forgotten him. For three years, the rotund pony had withered in the stinking stall. Alice came upon him, big bones sprawled across the urine-soaked straw, and her stomach twisted. She woke up in a cold sweat.

Her third dream was also about the pony. They were cantering across the smooth green grounds of the hunt club. Alice was allowed to ride there, but not to board her horse, because only members could board their horses there and there were no Jewish members. They cantered softly across the flat field used for shows and polo. Ahead of them was the "in and out," two fences with just enough room in between for the horse to land and immediately take off again. As they approached the jump, Alice leaned forward, her hands level along the pony's neck. They sailed over the first fence, her pony's neck arching and brushing her cheek, landed lightly and, as the horse's back hooves touched the ground, his front ones lifted again, drawing them easily over the second fence. It was a moment of exquisite, clean morning air and horsy muscles, and Alice woke up exhilarated, still feeling the cool sky on her cheeks.

Her fourth dream was about Simchas Fresser. Simchas,

Alice's mother, and Alice were at Coney Island. Alice's mother bought a hot dog, tore it in half, and gave half to Alice. Alice accidentally dropped her half as she opened her mouth to bite it; when she picked it up, it was covered with gray grit and some ratlike hairs.

"Yuck," she said, dropping it in a green trash barrel. "It's dirty."

And she opened her eyes, amused and blushing at the banality of her unconscious.

"You've got to eat something besides eggs," the tiny lady in the pink sweater said. "Too much cholesterol."

"Now I have to worry about cholesterol? Give me a break."

The nutritionist frowned. "I'll just have to fill in your menus myself."

Alice envisioned turkey and gummy gravy marked on that day's menu. "Eggs," she said.

"Salisbury steak." The nutritionist left.

For weeks Alice had eaten nothing but soft-boiled eggs and golden-pink cherries in heavy syrup, listed on the menu as Queen Anne's Cherries. Then her father came East on business and brought her Chinese food—hot bags of greasy spareribs and shrimp with snow peas—from the restaurant next to the garage where he had left his car. Her mother sometimes brought her Chicken Kiev from the Russian Tea Room or brioche from Dumas in the morning, and Stephanie began to go out every afternoon to get her knishes and popsicles from the street vendors.

Mrs. Trawling made her nightly rounds. She had a long face with eyes that smoldered in the dull, uninteresting way of the slag heaps Alice had seen in Scranton, Pennsylvania. Her hat flew back from her head in great starched gusts; her hands were always cold. To Alice, Mrs. Trawling was the awful, skinny symbol of her helplessness. That an intrusive withered old bag with a flashlight could disturb her precious sleep with impunity, could poke her and ask rude questions about her bodily functions, was a nightly humiliation she dreaded.

"Did you void?" asked Mrs. Trawling.

"It's on the chart," Alice answered, blinking into the flashlight.

"Why aren't you covered? And what's this?" Mrs. Trawling had turned her light on Alice's exposed flank. "Something is oozing!" she cried, hurrying out of the room.

She returned with three other nurses. One of the capped entourage flicked on the light switch. Alice watched them peering at her hip. Mrs. Orion snored peacefully.

"It's from the shot," Alice explained patiently. "I just had a shot, remember?" The flesh around her hips was so swollen from injections that it no longer absorbed very well. "Happens all the time."

The nurses were watching the few miniscule beads of thick clear liquid.

"It just doesn't absorb," Alice repeated. "Oozes. All the time. No big deal . . ."

"Call the resident!" ordered Mrs. Trawling. "Something is oozing!"

The resident on call was a sleepy girl with straight brown hair and a red pullover sweater. By the time she came in, a few minutes later, the oozing had stopped. She touched Alice's black-and-blue thigh, setting off a few spasms, and yawned. "I'll have to tell Dr. Witherspoons about this in the morning." She scuffled out in her white clogs.

"We have to go in," Dr. Witherspoons announced. It was nine. The oozing had not recurred since Mrs. Trawling's two A.M. sighting. "Emergency exploratory surgery. We have to find out if there's an infection."

Alice wondered aloud why we must find out if there was an infection when she was already being treated with massive doses of antibiotics as if there were an infection. "So why bother?" Emergency, emergency, emergency, the doctor kept saying. Her mother wrung her hands.

"The most expensive operation in history was performed on Louis XVI," Dr. Davis said. He giggled. "On his hemorrhoids."

"I imagine mine will cost considerably less. But still . . ."

"There's insurance, dear girl."

"It seems to have run out." The policy had been for seventy-five thousand dollars.

"Does your father mind very much?" Dr. Davis was lining up all the get-well cards on the window sill and knocking them down like dominoes.

"I think the family business is picking up the tab and writing me off on its taxes. Something like that. I guess he's okay. He still flies first class. He says the seats are too small in coach."

Rolling to the whirlpool, trailing tubes, Alice saw her neighbor Lawrence. Lawrence Darling, as she and her mother had begun to call him after hearing his girlfriend's greeting each night.

"Good afternoon," he said to Alice, leaning forward in what might almost have been a bow. "Good afternoon," he said to the orderly who pushed Alice's stretcher.

When Alice—hot, flushed, and enervated—returned from the basement whirlpool, she heard the unlikely sounds of a party. Glasses clinked, voices chattered aimlessly but pleasantly, laughter rose to little crescendos and fell off.

"He got married!" cried a nurse, scurrying by. "Right here! In his bathrobe!"

"Who?" Alice asked from her stretcher.

"Mr. Lawrence."

"The nice guy across the hall? I thought Lawrence was his first name."

"It is. Lawrence Lawrence."

How convenient, Alice thought. I'm glad I wasn't calling the old gent by his last name. "In his bathrobe? To the blonde?"

Alice decided to marry Dr. Davis in the hospital. She wondered how long it would take him to get a divorce. He would wear cutaways and striped pants and small, shiny black shoes. She would wear a white nightgown. He would carry the bouquet.

Her father would not be invited. Simchas Fresser would watch, his heart secretly breaking.

"Champagne!" the nurse said, walking to the floor refrigerator, where she deposited the two plastic bags of blood she had been swinging as she spoke. "By the way," she added, patting the dark bundles on the refrigerator shelf, "these are for you!"

Her mother gathered up the cards and envelopes sprinkled on Alice's bed. "Do you want your stationery?" she asked.

"What for?"

"To answer your father's letter."

"What for?" Alice held a card of a cat with a crutch and began idly to draw a handlebar mustache on the stricken animal's face.

"Alice, I think you should write."

"Mom, I think I don't want to write. I think he's too cheap to call. That's the only reason *he* wrote." But, as she said it, she knew it was untrue. If her mother romanticized pastry, imagining colorful Parisian streets with every bite, her father's vision of letter writing was of leisured gents scratching thoughtfully at heavy parchment. He had sent her letters while she was at camp that were full of wistful stories of his youth and began with lines like "Neither a borrower nor lender be." She had loved those letters, which made her feel adult, old enough to have her own memories to send on the return post.

"Okay, then at least call him."

"No. N-O."

"Why?" asked her mother. She began to water the plants with a Dixie cup.

"*Why?* Whose side are you on?" Alice said. "And don't tell me again that he's still my father and that he left you and not me."

"Well?"

The letter from her father had said,

Dear Alice,

I enjoyed visiting you, and seeing that you are in good hands. Your mother seems to have everything under control, which is a great relief to me, as you might imagine. Seeing you left me extremely sanguine with regard to your ultimate recovery.

My trip East was a trying one, as, of course, you of all people will understand, and so to unwind I am taking a holiday. I have chartered a little sloop. It is a cozy bark —sturdy and shipshape (so to speak), and the perfect boat in which to cruise the many picturesque islands in this lovely area. Perhaps this will help to knot the ravelled sleeve of care.

I wish you and William could join me on this voyage. But you two are growing up. In a way, moving out here is a testament to you and William, for I am going through many changes and feel that I am growing up a little myself. And sometimes it is better for children to have a little distance from their parents.

Give my regards to your mother.

Love,
Daddy

Alice reread the letter. Perhaps her mother was right. A letter like that should not go unavenged.

"Okay, Mom, I'll write Dad," she said, and she pulled out a pad and began:

Dear Dad,

I hate you and hope you drown on your holiday. In the United States we call it a vacation.

I'm sorry you had a trying visit. Of course, you know what they say about New York—a nice place to visit, but you wouldn't want to live here.

I will certainly convey your regards to Mom. She is at the moment emptying my bedpan, but when she finishes, I'm sure she will be eager to hear about your much-needed trip.

Deserting one's family in a time of crisis is an important step on the rocky road to adulthood, I agree. And of course I am deeply moved by such a heartfelt testament to myself and my brother.

Willie and I are both extremely grateful for the distance you have so generously put between yourself and us, and I think Willie's poor grades and constant visits to the guidance counselor speak for themselves as proof of the independence of spirit inspired by your move.

I hope the pajama sleeve of care unravels and strangles you in your sleep.

Love,
Alice

P.S. I'm having emergency exploratory surgery tomorrow. I guess I'll be pretty sanguine then, too. Get it?!?

Alice smiled at the letter, put it in her bedside drawer to
show to Stephanie Carter, and wrote another:

Dear Dad,
Thanks for your letter. It's nice getting a real letter
instead of all these get-well cards.
   Last night an idiot nurse came in and found some fluid
oozing from my hip. I told her it was from an injection
I'd just had that had not been absorbed, but she decided
it was an emergency and now I have to have an exploratory operation. It will kill some time, I guess.
   Well, that's all the news from bed. Willie is off to
Paris, as you probably know. The dog and cat have come
to New York because there's no one home to feed them.

                                    Love,
                                       Alice

   Surgery was scheduled for the next morning. A middle-aged
woman who spoke only Spanish and wore a blue uniform came
into the room with a cart. Alice thought she had come to mop.
Why is she taking out a razor? Why is she putting towels under
my legs? As the woman spread soap on her legs, Alice realized
that she had come to prep her for the operation.
   As Alice's legs jumped in chaotic spasms, the woman dabbed
and scraped with the razor and deftly avoided drawing blood.
She next began to soap Alice's pubic hair.
   "Oh no," Alice said softly. There is a limit. "Do you have
to do that? It's my *leg* they're operating on." She pointed to her
leg. "Not my *cunt*, for God's sake." She pointed and shook her
head. "Leg! Leg!"
   The woman shrugged and continued. Alice watched in dis-

belief, and as she watched she saw appear the vagina of a little girl.

"Leg," she whispered absent-mindedly, hopelessly.

She tried not to cry. Then she remembered splashing in the bath with her brother, her mother drying them with what seemed an enormous towel.

It will grow in all stubbly, she thought.

Dear Katie,

I'm sure it's very annoying to be chased around your bed by a nude roommate wielding sharpened No. 2 pencils. And I would be embarrassed to go to the symphony on a bus with patients who talk to themselves and froth at the mouth. But I don't think refusing to bathe is a very effective strategy to get out. Your doctors could easily interpret your protest as a symptom. Be careful.

What does a "low affect" mean anyway? Whatever it is, I hope yours get higher.

My doctors have finally come up with a possible diagnosis, too. I may have osteomyelitis, which means my hips are rotting from an infection. Or I may have aseptic necrosis, which means my hips are rotting, but *not* from an infection. Well! You can imagine how relieved I am to know what's wrong.

The doctors, hoping to refine this already precise diagnosis even further, performed an emergency exploratory procedure. Oh, dear. I'm beginning to talk like them. What I mean is, they cut open my hip to see if they could find some pus. They took the biopsy, and half the doctors think there's infection and the others don't. So we're back to where we were three months ago—my hips are disintegrating and no one knows why. A big scar on my leg—and I mean big—and a lot of post-operative puking for nothing. Oh, well.

My father's moved to Canada, so my mother is very unhappy, but brave. Willie is in Paris and I miss him terribly. He was my favorite visitor—he'd stretch out in a chair and tell stories about the dog and the cat while the nurses tripped over his legs. Then we'd talk about how much we hate Dad. He used to idolize Dad. So did I, for that matter.

Are there any cute boys in your hospital? There are no boys here at all. I have, however, fallen madly in love with a very cute, very old doctor. And he's not even my doctor anymore—the eye doctor. Remember? The one with the divine gray hair? If I could walk, I'm sure he'd take me dancing. He brings me presents all the time and quotes poetry and sings Cole Porter songs to me. I have always wanted to be a kept woman. I wonder if this counts. I guess my father is actually doing the keeping. Oh, well.

There's also another one—a crazy friend of my mother's who comes and hypnotizes me. No swinging watches, but it is pretty romantic to have someone tell you you feel like you're floating all the time. But I think he had an affair with my mother. Would that be incest or just gross?

Anyway, here I am in this stupid bed and everyone thinks I'm being brave, but I'm just being desperate.

Write again. Get Well Soon, as the cards say. And take a bath.

Love,
Alice

Alice's mother came with her mail: long envelopes from Bloomingdale's, Saks, Bergdorf's, and Altman's. All her charge accounts had been cut off.

"That son-of-a-bitch," she said. "What's the point of this?"

Then she began to cry. She left the room quickly so Alice wouldn't see, but Alice saw. The humiliating protocol of divorce bewildered her mother, who had become more and more involved in Alice's hospital routine and seemed surprised each time the divorce proceedings intruded on the life of bedpans and needlepoint.

One night her mother came back from dinner with a man in tow. He was short, wiry, much too dark, and Alice thought his hair was dyed.

"This is Louie," said her mother. "Louie Scifo."

Why is my mother bringing a greaseball into my hospital room?

"Hello there, Alice," said Louie, grinning widely. He had capped teeth. "I heard from your mother here about your terrible predicament. You know, my cousin Dominique Scifo is a big neurosurgeon here. And, see, they think I'm my cousin, Dr. Scifo. . . ."

"Why?" Alice asked.

"Well, because I told 'em I was, so if they don't treat you right, you just tell me and I'll take care of these jokers."

"Louie has a diamond ring," said Alice's mother, lifting up his dark little hand. "I thought you might like to meet a man with a diamond pinky ring."

"Oh, yeah, thanks. See you around, Mr. Scifo, thanks for your concern."

"Mom," she said when he had gone, "who was *that?*" Alice recalled his double-breasted cream-colored jacket with dirty cloth buttons.

"Well, I was walking across Sixty-seventh Street, the way I always come here, and I'd seen him on the stoop of one of the brownstones a few times before. He's seen me too, so he asked me where I was going."

"And you *told* him?"

"He's very nice. Italians are very warm, you know. He took me for a drink. I thought you'd like the ring."

"How come he's always sitting on Sixty-seventh Street?"

"He lives there. He owns a building—the brownstone."

"I think he just hangs around to pick up rich East Side ladies."

"Maybe," her mother said pleasantly, picking up one of her many unfinished needlepoints.

After her tray with its tea bags and sticky spoons had been carried off, Jeffrey called. She hadn't seen him since the afternoon he cried in her bedroom three years before. He had held and shaken her by the arm, his fingers digging into her as he begged in his best melodramatic manner that she take him back. Mucus gathered between his nose and lip, and as he squeezed her arm harder and harder, he had begun to scare her.

"Go away," she kept saying. There was no one else home and he refused to leave, pulling at his long hair with one hand and shaking her with the other. But Jeffrey is even more vain than hysterical, she thought.

"I'm calling Katie," she told him. "She'll *hear* you, Jeffrey. She'll hear you crying. . . . Hello, Katie? Hi . . . Terrible, actually . . . Well, Jeffrey is here and . . ."

"Fuck you," Jeff muttered, sniffling, leaving.

When she heard his voice now, the chaos and fear of their adolescent romance came over her like a sweat. He was so crazy, she thought. But he was her first boyfriend and she had often thought him simply intense. How naïve, she told herself, remembering his screaming in jealous rage, his kicking and pounding through the fiberboard walls of his attic bedroom.

Their courtship had been conducted after school, when they would hitchhike downtown to spend their allowances on records. Once they went to the Fillmore East to hear Janis Joplin. Alice wore a plaid kilt and navy-blue knee socks and penny loafers; her mother told her not to talk to any strangers.

Jeffrey was extremely ugly and extremely vain. So vain, in

fact, that his round, ridiculous features took on a certain dignity, as if he were of another race and only the truly liberated could transcend their petty prejudices and appreciate his beauty. His funny face and bad skin became a challenge to Alice, like a piece of avant-garde art. To love this arrogant, unlovable boy—and she realized one day that she did love him—would constitute pure passion, an emotion untainted by the contemptible considerations of good looks and pleasant personalities that occupied her friends. It was true that Jeff had the longest hair in the school and played lead guitar in a popular band and was considered terribly cool even by the seniors, but still, Alice had told herself, her feelings were unsullied.

Jeffrey never tied the laces of his white leather sneakers and his Levi's were torn—every pair—below the left knee. He was big and walked as if he were fat, as he had been as a little boy. His hair was long, but it looked like no one else's. It didn't flow down his back in stringy waves, or curl luxuriantly around his head. It stood out; it simply stood out.

"Mommy," said a little girl who passed them on the street one day. "That man has big hair."

He had older brothers and sisters whom he visited at Berkeley and Brandeis and Bennington, and Alice thought him sophisticated and profound. They talked about Life and the War and the Cream.

"I can't live without you," they told each other, feeling very serious and adult. An obsession, Alice told herself, overcome with happiness. None of their friends couldn't live without each other.

"I love you, I love you, I love you," they told each other. There were bumper stickers that said "Love" and love beads, and they felt part of all that, as if they had just come from Woodstock or lived in the commune above the Chinese restaurant downtown.

When Jeffrey first tore the phone out of the wall—because

she suggested the early Dylan was, in its way, more sophisticated than the late Dylan—she had marveled at his passion. This is emotion, she thought.

This is a little scary, she began to add at the end of Jeff's scenes, which he had more and more often, over increasingly trivial things. But then she would perk up: This is a *scene* we're having. Now he's enraged. And I'm trembling. Then we'll *brood!* And then we'll fly into each other's arms! And weep!

They went everywhere together, and when they were apart, they phoned and declared into the receiver their undying love. Alice called Jeff to tell him if she was going anywhere, even if it was just for the afternoon. She wanted to tell him how much she would miss him. And, of course, he tore his clothes in jealous fury if she didn't.

One day Alice's mother asked her to come into the city with her. "Come on, Alice. We'll go to a museum. We'll go out to dinner. We'll have fun." Alice wanted to go. But Jeffrey wasn't home and she realized she was afraid to go without asking his permission.

She began to sense there was something wrong, something unseemly, about such possessiveness. One afternoon, as Jeffrey flung her off the school bus and she skidded across the gravelly road on her stomach, she decided it was not only unseemly but obscene. It was a school bus after all, a yellow school bus full of children chewing gum. While her friends lied to their parents about their hickies, she made up excuses for bruises, and sometimes just blushed and let her parents think they were hickies.

On the day of the student strike, when the greasers called the demonstrators fags and the demonstrators called the greasers fascists, and everyone finally began simply yelling "Fuck you" at everyone else, Alice, screaming and jumping happily with the rest of them, suddenly felt a hand grab her arm.

It was Jeffrey, wild-eyed and sweating. "You can't lower the flag to half mast. What are you people trying to do? You'll start a riot!''

"Some freak you are. Anyway, we have *permission*," Alice said. "From the *principal.*"

"Lower that flag and we break your face," a greaser called as someone began to untie the rope on the flagpole.

"Stop it!" Jeffrey yelled at Alice. He shook her back and forth and screamed that she was irresponsible and committing thoughtless acts of violence. He dragged her around a corner and, as he threw her to the ground, she noticed Mr. Marcus, her progressive English teacher, watching from a window, shaking his head.

"Help!" she shouted.

Mr. Marcus continued to shake his head.

Does he think this is an encounter session? she wondered. Why doesn't he help me? My Latin teacher would tell me this is an unexcused absence, but she would help me.

But Mr. Marcus only looked pained, as if to say, This is what happens when you don't *open up* in class. Alice is a troubled girl, she could see him thinking as she hit the ground.

She looked away from Mr. Marcus and back to the raging Jeffrey. He thinks this is an encounter session, too.

"Jeffrey," she said. "Let go of me or I'll tell your mother."

Just then Mr. Marcus walked by them. He looked at Alice with deep concern.

"Are you a happy person?" he asked Alice. "I mean *really* happy?"

He walked away. Jeffrey followed him.

"Bourgeoise!" Jeffrey called over his shoulder.

And Alice allowed herself to admit what she had long suspected—Jeffrey was an ass. When he tore his room apart or had a tantrum in the street, he no longer seemed to be expressing himself. He didn't look like an uninhibited child of nature, as she had once seen him. He looked like a nut.

"But I love you, I need you," he cried when she told him he was a big baby and that she never wanted to see him again. Oh no, she thought. Oh no, he's tearing out his hair again. Now he's at my feet.

And when once she would've held his head on her lap and thought it a tender moment in the frenzied carnival of love, now she looked at him in disgust, as if he were covered with sores, or were himself a sore.

His voice over the phone, proprietary and solicitous, made her grit her teeth and crack her knuckles.

"I'm really sorry you're in the hospital. Are you okay? I mean, are you, you know, comfortable and everything? What can I do? Just tell me. Can I bring you anything? Any records? I'm so wiped out. This is . . . this is . . . tragic! You know? Can I visit you?"

"No," she said.

"Yeah, but . . ."

"Thanks for calling," she said slowly, with great effort to remain polite. "Gotta go now."

"It's all right," she heard a loud accent from the Bronx saying down the hall. "I'm Dr. Scifo. The big neurosurgeon. You know, Dr. Scifo."

Very convincing, she thought. What on earth is he doing here?

"Oh," said her mother, putting down a book cluttered with charts. "That's Louie. We're going out to dinner. Louie is really a fascinating man. Such an interesting background."

I'll bet, Alice thought, as Louie's patent-leather shoe swung into the room, followed by Louie himself. Definitely dyed hair, she decided. Capped teeth. I am a snob. I know I am a snob and I'm sorry for it.

Louie said, "I'm taking Mommy out for a nice Italian meal. She could use some nourishment. I'm taking good care of Mommy."

Well, maybe he takes her dancing or they go on long walks, she thought, watching her mother chew complacently on a piece of cake left over from Alice's lunch tray. Alice took a deep breath and decided to be pleasant for her mother's sake. Let's pretend we're nice, a friend's grandmother had always said while the rest of the family shrieked "Fuck you" and slammed doors. Alice pretended she was nice.

"No kidding?" she murmured when Louie suddenly announced he had attended medical school in Boston.

"Sure," he said. "But, you know, it just wasn't challenging enough. Now, see, when I went to India and studied with the guru Dhuri Bokhara, well, that was something else again, you know what I mean? See, the truth is I'm very much relieved to hear you have this hypnotist. This problem that you have, this osteopathics . . ."

"Osteomyelitis," her mother said.

"Generic term, Brenda, generic term . . ."

Alice was silent because she could think of only two words to say: Oh sure. But nice people are not sarcastic, she kept telling herself. Let's pretend we're nice.

When Louie and her mother left, she was exhausted by the effort and suspected she had not been a complete success. Perhaps her mother would grow tired of her trying friend before he decided to make another hospital visit.

Instead her mother began to see Louie regularly. "He's such fun. So warm and demonstrative."

Loud and vulgar, Alice thought, but she said nothing. Maybe it's good for her, Alice told herself. She's miserable and lonely and it's no fun to be dumped, even by Daddy. Maybe this Louie Scifo is good for her.

But he was bossy, opinionated, and wrong, all at the same

time. A conversation with him was like being trapped in a taxi with a talkative cabbie. He constantly said "Um-believable!" about perfectly credible things. He cornered interns and offered loud diagnoses peppered with incorrectly inserted "per se's" and warnings about drugs whose names he mispronounced. "You gotta laugh sometimes" and "I don't claim to know everything" were favorite comments. Alice's skin crawled when he came near her, and she suspected he was scouting for quick feels when he leaned over her bed to kiss her hello or goodbye.

Louie Scifo was always scurrying in or out, telling her mother where to park, where to eat, bringing her strange sunglasses found on the street—"They're perfectly good!" Tiny and fast, he scuttled like a cockroach escaping down the drain. Alice found she didn't believe anything he said, even something as banal as a complaint about a traffic jam on Lexington Avenue.

Why is he saying that? she would think. What will he get out of it? Maybe he does take her on nice long walks, she kept reassuring herself, imagining him scampering around her large mother. But every word he uttered seemed part of a strategy to mislead her mother, a badly tailored fabric of cheap lies that her shaken and vulnerable mother could not recognize.

At first he claimed to own a brownstone on Sixty-seventh Street. But, when Alice's mother asked to see it, he told her some friends were staying in his apartment there—movie people who wanted him to direct their next film.

"Isn't that exciting?" Alice's mother had asked her.

"Mom," Alice said.

While his friends worked on the screenplay, Louie explained, he was staying upstairs, in the apartment of one of his tenants, a faded, bibulous society lady who thought of Louie as a son.

"And open your eyes," Simchas said.

She opened them slowly, languidly. He stood by the bed looking down at her. His hand—pink and soft-looking and not very attractive—was on the aluminum bar. The room seemed hushed as they looked at each other. Only the small light in the corner was on, and the room was dim and hushed.

Simchas's cuff showed, cream-colored and starched. A gold cufflink shaped like a knot sparkled in the semi-darkness. His clothes were very expensive, she could see. They probably felt good—soft and substantial. She put her hand out and touched his jacket. Cashmere.

"You're very beautiful," he said.

About time, she thought. She had been expecting this, waiting for it.

He slowly put his hand on the side of her head, stroking her hair until he reached her throat. At the touch of flesh on flesh, both of them breathed in sharply. He had been hovering around her sickbed, watching her, wary. She had just waited, watching his pink hands.

"Did you have an affair with my mother?" she suddenly asked.

He pulled his hand back. "What the hell kind of a question is that?" he shouted. "Of course not," he said, squaring his shoulders. She decided to believe him. It would make life so much easier. "Of course not," he murmured, leaning down to kiss her.

"I've brought you a mango, my dear," Dr. Davis would say when he visited.

"Mmm-hmm," she would answer, not really hearing.

"I wonder if you have sufficient potassium in your diet," Simchas Fresser would say when he came by. "Do you hear me, Brody? Are you listening?"

Dr. Davis's mangoes and Simchas Fresser's advice were welcome parts of her day. When Simchas barged into Alice's room, insulted, affronted, abused by the weather, the stock market, the success of an enemy, she could pour out her own grievances. He reacted not with pity, or even sympathy, but with shared indignation, as if they were sitting at an extremely expensive restaurant in Paris and discovered the wine was corked. The humiliation of illness and weakness, the sense of profound failure that the failure of her body had caused, vanished when Simchas appeared. It was not she who had failed, but everyone and everything else. When Alice and Simchas complained to each other, her weakness became instead a kind of fastidiousness. She wasn't feeble and slowly rotting; she was refined and discriminating, persecuted by inept doctors, crude nurses, and foully disintegrating hips. Her surroundings were a sad disappointment to her well-bred, cultivated sensibility.

As for Dr. Davis, she waited for his visits as eagerly as she had once waited for phone calls from high-school crushes. She brushed her hair and, in lieu of wondering what to wear, since she wore her wrinkled cotton gowns, she wondered what he would wear and what gifts he would bring her, and she thought this must be what mistresses did. She lay in bed, pretending she was lounging, pretending she was Dr. Davis's mistress and not Dr. Witherspoons's patient.

Dr. Davis and Dr. Fresser occasionally met, and Alice would look from one to the other, eagerly searching for signs of jealousy. But she could never be sure. Dr. Davis held both of Simchas's hands in his own and thanked him for being such a comfort to Alice. Simchas generally reddened and snorted some short reply, and while Alice liked to think it was anger at a rival that caused him to turn color, she suspected it was simply a horror of having his hands held.

There were other days when she didn't care if they were jealous or not, days when she could think of nothing but sex.

In the mist of pain and drugs, her thoughts waxed porno-
graphic. There was nothing visual, only tactile. She imagined
naked men and felt her arms around a waist and her face pressed
against a warm neck; she imagined cocks and felt the warmer,
tauter skin.

The dreamy, perfectly dressed Dr. Davis and the noisy,
bullying Simchas Fresser seemed to disappear behind their own
bodies. When they entered the room, she saw them, spoke to
them, but her eyes were at crotch level, and everything else
seemed a blur, a memory. These two men and their organs
seemed to be the only things she had any control over, and she
would wait in her bed like a despot to exercise her power. She
could touch doctors and watch them make faces, instead of
always being touched by doctors and making faces herself, and
it made her feel almost healthy and strong.

Simchas usually called at 11:15, just before the hospital
stopped accepting incoming calls. He had trouble sleeping, and
after taking his Valium and sleeping pills, he would call Alice
to chat. The pills never put him to sleep, but they made him
groggy in the morning, when he usually took one of the am-
phetamines prescribed by his M.D. friends.

He and Alice would talk for hours, the sound of his television behind his voice, while Mrs. Orion snored erratically by
her bed.

"Snake Fingers missed his appointment today," Simchas
would say. Snake Fingers was an unhappy teenager who
thought his fingers turned to snakes when he showered.

"I charged him anyway," said Simchas. "Thank God for that
boy. Four appointments a week and usually shows up for only
two of them."

Simchas told his middle-aged lonely-heart patients to put
personals in *The New York Review of Books.* He took tips from

stockbroker patients that never paid off. He started an obesity clinic, a smokers' clinic, a headache clinic, and an orgasm clinic. A con man with credentials, he was never happier than when he suspected he had put something over on someone.

But at some level his cynicism cowered before a desire for respectability, and he could be very self-righteous. If Alice ever remarked on his contempt for his patients and suggested he was opportunistic and unprofessional, as she often did, he would bristle behind his black beard, and the wedge of hair would wiggle up and down with his eyebrows, and he would bellow, "I *help* these people!" Alice didn't doubt it, either. He had helped her. She just knew he would do what he did and charge what he charged even if it didn't help these people. There was something so utterly amoral about Simchas that she sometimes felt giddy just talking to him, as if he were a pirate with a foul-mouthed bird on his shoulder.

For the first few weeks, Simchas had refused to charge them. But he came every day and her mother said it was not right to take advantage of a friend. She insisted on paying him *something,* she said. He relented, and charged his regular $80-an-hour fee.

"My parents pay you eighty bucks so I can give you a blow job," Alice told him.

"I *help* you!" he hollered.

"And anyway," he said later, "I usually charge a hundred for house calls."

At least he never boffed my mother, Alice sometimes thought with a sinking stomach and little conviction.

"You're *sick.*" Miss Darty flung the remark over her shoulder like a long itchy scarf. She walked toward the door, where the two nurses who never got dates were standing.

"That girl is sick," Miss Darty repeated, nodding at Alice. The two nurses who never got dates stared at her. One had freckles, which she blamed for her inability to get a date. The other blamed her small chest. But Alice thought they were okay, except for their pastel pants suits, and couldn't understand why no one asked them out.

"Sick, sick, sick," said Miss Darty.

The two other nurses looked at Miss Darty as if to say, Of course that girl is sick. That's why she's here.

"She is *disturbed*," Miss Darty continued.

The younger nurses looked at each other in relief. That was something else again.

"I am *not*," Alice yelled from her bed.

"On her wall," said Miss Darty, putting her hands on her ample hips and pausing for dramatic effect, "in a frame, is a picture."

The picture was carefully clipped from the newspaper, a photograph of a famous transvestite languishing in her hospital bed surrounded by camellias. Although the patient had been scheduled for only minor surgery, she was convinced she wouldn't survive it and had arranged to have the picture taken as her legacy to her public. It was a romantic portrait, but it would never have made the papers if she had not been right. Alice had clipped it, framed it, and hung it by her bed.

"It's not healthy!" Miss Darty declared. "A transvestite!"

"You're a transvestite!" Alice yelled out the door after her. "You big he-she," she said more softly.

Then she counted up on her fingers her friends who had died. She left out relatives.

There was Katie's boyfriend, who drowned on a sailing trip; his body was never found. Then Jane, a determined fat girl, had contracted a rare blood disease and dropped dead, just like that, within the week. Rob Perry was tired all the time and the doctors told him it was because he was depressed; it turned out he had Hodgkin's disease, and he died slowly, shrinking and wasting with the chemotherapy. Don committed suicide—his second attempt—with pills. Three more bit the dust in car crashes. Jack Richie, Susan Miller, and Debby. And one friend was hit by a car when she was crossing the street.

By these standards, Alice thought, looking at the eight fingers splayed out on the sheet, I should probably consider myself lucky. There was blood on the sheet. An Indian resident had come into the room armed to the teeth with needles of vastly different sizes. He had been trying for half an hour to insert one into her arm to start a new IV.

"Oh my," he said, looking at her arm with the yellowish rubber tourniquet pinching it. "Such veins! Again and again such veins!" He undid the rubber tube from her left arm, put it on her right, and told her to clench her fist, which she did weakly. He poked her arm with his long fingers, tapped it, stared at it until it turned blue, said, "Oh my!" and then transferred the whole apparatus to her left arm again.

This time he stuck in a long needle, said, "Oh my!" when it missed the vein, then dug beneath the skin with his needle, probing blindly. "Such veins!" There were tiny red and white dots along the inside of her arms. The white dots were scars from the IV. The red ones were newer IV sites that hadn't yet formed scar tissue. She pointed them out to all her friends.

"Tracks," she would say, showing off, holding her long arm out.

"Ah," they would say, looking away.

"This is called a drain," she would say, lifting the sheet and revealing a long twisted tube running out of her hip. It was frothy with pink bubbles and liquid inside, like the clear curled straws she used to drink strawberry milk from as a child.

"This is called a pressure bandage." She would point to a thick white wad that swaddled her right hip. "I get oxacillin every six hours," she would add. "It stings and it's cold when it runs in."

She watched her friends squirm, pretending to be interested, and she took malign pleasure in it.

The only visitors she really liked, other than her mother and brother and Simchas and Dr. Davis, were not her friends at all. They were her mother's. They would come to Alice's hospital room because her mother wouldn't leave it, and they would talk and gossip as if they were home on the phone. One spoke through her nose and sometimes cried because her daughter was a lesbian and had brought a girlfriend home for Passover. Another, Lili Hoffman, reminisced about escaping Germany during the war and living in a French convent with bedbugs. Mrs. Hoffman brought Alice jars of homemade jam. One of Alice's favorite visitors was a small, sprightly lady named Annie Bech who came into town from Westport for singing lessons every Tuesday and Thursday. She spent most of the rest of her time exercising and lifting weights. Her eyes sparkled and her grip was iron when she greeted Alice. She could tap dance and often shuffled off to Buffalo on her way out the door. Alice would lie quietly, daydreaming and half listening to her mother's friends, as she used to when she was a little girl and her parents had parties and she would lie in the hall where no one could see her. She could remember the smell of the gold carpet.

"Feeling a little hostile today, dear?" her mother asked mildly, coming in and seeing the notebook on Alice's stomach. She had drawn a very crude but instantly recognizable caricature of Miss Darty brandishing a large dripping hypodermic.

"Uh huh," she said and drew a bubble over the cartoon nurse's cap wings. "No!!!" she wrote in the bubble.

"She wouldn't give me my shot before I went to x-ray this morning and then she said I was sick," Alice said, her lower lip pushing out farther with each word. "I hate her," Alice added. "It *hurts,*" she said a moment later. "It always hurts. *Everything* hurts."

Her mother opened a yellow bag she had brought in. "Raspberry tart," she coaxed. "Delicious raspberry tart!"

"Mommy, I'm so miserable," Alice said, taking the tart and pushing it into her mouth between sobs. She returned to her drawing, adding frown lines to the nurse's brow and a wart to her chin.

"Ooowwwww," she suddenly hollered, tears smeared all over her face. She hung on to the aluminum bars, her knuckles turning grayish white, her legs flapping like idiot wings.

Her mother stood by the bed, pushing her fists into Alice's thighs. "I've got it!" she cried at last as she pressed a knot of muscles and the spasm ceased.

"Don't let go," Alice whispered desperately.

Dr. Witherspoons walked in, stopped, and looked at them.

"Come here," Alice's mother said to him. Looking startled by her authoritative tone, he obeyed. Alice's mother stood with her hands pressed against Alice's thighs and a needlepoint under her arm.

"Put your hands here," Alice's mother ordered, and Dr. Witherspoons sat by the bed with his hands stuffed into Alice's thighs. Alice wondered if his hands were insured, wanting to break all his fingers.

"I c-c-can't stand it," she said, snuffling in the mucus, which she thought must make her look extremely undignified. "Help me," she said, the last word trailing off into a pitiful wail. "H-help. I can't stand it. Something stronger. Please, please, for the p-pain." Great reserves of self-pity found their way to the surface. "Please," she wailed. She couldn't stop, though she knew this was doing her cause no good. She had grabbed Dr. Witherspoons's arm.

"You see?" Dr. Witherspoons said, removing her clammy hand from his white sleeve. "You're begging. Begging for drugs. Do you want to become addicted to morphine? Think about it," he said, looking down at her and suddenly reminding her of Mr. Marcus, her English teacher. "If it were only for a few weeks, we'd put you on it," he said. "But we don't know how long this is going to go on."

Dr. Witherspoons's logic escaped Alice, who was thinking back to the morphine she'd gotten immediately after the exploratory surgery. It had made her feel as if she had no legs.

"Morphine, morphine," she said. "Can't stand it. Detoxify me when I'm better." And, when he looked at her severely, she imagined kicking him, lifting up the hopeless legs and landing blows on his jaw, in his gut, below his belt.

"You mustn't use drugs as a crutch, Alice," he said.

I wish I had a fucking crutch, she thought, so I could hit you over the head with it. Listen, you high-priced sadist, she wanted to say, help me or get me another doctor. But all she could do was cry.

"L-l-l-" she stuttered as if she were having a stroke. She finally gave up and wailed, at the top of her lungs, until Dr. Witherspoons, his nose in the air, said, "You see?" to her mother and left.

Stephanie Carter looked at her watch. "He's coming," she warned in a whisper from her lookout at the door. "I'll be right here," she added.

Dr. Witherspoons strode in, hands in his white coat. Often, when Alice imagined him, she pictured only the white coat and the healthy hands, each in its proper place on a body that only rarely appeared to claim them. The white coat and the tan hands, like a top hat on a ghost.

Without nodding or saying hello, the white coat moved to the foot of Alice's bed; her visitors always walked directly to its head. One tanned hand came out of one pocket of the white coat, the other out of the other. It was the same every day. Alice would watch the hands, fingers spread, move toward her spindly ankle. She would watch the strong fingers close around her ankle, would watch the hands rotate the leg outward, turning the foot toward the edge of the bed. First one leg, then the other.

She would shriek, sometimes passing out and sometimes not. "Don't do that, please don't," she had begged at first. The hips never actually moved and neither foot could possibly turn out toward the edge of the bed or in toward the other foot—her joints were unyielding blocks of bone. Why did he insist on twisting this inflamed solid mass? she asked. But Dr. Witherspoons never replied; he simply twisted.

She thought about it and thought about it, and finally decided Dr. Witherspoons was determining the degree of inflammation from the decibel of her screams. Alice considered this a primitive diagnostic technique, and as soon as Dr. Witherspoons stepped out of the door, Stephanie would be at her side, hypodermic in hand.

"I don't like him," Stephanie would say softly as she pressed the needle into Alice, who was moaning and wet with sweat.

"You're trying to escape from reality again," said a muffled voice.

Alice's head was sunk into a soft feather pillow, her face covered by another one molded over the bridge of her nose to leave her mouth and nostrils uncovered. The pillows were from home. They originally had soft white cotton pillowcases with pink scallops, but a nurse had routinely stripped them the morning after they arrived and thrown them in the laundry.

A mitzvah, Alice thought at the time. Some pitiful poor person who can't afford good pillowcases, stuck in a ward where the lights are left on all night, is drooling on them now.

But every morning, when her sheets were changed, she cast a sly glance at the laundry cart, hoping that like Lassie they had miraculously returned home. Her pillows were now covered by scratchy cases with SHADOW OF THE VALLEY HOSPITAL stamped on them in black.

I love my pillows, she thought, as the top one was pulled off her face.

"You're asleep," announced Dr. Witherspoons. "Again."

"So?"

"You are using sleep as an escape," said Dr. Witherspoons, looking prim and concerned, very much like her Latin teacher when she discovered Alice and Jeff necking in a car in the high-school parking lot.

I am using sleep as an escape, she thought. Exactly. "So?"

"It's a crutch," said Dr. Witherspoons, putting his tan hands in his pockets and furrowing his high tan brow.

Again a crutch, she thought. I should be so lucky. "An unfortunate metaphor, doctor."

"It's not healthy to sleep all the time," he said.

She put the pillow over her head again.

"You're escaping from reality," he said, pulling it off again.

So Alice propped the pillow behind her head and turned on the TV set.

"Okay?" she asked Dr. Witherspoons, who frowned and walked out.

Alice concluded that the daytime TV audience must consist of weak and sickly housewives, nauseated and achy from so much polishing. The ads for Tide and Duz and all the oddly named and oddly spelled household cleaning aids—ads she had expected, ads she remembered from her after-school daytime TV days in Westport—alternated with advertising for headache and diarrhea remedies. When she saw women in blouses grimacing over what she now regarded as piffling ailments, she became self-righteous and enraged.

"This is my wife," an earnest fellow would murmur tenderly, turning his head to show the hint of gray at his temple, one arm around a smiling woman, the other reaching for a bottle of Geritol. "She takes care of herself."

"So did *I,* you fucking asshole," Alice would scream, sometimes hurling a toothbrush at the tiny screen suspended from the ceiling. "Fucking hubris, you asshole. Stupid, fucking Geritol, who do you think watches this stupid station at this ridiculous hour? Sick people who took care of themselves, you smarmy snake-oil creeps."

Then "General Hospital" would come back on.

"We're doing everything we can," the cute young doctor would say as his assistant, his brother's wife with whom he was having a hot but troubled affair, snapped off her rubber gloves.

Alice would settle back into her pillows and her mouth would slowly hang open, as if she were sleeping on the train. The ten-year-old boy for whom they were doing everything they could was someone's half brother, she wasn't sure whose, and had been precariously hanging on for over a month. Alice hoped he would die soon. It occurred to her that she hoped all the characters would die soon and that perhaps was why she watched the show.

"Not here," the young doctor said to his sister-in-law, sultry and seductive in her operating greens.

"What are you doing?" her mother asked when she came in that afternoon.

Alice's four pillows were piled on her lap, the red hand mirror leaning against them.

"Nothing," she said. She had been squeezing pimples, an activity requiring two hands, and had cleverly propped the mirror up with pillows. "I wish I could sit next to someone. I can't sit next to people on a couch like normal people."

She felt cut off and remote, like the wrong species dropped by mistake among humans in this hospital bed. Any real physical contact was too painful, and the sexual gropings, or when her mother stroked her forehead or held her hand, seemed token contact—the tolerant humans periodically petting the creature. She looked at her mother over the bed bars.

"Anyone," she said. "An old lady on the bus. I'd settle for that. To be pressed up against an old lady on the bus."

"There, there," her mother said, taking her hand. "There, there."

"Will you take the cigarette out of your mouth?" Simchas Fresser asked. He stood at the end of the bed, his face behind a huge camera bearing every accessory Alice had ever seen. The camera was so tarted up with gadgets that he couldn't carry it and had screwed it to a tripod.

"Do you really need that cigarette hanging from your mouth, Alice?"

She thought it looked decadent and cool, and had it between her lips on purpose. But she didn't tell Simchas, who would have made fun of her. She paid no attention to him.

"All right," he said. "Stubborn." His camera whirred and clicked like a small animal. He dragged the tripod from spot to spot around the bed, then stood on the chair, leaned back against the windows, hung over the bed, switching lenses as he went. She blew smoke, looked serious, smiled, sulked, removed and replaced the cigarette in what she imagined were elegant poses. A Chinese vase Simchas had brought back from a hypnotists' convention in San Francisco stood by the bed holding yellow freesia.

She put her cigarette out carefully and suddenly felt cranky. Why was he taking pictures of her in bed? It was so stupid. Simchas's cologne filled the room and nauseated her slightly.

"I don't want to play anymore," she said. "Take your toys and go home." She turned her face in to the pillow.

"Dry up," Simchas said in his heavy Israeli accent, and Alice almost laughed. At least the film is black and white, she thought, feeling the pimples on her forehead. And there were two red, swollen ones on her chin.

For the next three days she dined on celery. Even the demure white eggs perched in their little dish turned her stomach. The dirty knishes Stephanie brought her from the street dripped and smelled as they had never dripped and smelled before. But the long stalks of celery, translucent and crisp in the big bowl her mother put out for her, looked cool and clean. The delicate pale stalks toward the center glistened with drops of cold water. Alice poured salt on the celery, stick by stick, held it in her hand, and chewed loudly, watching television or staring at the ceiling.

The dietician introduced a little plate of shriveled raw vegetables, proudly called "crudités" on the hospital menu. She was sure to include carrots and olives and cherry tomatoes, even though Alice wrote "Celery Only" all over her menu and refused to eat the other vegetables. The skinny celery sticks were a little dry when they reached her, looking whitish as if they had been sprinkled with powder, but Alice ate them. The tomatoes and carrots and olives sat in the crumpled cellophane, untouched, next to the plate of gray roast beef *au* gray *jus*.

Dr. Witherspoons tried to frighten her, presenting his white coat by her bedside and reporting on anemia and potassium deficiencies. Alice said, "I'm escaping from reality" and "If God wanted me to eat he'd have given me an appetite."

Her mother tried to tempt her with plump dainties from quaint bakeries run by little old ladies in little white aprons. Alice knew if she were quiet and let her reach the proper pitch of praise her mother would succumb to her own rhetoric and eat the cream puffs herself.

Simchas brought her a Polish salami that smelled like

feet, and Dr. Davis dangled exotic fruit that also smelled like feet.

"Go away please," she told them, sinking her teeth into a long green stalk studded with salt and ostentatiously tearing it away from a large bite in her mouth.

"Yum, yum," she would murmur as the salt dissolved on the yellow coat her tongue had worn since coming to the hospital. Sometimes she held the celery up to the window, staring at the light that came through.

Her mother asked her if she'd like a little chicken salad with her celery. No, Alice told her, although it had been three days without real food and she really wouldn't have minded. But, after the fuss she had made, she found herself too embarrassed to eat. They'll think I didn't mean it, she thought. And all night she battled against visions of creamy chicken salad surrounding little bits of her celery.

In the morning, her tray held oatmeal—a thick white bowl of steaming thick oatmeal. I really shouldn't worry my mother by not eating, Alice decided. How could I have been quite so selfish? she wondered, pouring four paper packets of sugar on the satiny cereal.

Louie Scifo's voice seemed the most menacing to Alice. Louie Scifo himself crawled in and out of her vision like a tiny, shiny shelled bug. But his voice seemed to Alice more like a deadly plant—a pulpy Venus's-flytrap, for example. The words made their thick way through a gummy throat, emerging, it seemed to Alice, with great difficulty and for the specific purpose of making her flesh creep.

"You know your poor mother has been pulling her hairs out over you," Louie would say comfortingly.

"Really our name is de Scifo," he once said. "Nobility, you understand? But a cousin stole the title." He pronounced it ti-ul.

"Naked," she heard her mother saying. "Stark naked on Lexington Avenue, and with no shoes!"

"Um-bee-lee-vable," said Louie Scifo. "You gotta laugh, you understand?"

"So big deal," Simchas Fresser said. "Naked? No shoes? What about my late wife?" That was what he called his ex. "I saw her on the street and she gave me her card. Sarah Fresser, Ph.D. Can you believe it? A judge who wrote her dissertation on George Eliot."

"When I was on the bench, they wouldn't even take women," said Louie de Scifo.

Alice realized she was not quite awake and didn't have to open her eyes or hear any more of their conversation. She drifted back to sleep as Simchas explained that, while his ex-wife's father had sent her through law school as soon as she left Simchas, he hadn't done one thing for them when they were married.

"Oh," Alice said when she woke up and Simchas was still there. "Isn't that lovely!" she said, patting the small gray object. She didn't know what it was, but she was sure it was meant well. The card said, "To Alice, the most cheerful friend I've worked with." Simchas had never expressed himself so tenderly before, and she was touched.

"Very useful," said Simchas. "It's a fan—a little battery-operated fan. I got it at Hammacher Schlemmer. You can put it by your bed."

"Very convenient," Alice said. "Thank you."

Simchas Fresser was the only person Alice had ever met who had actually bought something at Hammacher Schlemmer. He carried the catalogue in his briefcase, and not only had he bought something, he had bought many things—an electric towel rack, a battery-operated crumb vacuum for the kitchen table, hot packs that plugged into swirling foot baths, and electric shoe polishers with a black buffer to the left and a brown buffer to the right. He bought a traveling case with forty-five containers for pills held in by elegant leather straps. He even bought pens with flashlights on them.

Alice thought it was really no wonder that he felt so at home in her hospital room rigged with the intricate contraptions she had only grudgingly gotten used to. And then, as if not satisfied with the room's mechanical motif, Simchas began adding to it. He brought the little fan. He lent her the tape recorder that played his own deep voice. He brought her a white-sound machine that sounded like waves on the beach and made her want to pee.

"And you really should have a camera," he told her, as her mother would have told her to wear a hat in the cold.

"Uh huh," she said, not interested enough to argue. A camera. What nonsense. She had once had a Brownie. She had been six perhaps, or seven, and had taken pictures of the cat appropriately named Spotnose asleep in her dresser drawer. And, when she was fourteen, she had been given a cheap Polaroid, called a Swinger, that took, under her guidance at least, the same appallingly dull pictures of the same pet.

And now I don't even have a cat, Alice thought. Life without pets. And I never move. I'd have to take the same picture, over and over, like Andy Warhol. Twenty identical exposures to use up just one roll of film.

"What a stupid idea," she said, irritated now and wondering if Simchas was making fun of her. "Twenty pictures of my toes in traction. Brilliant."

"Portraits," Simchas said. "Portraits of your visitors. And never again call me stupid." He began to pack up his gear.

Alice was about to tell him she had called his *idea* stupid, and that she didn't want pictures of her visitors if she couldn't take pictures of pets like everyone else, when a real visitor appeared at the door.

"Well?" Simchas said to Alice as he left, as if this woman at the door somehow proved his point.

Her name was Colette and she seemed to take it seriously. She had short, curly brown hair, was generally accompanied by two snorting bulldogs, and maintained a thorough French accent after living in the United States for almost forty years.

Had she never wondered under what circumstances Jeffrey's phone had been pulled out of the wall? What, thought Alice, had Colette imagined the screams were, and the occasional thuds coming from her son's room? Once Alice had run down the stairs, weeping, terrified of the violence she elicited from the shouting, stamping Jeff upstairs. She saw Colette sprawled on the couch, reading the newspaper.

Oh, God, Alice thought in a vaguely hopeful way. Maybe she'll help me, tell me this is wrong, forbid us to see each other.

"My darling," Colette had said with her hoarse voice and rumbling "r." Alice, lying weakly on the couch, her head in Colette's lap, thought how wonderful this woman was, how romantic, how like a French novel. Colette called everyone, even the Gristede's delivery boy, "my darling." Alice's panic eased.

"My darling," Colette said softly, stroking her head. "Do you love him?"

"Uh huh," Alice said dully, the vague hope that Colette would help vanishing.

"Is he the man you want?" Colette said. One of the attendant sleeping bulldogs snorted liquidly.

"Uh huh," Alice said, with an uneasy sense that Jeff was not really a man and that she wasn't entirely sure what she wanted him for.

"Then you two will *sur*-vive," Colette said, the accent falling on the first syllable of the last word. "You will *sur*-vive."

"Okay," Alice sniffled, but *sur*-viving upstairs with the man she loved was something she decided to put off to tomorrow, and she walked home, kicking pebbles.

When she thought of those days now, they seemed like just another adolescent excess, on a par with love beads or a journal full of hysterical poetry, or Lawrence Durrell. Adolescent excesses are outgrown, and she was sure she had duly outgrown this one. But what a fool I was, she often thought, and then she squirmed with embarrassment at the memory as at phony dialogue in a play.

"My darling," Colette said now, her tiny hands and painted red nails on the aluminum railing, her curly head approaching dramatically to plant a delicate kiss on Alice's slightly sunken cheek. "How long your eyelash are, my darling! Is it because you're so pale? Your eyelash are quite startling."

"Really?" said Alice. Gee, she's not so bad, Alice thought.

"It is odd lying down always, is it not? You know, I was consumptive many years ago."

Consumptive! Alice thought. How romantic. She was probably delirious too. I wish I had a French accent.

"I spent some time in a sanitarium. Have you read *The Magic Mountain?*"

"Sort of," Alice said.

"It's so difficult to adjust when you get out, my darling. It's a syndrome," she said, her guttural "r" turning that clinical word into passion. *"The Magic Mountain syndrome."*

Alice had no idea what Colette was talking about. She thought of Colette as she had always seen her, languid on the couch with her two dogs snoring beside her, smoking French cigarettes behind a newspaper, domestic and decadent at the same time. To Alice, she seemed perfectly well adjusted. And the only thing Alice could remember from *The Magic Mountain* was some young man taking his temperature all the time.

"That's interesting," Alice said, thinking of what good salad dressing Colette made and how deftly she peeled pears.

"Jeffrey sends you his love," Colette said.

"I hate Jeffrey," Alice said, startled from her reverie, and realizing too late that it wasn't polite.

Colette seemed very worldly and said, "Still?" She patted Alice's pale hand. "You must have loved him very much to hate him so now," she said compassionately.

No, no, Alice wanted to explain. You don't understand! He hit me! But that would have been really ungracious, so she smiled weakly and said nothing.

"What you had was ver-ry special, my darling," Colette gurgled, and then, as if that were encouraging, as if she had said, Stiff upper lip, or *Nil desperandum,* or Sleep tight don't let the bedbugs bite, she moved toward the door. "Ver-r-ry special," she repeated reverently, and vanished.

He kicked me, too, Alice wanted to shout after her. And once he spit in my face. It was disgusting. And he blamed me for everything. Everything! Even the Vietnam War . . . But Colette was gone, so Alice turned on the soap opera in which all the women were named for liqueurs and days of the week, and waited for her shot.

Simchas was enveloped by chaos. He complained and missed morning appointments and made hysterical phone calls to his stockbroker and tried different combinations of anti-depressants and tranquilizers and tax shelters on himself. He had only unpleasant things to say about everyone, and he said them loudly and over and over again.

Sometimes when Alice looked at him, tall and snarling, she thought of a proverb she had once heard somewhere: A drowning man reaches for a snake.

"He's a snake," her mother once said, absent-mindedly pushing the wide blunt needlepoint needle through the hole and into her finger. "Ouch. But he's funny, isn't he? In an awful sort of way."

He was funny, as very small truculent children are funny, and Alice found his vast disgust sympathetic. The world was so troublesome to him that she felt less shamed by her own self-pity.

"Oy gevalt, Mrs. Pulman," they heard him greet that lady down the hall.

"Johnson," Mrs. Pulman replied irritably, and they heard the little slap of her bare foot on the floor.

"Ah, Brenda," Simchas greeted her mother. "And Longo the Magnificent!" he added, as if he were surprised to see her there. He sat on the window sill. "Brenda," he said, "I bought a few things at Saks and sent them to your house in Connecticut. It saves me so much tax. It's wonderful, your house in Connecticut."

"Actually," Alice's mother said, "I don't want your underwear sent to my house."

"It's not underwear!" cried Simchas. Alice's mother eyed him. She lifted her head slightly, tilted it back until her chin was in the air, opened her mouth, and laughed. How beautiful she looks when she throws back her head and laughs, Alice thought. Alice watched her mother proudly. And suddenly Alice wondered if she was flashing her open laugh and handsome profile for Simchas's sake.

"Simchas," her mother said, "I've been thinking. . . ."

"Mazel tov!" barked Simchas, laughing and looking from Alice to her mother, like the terrible eight-year-old wit at a seder. He wiggled his wedge of hair furiously at the absence of a response. The matching eyebrows undulated below. "Mazel tov, mazel tov," he repeated.

Alice's mother said, "Yes, yes, now listen, Simchas—about your little machines . . ."

"Some of them are *quite* large," he muttered.

"Why don't you try one of your nice little machines on Alice?"

"My machines!" Simchas cried. He jumped off the window sill in his excitement, his arms in the air. He waded over to Alice.

"My machines on Longo!"

Then he stopped short, his arms falling to his sides. "My machines," he said thoughtfully. "But why?"

"Yeah," said Alice, who thought she was sufficiently wired already. "Why?"

"Hook up electrodes and train the leg muscles to relax. It might help the spasms."

Simchas's small eyes glittered. He stood up straight and tall and threw back his head as if to swipe the ceiling with the black triangle of hair. "Electrodes on Longo's legs!" he said with dignity. "Electrodes on Longo's legs!" Then he picked up his briefcase, turned, and marched out the door.

Alice's mother said, "You know, when he leaves, I always think we should count the spoons."

The wires crisscrossed like highways. The thick white wire running between the box on the wall and the call button pinned to her bed; the clear narrow tube that ran from the sagging IV sack into her arm; the TV remote-control wire that stretched from the undersized set to her bedside table; the black rubber hose attached to the blood-pressure machine, a grim festoon on its dull metal stand; the radio cord; the bedside-lamp cord; the strings between her booties and the traction weights; the wire that ran into the small box of controls for the bed. Like a Chasid in phylacteries, Alice thought, looking around her. And, starting at the head of the bed, running the length of it to the foot, was an aluminum bar clamped onto two poles attached to the bed. Hanging from the bar was a chain that dangled a metal triangle, much like the ones Alice had hit self-consciously with a little wand in kindergarten. This triangle was called a trapeze and was there for her to pull, to lift herself up. Trapeze indeed, Alice would think, trying to lift herself up to facilitate a bedpan, and usually collapsing from weakness before the nurse could push the shallow pan underneath her.

Alice looked around the room, at the bottles and blankets, rolls of gauze, here and there an empty plastic hypodermic lying like a discarded shell case. She had never been neat. Her room had been strewn with toys when she was a child, with clothes and books when she got older. She thought fondly of that benign mess, turned the pillow around to hide SHADOW OF THE VALLEY HOSPITAL, and stared dully at the ceiling.

When Simchas pushed through the door, huge shopping bags hanging from his wrists, it was already afternoon. He lined up small walnut-cased machines on the wheeled table by her bed, plugged in twisted brown wires, and turned silver dials.

"Gonna play the top forty, Simchas?"

Headphones balanced precariously on the peak of hair, and he pointed to them, indicating that he couldn't hear her.

"You are such an asshole," she said slowly and distinctly. But he shook his head again.

Needles suddenly wagged back and forth across brightly lit dials while the machines beeped and bleated and clicked. Simchas's eyes were as wide as beady eyes could be. He bit his lower lip in concentration, the corners of his mouth turned up in a slight, unhealthy smile. He cackled twice, squeezed cold, glistening jelly from a tube onto her thighs, and cackled again. Alice wondered if his pleasure were at all related to her parted thighs and decided with regret that it was because of the machines and the machines alone.

Simchas pushed minute electrodes onto the goo and taped them down. They were attached to his machines by slender wires. "When you move your arm—go ahead, move your arm," he said.

Alice lifted her arm and the machines blinked and beeped.

"You see? When you move your arm, you tense the muscles in your thighs. You don't have to do that to move your arm. It's tension. You see? And that of course makes you have spasms." He was speaking in his professional voice, resonant and reassuring and respectable, so different from the petulant whine he ordinarily used. This foreign, knowledgeable voice impressed her more than she cared to admit. She took his hand and kissed it. He patted her head lightly in acknowledgment, then put his hand back on a walnut case.

"So you see, if you tense the thigh muscles, the electrodes will pick it up and the bells will go off and the dials will spin." He patted another of the machines. "That's biofeedback," he said.

"What is?"

"The *bells*. The *needles*. How else would you know if you weren't relaxed?"

Alice looked at her legs, splayed, bare, and pocked with electrodes. She put the headphones on. She could hear the bells perfectly well without them, but Simchas seemed to think it would be better form with. Then she moved her arms. The needles flew across their dials, boxes beeped, and her legs went into spasms.

"Never mind," said Simchas, still determined after their fifth attempt. "We'll try again tomorrow."

He packed the quieted boxes into the shopping bags, began a long account of demands from his little brother in Israel for Keds, and then, idly fingering a hypodermic that had strayed to the window sill, stabbed himself in the thumb.

"My hand, my hand!" he cried. "It's bleeding! I'm bleeding!" And he ran to the emergency room, the wound wrapped in his white handkerchief.

"In a hospital no less," he said when he came back for his machines. "Very dangerous. Full of germs."

.   .   .

Her friends from college didn't like to visit and accordingly didn't often come by. One friend, a graduate student in classics, came and read Tacitus with Alice at her request. Alice had never been able to read Tacitus. She was a poor student and Tacitus had the unsettling habit of leaving most of the words out. Drugged and preoccupied, she fared no better now. But, as Anne stood over her bed and read the spare little sentences dispensing with great men, Alice stared stupidly at her own copy and was soothed, as if the words were prayer.

Another friend, an earnest Quaker who had once given her a recording of Mahler's First Symphony because the lopsided waltz of the second movement reminded him of her—awkwardly elegant, he said—drew a delicate pencil drawing of her face in profile. But she wasn't very nice to him and he never came back.

When her friend James Wellington came, he casually put his feet on the bed and she winced. He took them down immediately, but she lay miserably aware of the strain, the remoteness of a once easy friendship.

The nurses who wandered in to take her temperature and blood pressure stared at James in his orange jumpsuit. He was from an old Boston family, the maternal side of which was named James, and everyone in his family had last names as first names. He lived off a huge trust fund invested for some obscure reason at the anachronistic rate of 4 percent, and with his chiseled, even-featured face, slightly pursed lips, and streaky makeup, he looked, Alice thought, like the last figure in a tableau vivant called "The Decay of the American Family." She had always thought James exotic, but now the colorful figure leafing through her magazines and trying to introduce amusing anecdotes into the uneasy silence seemed garish and out of place.

Her other friends seemed equally irrelevant.

"Do you think," asked one, "that it's terrible to put all the books by professors I've slept with on a separate shelf? They've all written a little note on the flyleaf and signed them."

"Do you think," asked another, "that raspberry-flavored spermicide is obscene?"

"Should I mention in my applications to medical school that I've wanted to be a doctor since I was five?"

"Is it okay to wear a blue shirt with black pants?"

"I can't keep the cat from pissing in my plants."

Hundred-dollar phone bills, muggings, acting classes, affairs, term papers on Tasso, new boots, Smokenders, grades. Alice didn't care so very much. She hung up the phone, turned on the soap operas, and wished that she were better.

She noticed that she had not only slipped into hospital jargon—voiding, drinking cc's of water instead of glasses of it—but that she had become interested in her body in a new, technical way as well. She cared how many cc's she took in and let out. She followed the nuances of her fever closely. She insisted on seeing her x-rays and having them explained to her, and watched the gray canyons and plateaus slowly erode with intense yet almost detached professional interest.

"Can I see my chart?" Alice asked Dr. Witherspoons one day. He was holding a folder with her name on it. But it turned out that her chart was actually a pile of papers occupying a corner of the nurses' station, a four-foot tower of yellow, green, and blue sheets that expanded as reliably as a population and was viewed by the nurses as a heinous imposition.

Alice had realized some time ago—and it was with something of a jolt—that her doctors truly had no clue as to why she was sick and had no real idea what to do to make her well. They treated symptoms because symptoms were all they could find. They ignored the most obvious symptom, pain, but the pain had by now become like another sense, like seeing or hearing or tasting. They treated the other symptoms in as many ways as they could think of—antibiotics, anti-inflammatories, traction, muscle relaxers. The antibiotics were changed every two weeks and they never made any difference, but Alice wanted to know their names.

"Sorry I haven't come to see you," her friends would call and say. "But hospitals give me the creeps."

"Yeah, me too," said Alice, although it was no longer true.

Sneezing, Alice had always maintained, was a hostile act. When her grandmother sneezed—little mincing cries of "Hetch! Hetch!"—the dog jumped into her aged lap and barked hysterically. Her grandmother finally learned to run to the bathroom, where she would hurriedly lock herself in before each outburst.

A psychiatrist had told Katie that an orgasm was like a sneeze. But Alice thought the analogy a little forced. Once she and Jeffrey had been making love on the beach, in the cold autumn air under the bright autumn stars, waves lapping quietly along the shore. Alice was shivering and uninterested but didn't want a scene and so lay passively on the hard, wet sand. And then, in the middle, she sneezed—a great bugle of a sneeze that sent Jeff flying a foot in the air. Alice laughed uncontrollably, rolling across the beach, getting sand in her mouth. He was insulted, and she was glad.

When she sneezed now she no longer laughed. Her legs whipped through the air just as poor Jeff had done that night.

"Are you all right?" Dr. Davis asked. She was rubbing the top of her nose and muttering, "Grapefruit, grapefruit, grapefruit."

"Going to sneeze," she said. "Very . . . grapefruit, grapefruit . . . painful. Told this helps."

"Ah," he said. "Perhaps a Kleenex would be more useful?"

The sneeze suddenly broke through the incantation of "grapefruits" and Alice's legs spun. Dr. Davis held her hand and wiped her nose with his handkerchief.

"I think you're infantilizing me," she said, using a word she had recently heard her mother employ. Dr. Davis had gallantly given her his handkerchief as a present.

"Nonsense," he said and began playing Piggy Went to Market on her fingers, as he didn't dare touch her toes. He was sitting lightly on the chair, elegant as an egg in a nest, and his legs were crossed. One of his socks showed casually beneath a trouser leg, unwrinkled and a soft beige color. He began to tell her how to make coarse Tuscan peasant bread.

"It has no salt!" he kept saying in amazement. He had just left his Italian cooking class. "It has no salt!"

"How old are you?" she asked him. She knew he was somewhere between her father and her grandfather, but she wanted to know where.

"Why, sixty of course," he said airily, waving one arm as if it were trailing chiffon, and he continued with his recipe. Sixty, she thought. Not fifty but sixty. Her father was forty-seven, her grandfather sixty-seven. No wonder she could not call Dr. Davis by his first name. She always called him Dr. Davis when she spoke about him. When she spoke to him, she avoided calling him anything. His daughter was over thirty.

"It has no salt, and in Tuscany people put olive oil on it instead of butter!"

He's old enough to be my grandfather, she thought. Not my father, my grandfather. But he looked so elegant, perched on his chair, boring her. Well, he doesn't look sixty, she decided. He looks only fifty.

"You don't look sixty," she said, interrupting him.

He smiled, pleased that she was thinking about him instead of the saltless bread.

"Would you like some lunch, angel?" her mother asked her brother.

"Um, Mom," said her brother, twisting in his chair, his face screwed up. "Mom," he began again.

"Yes, angel?"

Her brother was chewing on a stiff piece of French bread smeared with Brie. He had come back from a month in Paris an insufferable Francophile who peeled his fruit and drank his morning coffee in a cereal bowl. He brought Alice the Brie and bread and a bottle of wine for a picnic in bed. Little chunks of the crust nestled in the folds of his sweater.

"Mom, do you think you could stop calling me angel?" he said, wrinkling up his nose even more.

"All right, dear. I'll try."

Her brother sighed with relief and pushed more bread into his mouth, chewing and smacking his lips in a loud and decidedly un-Gallic manner. As a child he had devised an efficient if unlovely method of dining—lowering his face to the level of the plate and pushing the food directly into his open mouth. Although this method eliminated the risk of stray rolling peas and slippery leafs of lettuce hitting the floor, he had abandoned it about the time he reached puberty. But his excessively noisy and energetic chewing had continued, and Alice wondered how it had gone over in Paris. Normally she would have pointed it out to him and told him to stop, but he had brought her the Brie and wine and a collection of tiny toys—little blocks stored in a matchbox, a plastic rabbit, with a spring and suction cup, that leaped off her bedside table.

Alice had played baby with her brother—putting him in a carriage and pushing it around the house.

"You be the baby," she had instructed him.

"Gah-gah-goo-goo," he would, answer, because he was a baby, the carriage was his, and that was all he could say. And now even he, her little brother, was bringing her childish gifts. And she was playing with them, shooting the rabbit at the TV screen, building a toy city and knocking it down again.

It's because I'm not tall anymore, she thought. I'm only four feet tall, the height of this bed, the height of a child. Or worse, a midget.

"Shall I peel you an orange?" her mother asked her, and then peeled it and absent-mindedly ate it herself.

"Mom," Alice whined.

"Oh, Alice! You look exactly the way you did on the boat!" her mother said, chuckling. Alice scowling against bright blue skies and full white sails was a family joke. And she was usually worse when her mother was not aboard.

"Do you mind?" her father would ask her, stepping across her, untying the halyard and trying to gather the flapping jib in over her head.

She would wince as the white nylon smacked her across the face. Why do they make me come on these trips? But she would never say anything aloud, ostentatiously continuing to read instead, thinking, I'll show them, although she was never sure what she would show to whom.

Then the jib would sprawl, as if suddenly dead, across her open book.

"She's not even reading," her brother would complain from the tiller. "She's just pretending. She's stupid."

"Do you think you could move for a minute, just for a minute, so we don't all drown?" her father would ask, his arms full of sail.

"T-t-t-t," Alice would cluck in disgust and walk sullenly back to the cockpit, which was padded with blue cushions, her brother, Eileen, and Eileen's two small sons—all of whom she hated. She hated Eileen most of all, and with her mother not present, Alice regarded this perfectly ordinary summer neighbor with suspicion as well.

She really thinks she's a hot number, Alice said to herself, eyeing Eileen over her book.

Eileen was small but not delicate. Her little limbs and short-waisted body were dwarfish rather than petite. She was small-breasted, but how those poor, mean mammaries were pushed and squeezed until they peeked, as hard and unappealing as two bald heads, over her low neckline. She was a respectable New Yorker with a house in Westport, a respectable husband, and dyed blonde hair, but those tits, Alice thought as she stared at them from behind the protective volume, those tits spell trouble! Eileen is as repellent as a pug, but the pug is panting, Alice decided, wishing she had stayed home, or at least driven to Montauk with her mother instead of sailing there. Her pretty smiling mother with a normal chest.

"Don't yell at your brother!" Eileen screamed at her son with wildly buck teeth who was yelling, "Stop it!" at the cuter son with straight teeth, who'd been teasing him.

The cuter son, the younger son, began exclaiming that the water was "exquisite," the sky "divine." He was five. He sounds like my grandmother, Alice thought. His mother patted him on his silky head. Alice wanted to smack everyone.

The boat bobbed on the windless water, content to move in no direction but up and down, and Alice realized she was thoroughly seasick.

We'll never get out of here, never, she thought, as if she were in a flooded elevator instead of the bright, wide sound. We're stuck. Stuck here forever. With *them.* Her stomach twisted and wallowed in nausea. Eileen sat next to her father, who manned the tiller with great dignity, and fed him Ring Dings.

I'm going to be sick, Alice thought, and hurried down the steps, backward, as her father had taught her, through the cabin and into the head.

"Be calm," she said softly, sitting on the toilet with her head against the wall. "There are hours left." Then she saw her underpants. They were dark with blood. Oh, great, she thought. My first period. She wanted her mother, but there was only Eileen, suggestively feeding her father.

Alice dried her eyes, wadded up some toilet paper, and sat strangely guilty, as if toilet paper were bad manners.

Now Alice looked at her mother, who was peeling another orange. She's awfully disorganized, Alice thought, watching her mother absent-mindedly throw the peels into her pocketbook. But she's here, she changed my room, got the private nurses.

"Mom," Alice said gently, pointing to the pocketbook.

"Oh!" her mother cried, placing the half-peeled orange in an overflowing ashtray while she emptied the bag.

"Oh!" she cried, glancing at the ash-covered fruit.

"That's okay, Mom," Alice said, thinking of her mother meeting them at the end of that awful sail to Montauk. She had immediately taken Alice to a drugstore, where they bought every piece of equipment even remotely related to menstruation. Tampax and Kotex and belts and Empirin and shields and carrying cases and special bags to throw it all out in had made Alice feel legitimate, and she thought fondly of it now. "You can peel me an apple instead."

Then her grandmother walked in, tall, in a stylish red dress. She had a pale, delicate complexion and large feet.

"Oy!" she grunted, sitting down. "I'm weak as a cat."

"Kitten, Grandma. You're as weak as a kitten," Alice said. But she knew her grandmother was right, that she was as weak as a cat and that cats are not weak.

"Garbage, poison, drek," her grandmother said. "Hideous, nauseating, vile."

"What?" asked Willie.

"That dirty Forty-seventh Street," said Grandma. Every earring in the diamond district was "fit for farmers," she explained. Every earring but the two she had bought, which were "exquisite, magnificent *gems* fit for royalty and *VIP*s."

"They're very big," Alice said. Her lunch had just been served; the earrings were the size of her potato puffs.

"Simple, understated elegance," her grandmother sighed, cradling the great gold-and-diamond edifices in her hands, rocking them slightly, fixing them with a tender gaze.

"Oh, Mother!" said Alice's mother in embarrassment.

Alice's grandmother said, "God willing, your mommy will wear these someday, and then you, when I'm gone . . ." The word, the idea, caught somewhere in her soft, white throat. A tear trembled in the corner of one eye.

"What about me?" Willie asked. "Don't I get anything?"

"They're beautiful, Grandma," Alice said quickly. "You have such good taste . . . luxurious but not vulgar, chic but classic."

Her grandmother perked up. "Nothing vulgar."

"No, never vulgar."

"Where's Mommy?" her grandmother asked. Mommy had slipped out the door. "I want my beautiful daughter to look at my beautiful jewels. My gorgeous Brenda. Alice, your mommy has a face that could haunt a thousand ships."

"Launch, Grandma. Launch a thousand ships."

"Yes," her grandmother murmured. "A thousand ships."

Alice looked at her brother. He lit a fat unfiltered cigarette. Willie had been a petulant child who collected heavy rocks on vacations, forcing his father to lug suitcases filled with rubble through airports, train stations, and faraway city streets. When Alice had been forbidden to tease him, she had explained to Willie that whistling was now teasing and should therefore make him cry. When her parents caught on, she changed the signal to winking, then tapping, humming, braiding her hair. It didn't matter what it was. It always worked, sending him wailing to their parents. "Alice is *braiding*," he would cry.

Alice looked at Willie now. She began to hum.

"Hmmm, hmmm, hmmm . . ."

"Alice, quit it." He sat behind a cloud of Galloise smoke. "There is a French saying that in every love affair there is the lover and the loved," he said, hopefully examining his fingers for nicotine stains.

"Yeah?"

"So which do you think Dad is?"

"Neither." She began to wink.

"Quit it, Alice," he said, throwing the blue cigarette box at her.

"Hey! Quit it, Willie."

Willie and Alice chatted and gossiped about the girls Willie was in love with and the teachers he hated, Alice complained about Dr. Witherspoons, and they expressed disgust at the impending divorce. But most of the time they just sat quietly. Alice loved to see him there, munching potato chips and reading *Le Matin.* His face, his posture, the shape of his hands were things she knew from home, things she had always known, and they comforted her.

It was eight o'clock and the ever-cheerful Holly had already filled the room with humming and, opening the blinds, bright sunshine—much to the annoyance of Alice, who piled pillows over her ears and eyes. But, when Holly began intrepidly to bathe her with a washcloth, Alice felt childish and came out to face the animated nurse.

"Good morning, Alice!"

"Good morning, Holly."

Alice sipped her weak coffee and tried to overcome her momentary dislike for the happy Holly. Holly was a quiet, efficient nurse, beautiful and even-tempered, and Alice attributed her occasional distaste for such an unobjectionable person to jealousy. One could only admire or resent someone like Holly, and Alice alternated between the two.

"Here's your mail!" said Holly.

"Oh, thanks a lot, Holly. Mail. That's great. Thanks." There was a get-well card with a sad puppy, another with a crude cartoon and a joke she didn't get, a postcard from a friend traveling in India with so many stamps on it that she could read only the friend's signature, and a note from Jeff.

"Ick!" she said, startling Holly so that she dropped Alice's pills on the floor and had to go get another round, something that gratified Alice tremendously.

"Ick," she said again, looking at the note. Even Jeff's handwriting repelled her—the hysterical scrawl of a psychopath sending rhyming death threats. Colette's surprise at her continued strong feeling for Jeff had embarrassed Alice, who for some time after that visit protested inwardly that she didn't care one way or the other about Jeffrey Klein, that she never thought about him at all. In fact, memories occurred to her, vile little things, as unwelcome as old gum wads touched under a coffee-shop table, and she would shudder and quickly pull her hands away. Jeffrey had tricked her. He had been unreasonable and unpleasant and had tricked her into thinking he was interesting. She had been a fool, and for this she would never forgive him.

I hope he gets hit by a cement truck, she thought now, although the little note only wished her well.

How, she wondered, could he have caused her pain? How could she have allowed it? Life is short; you live only once; *carpe diem*—not *carpe* melodrama. And how could anything have upset her when she was normal? How could anything disturb anyone who could use a real toilet and sleep on his side?

Pleased with this Olympian view of things, she settled back in her pillows and waited to *carpe* Simchas Fresser or Dr. Davis, whoever arrived first.

"Can I have my shot now, Holly?" Alice asked the pretty little vision in white, with whom all the residents were in love.

"Why, of course!" said Holly, although there were really ten minutes to go. She administered it painlessly, whistling softly, and retired to a corner of the room, where she effortlessly completed a needlepoint Alice's mother had struggled with for weeks and finally given up.

Simchas came later in the day to hook her up, and the room rang with the bells of the row of little machines. As he was packing up to leave, Dr. Davis came in with a bunch of black-eyed susans.

"What a marvelous picture of Alice you took!" Dr. Davis cried, and in his enthusiasm he took Simchas's pink hand in an almost flirtatious, feminine way. "It's hanging in my office."

The photograph was black and white and very sultry. Alice had been flattered but startled when she saw it. Do I really look like that, she wondered. Lust written all over my face?

"Thank you," said Simchas Fresser, deepening his voice to sound dignified.

"He's a fag," Simchas told Alice the next day. "A raving, flaming fruit and I can't imagine what you see in him."

Dear Katie,

Do you realize we've been in the hospital for three months? And I've been in bed for four? I'm glad the Thorazine is helping you. I think I took that once. Or maybe it was Stelazine. I think I was depressed or something. Anyway, now I'm really depressed. Before I went to Italy last year, my mother said she hoped I'd see more than the ceiling. Ha ha. And look at me now.

My parents are getting a divorce and my father is being horrible to my mother, although he is as good as good can be to me. Nothing is too good or expensive for me—private room, private nurses—but with my mother he's really tight. And unfeeling, I think. He insists on going to court. Do you remember "Divorce Court" on TV, with wailing children and misused husbands and wan wives? Do you think it will be like that? With my father, tears in his eyes, saying my mother undercooked the bacon, and my mother saying my father wanted his underpants ironed?

You would think my father could wait until I got better before subjecting poor Mom to that humiliation. She is not what you'd call carefree at the moment. But there must be another woman. And he probably thinks I'll be sick so long that she won't wait for him, will desert him for another mournful man with a mustache. I say, if she won't wait, she's not worth having!

As to how long I'll be sick, whenever I ask, the doctors cough and talk about the progress of my bedsores. So we've decided to call in some specialists. My odious orthopedist took it as a personal affront, which was fine with me. And of course it is in a way. I mean he hasn't done anything, has he? Except that exploratory operation that left one leg shorter than the other. The only thing I like about Dr. Witherspoons is that he has a nagging witch of a wife. Or so I've heard.

I'm glad your recurring dream has stopped. No, I have never dreamed that my entire family was burned to a crisp in a raging fire. Are you sure it means you're hostile? Maybe it means you're concerned about them? I'm concerned about my Mom—she has an awful boyfriend.

I have two awful boyfriends—the old gent and now this hypnotist. I've never had two boyfriends at the same time before. They don't seem to mind. I'm sick, you see, so any little thing to divert me is welcomed by family and friends. (One could become a tyrant of sorts if one weren't always passing out or wetting one's bed.) And there really isn't much else to do here, you know, except cry and complain. Which I do all the rest of the time. I'm glad I don't have to visit me. I'm pretty insufferable.

Love,

Alice

The first specialist was from New Haven and, because of a widely used textbook he had written twenty years earlier (a definitive study of prosthesis cement), was something of a celebrity in the little white-coated world of Shadow of the Valley Hospital.

"Dr. O'Solomon? *The* Dr. O'Solomon?" the interns asked. "The Dr. O'Solomon who wrote *Cement and the Orthopod?*"

They milled around Alice's door all morning in anticipation of meeting him. When Dr. O'Solomon arrived, he shook their hands amiably, greeted Alice amiably, examined her x-rays with the same pleasant manner he had when he declined to examine her in the flesh, and then, smiling agreeably, pronounced himself baffled.

"He's so *friendly,*" exclaimed the interns after Dr. O'Solomon had caught the next train back to New Haven.

Specialist No. 2 traveled a shorter distance and drew less of a crowd, but Alice liked him because he limped. When Dr. Onnen announced he would like to examine her, Holly began to prepare a needle and Alice dutifully gripped the bars of the bed.

Dr. Onnen tentatively twisted her right leg, slightly outward.

"Uh," Alice groaned, determined not to scream.

"Does it hurt?" asked Dr. Onnen. "Inward rotation too? Both legs? I'll stop."

"But you have to examine me," Alice said, not wanting to impede the course of science and the chance of someone discovering how to make her well.

"I just did," said Dr. Onnen. "I don't have to torture you."

"You don't?" she asked in great confusion.

"Of course not," said Dr. Onnen, limping to the window.

Maybe he's giving up on me, Alice thought. Maybe it's hopeless.

"You're sure?" she said. "I mean, if it'll help, please go ahead."

Dr. Onnen, somewhat patronizing, as if he were addressing a very old, very young, or very stupid patient, explained to her that it wouldn't help, that the degree of pain was revealing enough.

"It is?" she asked.

"It is." Dr. Onnen asked her a few routine questions which she answered enthusiastically and in detail, and then he went to join Alice's other orthopedists, rheumatologists, internists, immunologists, and her parents in a meeting called for that afternoon.

All doctors should be crippled, Alice thought. It makes them so much more understanding. She spent the rest of the afternoon mentally assigning crippling diseases to various doctors for the good of their profession.

From her window she could sometimes see the moon. That night it was full and flat, as if it had been smudged by someone's thumb, not really round at all. She remembered once telling someone from Cleveland that that city was just a dark smudge on the map, and she had never even been there. It was probably a perfectly decent city.

What happened at that meeting? she wondered. It had broken up late and no one had told her anything. She stared at the white moon until it disappeared behind a building, watched the fuzzy nimbus follow it, then fell asleep.

She awoke the next morning to the imposing white coat of Dr. Witherspoons looming above her. She shifted slightly and her equipment rattled.

"Dr. Onnen says you are in great pain," said Dr. Witherspoons in his monotonous voice.

Hooray! she thought.

"He has prescribed fifteen milligrams of morphine for you every four hours."

Hooray, hooray, Alice was thinking, when Dr. Witherspoons added, "Dr. Onnen also suggests we remove your hips."

"Remove my hips?" Alice asked. "How do you walk without hips?"

"You don't," said Dr. Witherspoons.

When her mother came later, the wretched wails were circling the hall like a litter of lost dogs.

Alice wailed all afternoon. She howled all evening.

The floor nurses closed her door. She cried after them.

She yowled at the ceiling. A real cripple, she thought. Too old to do Easter Seal ads, unable to do anything else.

She cried into the night.

A conference room decorated in the hygienic-cheerful manner—fiber-glass chairs around a walnut-Formica table enclosed by bright pink walls selected by a panel of psychologists after extensive government-funded tests—was manned by gray-haired doctors, most of them wearing white coats over their dark suits. Also at the table was a big man slumped beneath his mustache, and a red-haired, round-cheeked woman with a notebook and pencil.

"I'm a little forgetful," said the woman. "You don't mind if I take notes, do you?"

The doctor in the darkest suit and whitest coat addressed her. "Your daughter is seriously ill, Mrs. Brody."

"Yes, we realize that," she said, writing it down in the notebook anyway, on the off chance it might slip her mind later.

"She is in tremendous pain. Unbearable pain, I should say. Alice is undermedicated and she is suffering terribly."

"Yes, Alice has said almost the same thing, Dr. Onnen," said the droopy man.

"With Dr. Witherspoons's consent, I will prescribe morphine immediately," said Dr. Onnen.

Dr. Witherspoons mumbled what everyone assumed to be his consent.

"The inflammation is raging," continued Dr. Onnen. "Antibiotics have had no effect. The biopsy was inconclusive, so we don't even know if it's an infection causing the inflammation. Frankly, we don't know what is causing it. We don't know how to cure it. And we don't know how long it will last. I suggest, therefore, that we do what we can to relieve Alice's pain. I believe this is an emergency, and I suggest we surgically remove the patient's hips at the first opportunity, thus removing the inflammation and stopping the pain."

Mrs. Brody was scribbling furiously on her pad. Mr. Brody sank a little deeper in his chair.

"Alice will be somewhat disabled," said Dr. Onnen. "But she will still be able to live a full, rich life. Why," he said, pulling out a pipe and banging it empty in the ashtray, "I have another young patient, a lovely young girl, who recently had both her legs amputated. She's made a *remarkable* adjustment."

Mr. Brody and his mustache fell suddenly sideways onto the floor with a thud.

"Thank you so much, Dr. Onnen," said Mrs. Brody, fanning her estranged husband with her notebook and waving under his nose the smelling salts a nurse had brought. "We'll think seriously about what you've said."

Alice stopped crying as soon as her mother told her the story of the meeting and assured her there would be no surgery until other doctors had been consulted. Crippled doctors, Alice had in the meantime decided, were not ideal. Undoubtedly more understanding, Alice thought, but perhaps not sufficiently squeamish. Dr. Onnen was only condemning Alice to a fate that he, after all, had himself met quite successfully.

It was a relief, during the following weeks of consultations, that the specialists were all healthy and whole. None of them was much help, however. Alice wrote a list of questions in a notebook supplied by her mother. When each new doctor came, she would begin hopefully at the top.

"What is wrong with me?" she would ask, moving on to inquiries of why she had a fever; why the inflammation was in her hips instead of her elbows, for example, or in one hip and one elbow; what made them think it was an infection; what made them think it wasn't; and finally winding up with "So, what is wrong with me?" No one knew.

"No hip removals yet," one doctor finally decided. "Why not give the antibiotics another try? You've waited this long . . ." And he ordered massive doses of a new antibiotic.

"Wait six weeks," he said. "Then we'll see. What's six weeks? You've waited this long."

"You said that already," Alice said. But she waited.

The days dragged, and to everyone's surprise the inflammation gradually subsided. The pain persisted, blunted by the morphine, but the fever went down.

"Is that from the morphine?" Alice asked Dr. Witherspoons one morning after a night in which she found herself twitching like a junkie—short convulsive shudders in her arms and shoulders. "Am I addicted? Was that from withdrawal? Did I need another shot or something?"

"Yes," said Dr. Witherspoons, not without some gratification, Alice suspected.

How embarrassing, Alice thought. How infuriating that this repellent doctor was right.

"By the way," her physical therapist said when they were rolling toward the whirlpool later that day. "You might have some spasms from those new arm exercises we've been doing. You haven't used those muscles in a long time, you know."

At the urging of the staff nurses, who didn't like to see anyone idle, Dr. Witherspoons soon ordered Alice to sit up in a wheelchair. But when Miss Darty, Holly, and Alice's mother eased her off the bed, they discovered she wouldn't fit. Her legs stood out straight before her, long and stiff.

With Holly's pretty fingers digging into her armpits, Miss Darty manning her waist and thighs, and her mother struggling with her feet, Alice was lowered toward the chair and tilted with energy and imagination. But to no avail. The wheelchair's angle was not hers and neither could accommodate the other.

"I'm not enjoying this," Alice occasionally interjected into the strategies and schemes discussed by her handlers.

"Wait. Let's try just one more thing," they would say, eyeing the dull green wheelchair as if it were a narrow corridor and she a mahogany piano.

Miss Darty finally wheeled in a geriatric chair, which had the advantage of being longer and higher off the ground and allowing Alice to lean against it in a position that resembled sitting. But the geriatric chair was designed for souls in their dotage who either couldn't, or couldn't be trusted to, propel themselves, and so it had the disadvantage of tiny wheels beyond Alice's reach. Stephanie wheeled her through the halls, and Alice stared at everything from her new perspective. Dragging Stephanie and the clattering IV pole behind her, she chugged along, her legs pushed out in front of her at the angle of a cow catcher. She was wheeled to the windows to watch old ladies walk small dogs below.

Alice's aunt, who had spent her entire adult life stalking Loehmann's, brought her the most recent fruit of her endless search for bargains—nightgowns in the dusty pastel colors that were stylish that year, which Alice tried not to stain with blood or strained peas. The crinkled hospital gowns were almost entirely abandoned. The traction was dismantled and carted away by orderlies. As the inflammation lessened, the pain slowly lessened, too.

There seemed to be a general expectation that now that Alice *could* sit up she would. She was encouraged to struggle into the geriatric chair to eat her pink junket, to watch soap operas, to receive the heartened visitors. But Alice, who had once considered the electrically controlled bed the most immediate source of all her misery, realized she had gotten used to it. It seemed less like a prison when compared with the elongated geriatric chair, and more like a retreat.

"Anyway," she told the people urging her to move, "I'm used to eating in bed. I digest better."

One day they tried to wash her hair in the geriatric chair. It had been done on the stretcher before, with buckets and basins.

"This will be so much easier," the eager Nurse Darty said, determined to get Alice up and have her like it.

But the back of the chair, designed to keep gray heads from lolling, stood, an invincible barrier, between Alice's head and the sink.

Alice's toes wiggled under the white cotton blankets. Her bedsores formed scabs. "What now?" she asked her doctors. "What now?"

But the doctors seemed to duck the question of what to do

with her. They ducked behind details of her recovery, which had sprouted and flourished beside details of her illness. There were the growing number of days of a normal temperature, the shrinking amounts of morphine, the minutes she spent sitting or rolling about, the rising red blood count. Things were counted and recorded in her chart, the earliest volumes of which had been put in storage. But what they were to do now the doctors wouldn't say.

"Let's just worry about the present, shall we?" they all said. "Let's not rush things," the nurses and interns and residents would add. "You're so much better."

Alice hated to seem ungrateful for her recovery. The gradual evaporation of the terrible pain had left her deeply moved, as if someone had been kind to her. But, even so, twenty minutes a day in a geriatric wheelchair with absurdly small wheels did not conform to Alice's idea of health. It did not appear to her, as it seemed to appear to the doctors, as the end of the road.

In spite of the abject helplessness of her doctors over the past five months, she still harbored the belief that they would make her well. She attributed that simply to the light-headedness of relief from pain, but the unrealistic idea recurred to her again and again. The agony had languished daily into discomfort, she decreased the morphine gradually and uneventfully, and her doctors seemed content. But Alice became more impatient than ever.

Candles flickered for her in upstate churches. Her mother's father, a traveling salesman of plumbing supplies, had alerted the plumbing and heating establishments on his route to his granddaughter's plight. Ruggieros and Bianchis and DeMattios paid pennies for candles in Albany, Syracuse, and Poughkeepsie. Masses were said. Cards from B & G Radio Despatched Sewer Cleaners and Corbonaro Prompt Plumbing Repair came to her hospital room. The Scuchini's of Ithaca sent her a St. Christopher medal.

"Grandpa, I'm not going anywhere."

"You don't like it?" he asked. He sat by her bed and kept kissing her.

"Grandpa, Saint Christopher is the patron saint of travelers. I'm just not going anywhere, that's all."

"Mmmwwaahh!" went the kiss. "I think it's a beautiful sentiment," he added. "Mmmwwaahh!"

"It's very nice, Grandpa. It just seems a little silly, you know, since I'm not going anywhere."

"Mmmwwaahh! Mmmwwaahh!"

"Mmmwwaahh!" She loved her grandfather.

"You want another kind?" he asked. "A different saint? I don't know, Alice, they all want to send you something. I think it's a beautiful sentiment."

Alice thought for a minute. On her trip through Italy the summer before she had been struck by a skinny saint who stood on panel after panel, lifting his skirt, pointing to an oozing black sore on his thigh, while a small dog sat beside him holding a slice of bread in its jaws. Swooning St. Sebastian and San Lorenzo clutching his grille had interested Alice, but this odd fellow, shamelessly showing his sore, had struck her as an unlikely iconographic figure. He turned out to be San Rocco, a rich young man whose only claim to sainthood was an indefatigable determination to get the plague. He had never helped anyone, never written anything, never preached or had a vision. San Rocco, thirsting for a martyr's death, had wandered through Italy, diligently checking his armpits, and when he finally saw the black bubos, he crawled off happily to a ditch to die at last. But a stray dog brought him food every day, and he recovered.

Now that's a saint you can identify with, Alice thought. "I'd love a San Rocco medal, Grandpa."

And the San Rocco medals poured in. At about the same time, two silver mezuzahs arrived from distant relations and she put them all on together, thinking they would perhaps cancel each other out. The tinkling collection of religious medals of questionable design sometimes wrapped too tightly around her neck when she slept, and she woke up, coughing.

When her grandfather's customers heard she was getting better, letters congratulating her on her miracle arrived in company envelopes.

"Your grandfather very happily told me of your miraculous progress, and also of your great faith in Saint Christopher and San Rocco, and in the Mazzuza," said one letter that made her particularly uncomfortable.

"Faith such as yours can and should renew faith such as mine," said another.

Oh dear, Alice thought.

There were poems about Flames, Our Father, and His Helpers. The letters told her she was blessed; sometimes the B was capitalized.

One day her mother said, "We thought the Manhattan Institute might be good."

Her father said, "They pioneered the field of rehabilitation."

Her mother was sent downtown on a reconnaissance mission. Did everyone drool? Was every patient missing at least one limb and unable to move the others? Were there many small children with flippers? Alice was convinced the answer to all her questions was yes, and after her mother left with them carefully recorded in her notebook, Alice waited, her eyes glazed over.

An institute that isn't a summer school, she thought miserably. An institute for disabled people. I am disabled and I'm going to an institute.

She said, "It will be very depressing. I know it."

Her father, who had stayed behind, said, "Rehabilitation is
a wonderful thing. A wonderful thing. Why, people used to be
locked away in closets, not let out of the house. Like your cousin
Benjy." Cousin Benjy had a pool table in his dining room and
orange peels on the carpet. That was all she remembered of
Cousin Benjy. She had met him only once, in his dark house
scattered with dried orange peel. But, her father told her,
Cousin Benjy was not really badly crippled at all. His parents
wouldn't let him out of the house because they were ashamed
of him. "No one liked to look at his brace," her father said.

"I don't like looking at braces," she said. "It will be very
depressing."

Her father picked at his thumbnail and did his best to be
amusing, telling her of his new apartment in Vancouver and
how much it rained there. But she could think only of Cousin
Benjy and his dark, musty house littered with orange peel. Why
did he eat so many oranges? She had never realized Cousin
Benjy was crippled, had always thought him a half-wit.

"There was no physical rehabilitation in those days, and
look what happened to him—his condition was neglected and
got worse and worse until he really *was* a helpless cripple. And
of course he did become a little eccentric after being locked up
all those years," her father said.

"Did he play pool?"

"Pool?"

"Pool. Did he play pool? He had a pool table. Did he play
pool?"

"I don't know if he played pool. What difference does it
make? How should I know if he played pool? He was a pathetic
man whose parents locked him up and he would have been
much better off if he'd gone to some place like the Institute."

They waited in silence. Alice watched the IV drip, the solu-
tion stretching toward the bottom of the plastic chamber between the bag and the tube, stretching and hanging until

it swelled into a drop that made a little plink when it landed.

Her father cleared his throat.

Her mother came back.

"It was lovely!" she cried, clapping her hands together. "Just lovely! Everyone was dressed! There was a handsome, bearded young man on crutches! And everyone was so friendly!"

Alice imagined the halls lined with fully clothed Mrs. Pulmans, slipping from their chairs, incanting aphasic greetings from the floor.

"A few of them drool, dear," her mother said. "But not all. And the amputees are on the second floor. You'd be on the fourth, so that's all right! I guess the children with flippers are on another floor too. At least I didn't see any. Your floor . . ."

My floor? *My* floor! Alice thought with horror.

". . . your floor had some elderly people, of course, but they seemed quite nice. And there were a surprising number of teenagers! I think it's just the place! It's so cheerful!"

"I don't have any clothes," Alice said. "I can't go."

"Why, angel, we'll bring you some clothes. Oh, I hope you can get in! There's actually a waiting list! I think one of the Rockefellers was there. Or was it a Roosevelt?"

Dear Katie,

MORE GOSSIP, SLANDER AND CHAT FROM . . . TATTLE-TALE GIMP! I was just sitting down to an inspired Salisbury steak with carrots and peas last night when the dashing WILLIE, brother-about-town, walked in and joined me. WILLIE is in town on a visit to ME but he took time out to buy a sweater at BROOKS BROTHERS and he looked elegant indeed as he discussed his upcoming semester and the difficulties he anticipates in looking after POOKIE, the luxurious collie he is often seen squiring about.

Also present in Room 903 were MOMMY and DADDY, who, as I mentioned in my last column, were "re-examining their setup." I have it on good authority that the illustrious and well-turned-out parents are going ahead with their plans for a divorce, something that has caused quite a sensation in family circles! Good luck, MOMMY and DADDY!

There was a cameo appearance by the world-renowned surgeon, DR. WITHERSPOONS, who dashed over to my table for one or two words and an enthusiastic twist of my ankle, but unfortunately didn't have time to stay. DR. WITHERSPOONS, by the by, has recently been seen at MORRIS'S DELICATESSEN on the POST ROAD in WESTPORT helping a snarling woman with long fingernails out of a brown Mercedes. The taloned lady in question is rumored to be MRS. WITHERSPOONS. Good luck, DR. and MRS. WITHERSPOONS!

Meanwhile, with the excitement of the dinner and the company, I fell asleep. I, in case you haven't heard, will be trying something completely new in the fall. Branching out from past projects (my best known are Going to School, Getting Sick, and Recuperating), I will begin Rehabilitating. Rehabilitation is scheduled to begin this October, on location at the MANHATTAN INSTITUTE. Good luck, ALICE BRODY!

Love,
Alice

While Alice waited impatiently to get better and patiently to move to the Institute, both Dr. Davis and Simchas went away on vacations. Dr. Davis spent three weeks in Portugal and sent her letters full of mildly amusing observations. ("After the pharmacia gave us change in Band-Aids, we wondered if the butcher would give us a bone, the iron monger—and the bordello!—a screw, the medico an extra suture in the wound.")

"Dear Little Alice," the letters began. "I think of you daily," they concluded, "and feel like a rat for leaving New York. I miss you almost palpably and painfully. I love you very much." In the middle were appreciations of the local fruit and quotations from Shelley's "Ode to the West Wind" that she couldn't quite make out.

Why *almost* palpably and painfully? she wondered.

Alice spread the most recent of Dr. Davis's letters on her stomach. It was written in a beautiful hand in fine black ink on pale blue airmail paper. The number seven in the return address was crossed in the European style. She held it up to the light and thought what a lovely shade of blue the paper was, that it was altogether a lovely letter, that everything about Dr. Davis was lovely, even the songs he sang to her from *Kiss Me, Kate.* Sometimes he sat by her bed chatting about how much fun it must have been to live in the Renaissance and wear tights. She looked at the willowy black ink on the frail blue paper and paid no attention to what the letter actually said. If only it had been scented. She was a little surprised it wasn't.

Simchas sent her a letter from Norway. She had gotten a letter from him once before, from Texas. That one had said, "Dear Alice, I hope you are better. The weather is unbearably humid. The convention is boring. I have ordered a more sensitive EMG machine for you. It should be there next week. Simchas."

The letter from Norway was written on hotel stationery with what Alice knew to be an enormous and absurdly expensive fountain pen, claimed as a tax deduction. The hotel's logo, printed at the top, included a cartoon of dancing frogs. Simchas had drawn a picture of another frog, this one lying on a bed with an ice pack on its stomach. At first glance Alice thought it was meant to be her, and smiled. But then she saw it was labeled

"Simchas." The letter was addressed to Alice Brody, Model Patient. It said he had thrown up on the plane.

She looked at the letters and began to cry. Simchas and Dr. Davis were gone and she was a diseased cripple sweating in a narrow hospital bed. She used a blue plastic bedpan, her food came on a pinkish plastic tray, she was attached to dripping bottles and rode around in a geriatric chair.

Alice kept the letters in the drawer of her bedside table. For the next three weeks, she cried because she wanted to walk; she cried because she was afraid she never would; she cried because she was feeble, because she had pimples, because she missed Dr. Davis and Simchas Fresser. But when she cried for them, she felt almost happy. Healthy people cried for their lovers, too. She would sob and play Billie Holiday records on her record player, clutching her letters under the covers.

When Simchas got back, he showed her pictures, which he had taken, of a woman undressing in a hotel. She was going to be married in two weeks, and he had picked her up on the train. She was blonde, a little sinewy, and had traces of a bikini surrounded by a tan.

The next day Simchas brought two photograph albums to show her. One was filled with color pictures of trees and city skylines.

"That's nice," she said. "Very nice."

The other was peopled with women, all ages, all kinds, on page after page. The Swedish woman with bikini lines had been inserted toward the back, one page past the sultry black-and-white picture of Alice looking up from her hospital pillow. In the middle of the book was a beautiful picture of Alice's mother, her sunglasses pushed up on top of her head, her head thrown back in laughter.

"Take my picture out of that book," said Alice.

"Why? It's one of my best. It's a wonderful picture."

"I'll take it out. And don't put a copy in either. You *are* a vile man."

Simchas paced up and down in protest. "It's not a trophy book. What do you take me for?"

"You *wish* it was a trophy book," she snarled, folding her arms on her chest, holding the picture.

"It's just *friends.*"

"They're all women."

"Women are prettier than men. It's just my friends. Why, your mother is in there."

Yeah, Alice thought. My mother is in there.

"Take her picture out too," Alice said.

"You have such a filthy mind. I mean, really."

Alice looked at him and thought, Lie down with dogs, wake with fleas.

Then he told her a story about an eight-year-old patient who asked Simchas's doorman if he "fucked his wife at night." The doorman said he wasn't married. When Simchas, as part of the boy's therapy, asked him to finish a story that had begun, "A boy was walking down the street on a cool fall evening . . ." the boy had said, ". . . and he stepped in dog shit. The end." When Simchas said, "It was Christmas Eve and the boy heard a noise on the roof . . ." his little patient continued, "Santa had shat and all his reindeer had farted."

Simchas was delighted with this entertaining new patient. There was nothing wrong with him, so there was no chance of his getting well. Moreover, he came three times a week.

Simchas left Alice clutching her photograph and demanding the negatives. When he was out of sight, she hid it in her bedside drawer and turned on the radio. A man urged her to enter the Cricket Quiz. Who would win the series between West Indies and Pakistan and by how many runs? Alice wondered how many games were in a series and how you got a run in cricket, but she sent in her postcard anyway. It was a picture postcard of the red brick hospital, and she voted for West Indies, thinking that Pakistan was often involved in wars that might tie up the really good players, and would certainly leave West Indies more time to practice. The prize was a trip for two to the Caribbean. The man on the radio didn't say where in the Caribbean, but Alice pictured herself lying on a beach first beside Simchas, who was so pasty and thin that she shifted to Dr. Davis, who wore a bikini bathing suit.

Stephanie mailed the postcard immediately. In case of a tie, the earliest postmark won.

A week later, Alice poked through her get-well cards, looking at the return addresses, throwing out the ones she knew would be maudlin. The one from Aunt Leona. Two from upstate New York. And then she saw an envelope from WLBB.

"From the radio station!" she said.

"That's nice, dear," her mother said, looking up from a book.

"I won! I won!" Alice shouted, waving the letter. "Mom, I won!"

"That's wonderful, Alice! Won what?"

"The Cricket Quiz! West Indies beat Pakistan by fourteen runs! That's what I wrote! I won a trip to Gumbo! *Gumbo?* Anyway, can I go?"

Her mother said, "I don't think so, dear. Maybe next time."

"But there won't be a next time. I've never won anything before in my life. I've got to go. They're taking me off the IV soon. I can sit in a chair. . . ."

"Alice . . ."

"I never get to do anything. I don't want to go to the Institute. I want to go to Gumbo. It's my prize. I get to go."

"Alice . . ."

"Oh, come on, Mom . . ."

"Alice. You've been seriously ill. You're still getting intravenous antibiotics, for heaven's sake. You take morphine. You can barely move. I mean, I can't believe what I'm hearing. . . ."

"I wanna go to Gumbo."

"Alice, really."

"I never get to do anything."

So a woman named Mattie C. Ballou from Francis Lewis Boulevard went instead.

Holly sat, small and quiet, in her chair by the window. The blinds were open. It was the first thing Holly did each morning, and now the sun slanted through them, one stripe of white falling across Alice's foot. Alice looked at the foot, colorless flesh poking out of the covers, and it seemed far away, remote, an acquaintance. She could hear the little herd of doctors and interns making their morning rounds, seeping from room to room, the scuff of soft shoes and the sounds of white coats rustling against each other as they passed through the doorways to see a man with a bad liver, a roomful of stroke victims petitioning them with incomprehensible requests, a woman, moaning from abdominal pain, whose roommate had brown spots.

An eclectic floor, thought Alice.

She watched the janitor follow his mop in, and the room filled with the stinging smell of ammonia. Holly lifted her little feet while the mop slid beneath them and back. There was a rattle as the wastebaskets were emptied in the hall, and Holly looked up and saw Alice was awake. She immediately began to move around in a helpful way; basins and towels and toothbrushes fluttered to Alice's side like happy birds.

"La-da-da-deeeee!" Holly sang to herself as she dipped the thin washcloth in the kidney-shaped basin. Alice hated all the basins. They were formed of pale blue plastic that never looked clean to her even when the little tubs were first unwrapped from their plastic bags. She hated to brush her teeth and spit the used foam into a small moon-shaped basin held under her chin, to see it sloshing like the slime of pollution in a stagnant pool.

The interns slowly came into the room.

"I voided, I moved my bowels, I took in my intake and put out my output, I turned, wheeled, and sat. Okay?" she said.

"Okay, okay," said one, turning and leading the others out. They had little interest in a patient with so many specialists, and one who had gotten better even though they had never figured out what was wrong. One young doctor's stethoscope caught on an IV pole as he turned, and he untangled it with dignity and followed the others.

Alice settled back in her pillows wondering how she could possibly last through the six hours before "One Life to Live" came on. She wasn't looking forward to seeing her mother, whom she had told the day before to hire a private detective.

"Send him to Vancouver. I'm telling you, he's got a girl-friend."

"Oh, Alice," her mother had said. But Alice was sure of it. A woman with a child. Her father had asked her mother to send him the book about the rabbit that had been his favorite as a child, a book he had given to his two children to read as soon as they were old enough.

So it must be a woman with a child, Alice thought. Probably a nine-year-old son. Her father loved nine-year-olds. He had been wonderful to Alice and Willie when they were nine. It seemed futile for him to start with another nine-year-old, though. Even a Canadian one. It was bound to become ten sooner or later, and then eleven, and then twelve. It would go out with girls and come home late and might even call him an asshole in a fit of adolescent rebellion. Poor Daddy, she thought. This can only end in tears.

Alice sat in a sullen reverie all morning, wondering what this nine-year-old boy was like, deciding he must be towheaded and polite. When Stephanie arrived that afternoon and Holly gave them a chipper "Bye-bye," Alice barely said hello.

Stephanie sat on one chair, her feet on another.

"I guess I should polish my shoes," she said, turning them

to show their gray sides and turning them back to show their dingy laces. "At least I don't have to wear a cap."

Alice offered her a cigarette and they smoked, not saying anything. The door was closed, and the only sound in the room was the murmur of the air conditioner, muffled by the blankets stuffed into the vents to cut the chill flow.

"I'm glad you're coming with me to the Institute," Alice said. Holly was also coming, and looking forward to it. Mrs. Orion, however, declined. She objected to the atmosphere, she said. And Alice didn't really need a night nurse.

"Me too," said Stephanie. "I hope I don't have to wear a cap there."

"I think it's very informal."

Stephanie told Alice her husband had stayed out for the third night in a row. She had finally gone out with the doctor at the cancer hospital, she added.

They became silent again, Stephanie taking off one of her shoes and examining it.

"I'm glad I'm leaving," Alice said.

"Yeah, this place is a dump."

"But what if the Institute's a dump, too?" asked Alice, who was already convinced it was.

"I've heard it's nice. Want a dirty dog from the street?"

"No, thanks."

"Jell-O?"

"No, thanks," Alice said, thinking about a towheaded child putting his fingerprints in her books.

"Is your witch doctor coming today?" Stephanie asked, referring to Simchas.

"I guess so," Alice said, now imagining the drab halls of the Institute. She sighed.

"Should I leave my husband?" asked Stephanie.

"I guess so," said Alice, too overcome with self-pity to listen. How dare her father give books to a strange blond child when she had to go to an institute?

Stephanie said, "I will when I have time."

"What?"

"Leave my husband."

Then Alice read an article announcing that everyone was writing screenplays, so she began her own. "I Was a Teenage Gimp," she wrote at the top of a sheet of paper. She crossed that out and wrote "The Magic Molehill." But she could think of nothing else to say and filled the page with barely recognizable doodles of doctors sawing each other's legs off. She asked Stephanie to hang it over her bed, next to the picture of Miss Darty brandishing her hypodermic.

"This one's not very good," Stephanie said, standing back and surveying it.

"It's abstract," Alice said.

On the day she was supposed to leave for the Institute, Alice peered past her legs at shoes.

"I'm not wearing them," she said.

Her mother said, "Why not?"

"I'm not wearing them," Alice repeated, on the verge of tears. She stared at her feet, puppet feet, dangling at the end of stiff legs, in puppet loafers that never touched the ground. She stared at them, neat and shiny, in horror.

"I'm *not* wearing them."

Her mother slipped them off—"I hope you don't catch a cold"—and put them in a bag. All her belongings had been stuffed into big green garbage bags, which were piled on an extra stretcher, as bulky and misshapen as chubby little corpses.

Alice had not been sure what was considered suitable attire for a rehabilitation center and had finally decided on blue jeans. But shoes on a stretcher she knew could not be right. Purely decorative shoes, like false pockets in a jacket, she thought, still shaken from seeing them slide onto her feet.

While they waited for orderlies to wheel her down, her

mother and Stephanie chatted. Alice shifted uncomfortably in her clothes, although it was exciting to be dressed again. The collar of her shirt pressing lightly against her neck was as unfamiliar as the sheepskin booties had been five months ago. She had wriggled into her jeans and rejoiced in how heavy, how substantial they felt. No more flimsy nightgowns in the middle of the day like a depressed and idle housewife. She could feel the seams of her pants beneath her, and the cuffs of the shirt clung too tightly to her wrists.

An aide in bedroom slippers walked in and began to change the bed Alice had just vacated. Alice watched her silently pull the bottom sheet flat, square off the corners, spread the top sheet, and fold a clean white blanket across the foot of the bed. As the ambulance attendants wheeled her away Alice watched the aide push the pillows into their cases. Fresh white cases with pink scallops.

"Hey!" Alice cried. "Those are mine!"

The aide turned her head slowly and watched Alice disappear down the hall. The orderlies pushing her stretcher tried to quiet her.

"My pillowcases!" Alice called. "Stop! My pillowcases came back!"

"It's okay, kid," said one orderly. "We're taking you to a nice new hospital where you can have nice new pillowcases. All the pillowcases you want."

"Mine, mine, *my* pillowcases," Alice said, gesticulating under the tightly tucked blanket.

Her mother and Stephanie were out of earshot, wheeling the stretcherload of garbage bags and plants.

"Mine," she whimpered to the nurses she passed.

"Why, don't cry, Alice," they said. "The Manhattan Institute is every bit as nice as this place."

II

The cold air made her eyes water. Sirens wobbled hysterically and red lights flipped across the waiting white ambulance.

I'm outside, she told herself. But it seemed more likely that she was in a World's Fair exhibit attempting to simulate different environments. This would be called "City Emergency" and now she would go on the Ambulance Ride.

The ambulance was the same size as the one in which she had motored to the hospital. She pushed aside the white curtain and stared at the traffic. A Chevrolet in the next lane was long and dented, filled with children who stared at her. When she waved, they ducked.

They drove down Park Avenue, past islands of dying flowers.

The room was as white as a new sneaker, the bed narrow and high as a tree house. Across the street was a billboard—Santa Claus with a shining red face drank a bottle of Coca-Cola while cans floated aimlessly in the upper right-hand corner. The billboard had been changed last night, or perhaps very early this morning. It was only seven now. Yesterday the billboard was a mass of autumn leaves cradling the bottles and cans of Coke. Yesterday had been Halloween. Moved into the little room,

Alice had stared at the billboard until it was too dark to see, and then had turned on the TV. Stretched out in the little bed, she watched the local news. Small deformed children waddled, wheeled, and thumped through the halls of a hospital. Some were lying face down on stretchers, turning the wheels with their limp hands. They were trick-or-treating. They were, Alice realized as she stared unhappily at the television screen, downstairs.

She looked around the narrow little room. Someone had already come around to straighten up. Her hairbrush had been put neatly in her empty water glass. She could see the bristles and hairs pressed against the glass like little faces against a window. Her radio had been moved out of reach. Her view comprised the Coke billboard, a great expanse of muddy sky, and then suddenly, the startling Chrysler building.

"I'm tired of looking up to the Chrysler building. Let's fly away . . ." She stopped singing when a nurse came in. The nurse pushed a vehicle that vaguely resembled a chair. It had a hole in what appeared to be the seat, like an elaborate rolling toilet.

"Good morning," said the nurse. "Did you sleep? I've come to take you to the showers."

The showers? Showers? Plural? The kind with other Jews, or the kind with other girls—nasty buxom girls imported from the local high school?

"Listen, I have a private nurse, so, you know, I don't want to keep you from your other patients," Alice said. Go away, she thought. Your very odd chair frightens me. "And, um, I'm not sure I'm supposed to go to the showers just yet. Listen, I can hardly sit up, so I'll just have a sponge bath when my private-duty nurse gets here, which should be any minute, it's almost eight now. . . ." She babbled desperately until the nurse went away and took her chair with her. Oh, Alice thought, woe is me. Even the chairs are deformed here.

She heard small whirring noises outside her door. The electric wheelchairs. She couldn't see them, and for this she was glad.

When Holly finally came, she carried Alice's breakfast tray, which looked very much like the breakfast tray at Shadow of the Valley the morning before.

"What's it like out there?" Alice asked. "Creepy?" She had been whisked up to her room yesterday and had seen very little.

"It's very nice," said Holly. But Alice didn't believe her for a minute. The swarming insect noises buzzed past her door with alarming frequency. How many of them are out there, she wondered.

"Yeeeee-haaaa," she heard someone shout. "Head 'em up and move 'em out!"

Alice watched a helicopter fly past the window as Holly washed her feet.

"Welcome."

The doctors sat in a semicircle, facing her. The same nurse who had tried to transport her to the showers in the strange chair had come back into Alice's room with a conventional wheelchair and asked Alice to "climb aboard."

"I can't," Alice said.

"She can't," Holly said loyally.

"Leave it to me," the staff nurse said, and Alice was pulled up in bed, her feet were put on footrests, and the rest of her was twirled until her shoulders pressed against the back of the chair. She seemed to be sitting, but was actually several inches above the seat.

The nurse said, "There!"

Alice, rigid, resembled the figure in the middle frame of a film strip depicting "The Ejector Seat in Action." She was piloted out the door and down the hall to the room where the semicircle of doctors waited. She wobbled, but did not speak until the doctors said, "Welcome."

"Thank you," she said, putting both hands in the space between her behind and the canvas seat. Six fingers. Three inches? Four maybe. She began to cry.

"I'm a little uncomfortable," she said, hoping she wasn't making a bad impression. The weight of her body pulled down on the unyielding hips, and she was afraid they might snap, letting her down on the seat with a plop.

Oh, God, she thought. I didn't get dressed. You're supposed to be dressed. They'll think I have a bad attitude. She sniveled pitifully.

"Go back and rest now," said the doctors.

As the nurse rolled her back to her room, with Holly following at a respectful distance, Alice was dimly aware of the motorized wheelchairs whizzing past her on both sides, while she, in turn, seemed to whistle past the manual ones, whose occupants pushed their limp hands against the wheels. Alice was dizzy and noticed the floppy hands, but saw no faces, no people really. Just the rhythmic hands and the movement of traffic.

"Watch where you're goin', will yuh," someone shouted after a flurry of clicking and squeaks.

"Then quit hoggin' the hall," someone else hollered.

Zoom, zoom, zoom went their motors.

Alice wondered how she would sleep in such a noisy institute. The hall began to spin slightly, and she felt herself surrounded by vehicles, monstrous and wheeled. She was lifted into bed. The noises faded. The vehicles dispersed. She slept.

Her mother brought the various twisted needlepoint canvases, threads hanging from tigers' ears and flower petals, and tucked them into new corners and cracks. The refrigerator was plugged in, well stocked. An extra armchair was squeezed between the foot of the bed and the window.

"Just like Albert Schweitzer's hospital!" said her mother, settling in. Her mother used to shake the bottle of milk before pouring a glass for five-year-old Alice, and when it came out white and frothy, would say, "Just like Heidi's milk! In the mountains!"

"Just like Albert Schweitzer's hospital in the jungle, where the families come and sleep on mats!" she said, arranging plants and plumping pillows. "What fun!" They prepared for a new siege, for long desultory days, waiting for shots, for spasms, for night. But when her mother came the next day Alice was gone.

"It's only nine. Where can she be? I thought she'd be asleep."

Holly, who had wheeled Alice to a gymnasium at eight and was told to pick her up at ten, said, "She's in therapy."

At that moment, Alice lay on her stomach on a table. Her legs were trussed behind her and hung from the ceiling like a ham. "Get me outta here," she called occasionally.

While she hung, curious patients wheeled up, braking expertly, with little screeches of the tires. There seemed to be only teenagers and old people at the Institute. It was as if an entire generation had been swallowed up, or had emigrated, leaving ungrateful children with their ungrateful grandparents. The old people muttered and shook, had Italian or Jewish names. One man sat at her side, muttering, "Jesus Christ, Jesus Christ," over and over again. She politely asked him why he was there, how long he'd been in, what was his name again, was he from New York? He nodded agreeably and said, "Jesus Christ." All the old people were stroke victims.

The teenagers had been in car accidents. They wore blue jeans and T-shirts bearing the names of bad rock groups, and they put decals and bumper stickers on the backs of their wheelchairs. They were disheveled and unclean in the way only teen-agers or sick people are, and since they were teenagers *and* sick, the grubby, slouching disorder seemed intensified, almost threatening. At first, Alice was a little frightened of them. But then a girl in denim—"Led Zeppelin" spelled out in silver studs across her jacket—parked alongside and began to tell Alice stories of the Quad Squad, a legendary group of quadriplegics founded by a crippled, and since released, policeman. But the Quad Squad lived on, and Lynn, the girl in denim, was now its leader.

"What does the Quad Squad do?" Alice asked.

"Cruise," said Lynn, and Alice decided she was harmless enough.

"Hey, man," Lynn said, flicking ashes onto her jeans and rubbing them in. "What are you gonna do when you grow up? You know, and get outta here?"

"I don't know," said Alice. "Graduate? Then go to graduate school, I guess."

"I'm gonna marry off. See you later." Lynn whisked back-ward out of the room.

Alice was finally cut down and taken to the whirlpools, where she sat in an antechamber, waiting for a free tub. Holly accompanied her and sat reading a magazine.

"What are you here for?" a lady asked Holly.

"I'm a nurse."

"Yeah," said the lady. "A lot of people have trouble with their nerves."

Later, Alice was evaluated. An enormous physical therapist, looking out from under eyelids heavy with blue shadow, came for her.

"Nothing to be afraid of," she said in what Alice thought was an excessively hearty manner. "Let's roll!" cried the therapist, who had thoughtfully come equipped with a wheelchair so large, with footrests so extended, that Alice could actually sit in it. Must have a big inventory, Alice thought.

As she was pushed through the hall, Alice noticed a room with four beds; inside, hair dryers and fluffy slippers. Farther down the hall, in another room with four beds, Alice saw a dartboard. The girls' bunks and the boys' bunks, she thought, but where are the boys and girls?

When they passed the nurses' station at the end of the hall, six wheelchairs whipped around the bend in front of Alice's caravan. The drivers hollered and whooped, cigarettes dangling from their mouths; some wore funny hats.

"The Quad Squad," said the therapist.

Down another long hall, Alice was wheeled into an L-shaped room filled with what looked like the results of an undisciplined child's afternoon with an erector set. Machines with pedals, steps, straps, and pulleys stood beside parallel bars and gray, rolled-up gym mats.

"Rehab," said the therapist.

"Karate Kung Fu!" cried an aide, executing a questionable scissors kick.

"That's Moses," the therapist said. "And this corner is PR exercises."

"Puerto Rican!" said Moses, delivering a decisive blow to an unoccupied wheelchair, which spun across the room, hit an exercise mat, and stopped still.

"Physical rehabilitation, actually," said the therapist.

"Well, we're all Puerto Ricans here, man." Moses was bobbing a red rubber ball on his head and shoulders.

"Das right, man," called all the other aides, who did indeed seem to be Puerto Rican. They wore white shirts with short sleeves and buttons on the shoulder like a dentist's shirt, or Dr. Kildare's.

"Hot pocks! Hot pocks!" Moses announced, pushing steaming hot packs under the shoulders of patients lying on tables against the wall.

The therapist lifted Alice onto a table and took from her uniform pocket what looked like an elementary-school protractor. She held it against Alice's hip and tried to move the leg out to the side. "It doesn't move."

"No," said Alice.

The therapist then lifted the leg up and tried to rotate it. "Doesn't move." She wrote a zero on a chart she had next to her. She took out another chart, tried to move Alice's other leg, and marked additional zeroes. "That's it."

"That's it?" Alice asked. "That's evaluation? I get a zero?"

"That's it," said the therapist. "Zero degrees. Zero range of motion." Alice was put back into her great, wide wheelchair and returned to her little bed.

Sometimes she felt as if she were riding a grocery cart. "Mommy! Mommy! Frosted Flakes! Twinkies! Mommy! Mommy! Disabilities!"

The rehabilitation hours were eight-thirty to four with an hour break for lunch. Alice was never in her room. "8:30, Rm. 201 HT," her schedule said under Mon., Tue., Wed., Thur., and Fri. Holly would apologetically wake her at eight, roll her onto a stretcher, and deliver her to the basement. In a large yellow locker room, Holly would select a dreary blue bathing suit from a dreary blue pile of sagging, dull cotton-knit garments the likes of which neither Alice nor Holly had ever seen. If they had carried labels saying, "Institutional garment, guaranteed to fade accordingly; may not be worn in the outside world or purchased in any store," the bathing suits could not have been more obviously the costume of some hospital or prison—at best some obscure branch of the armed forces. Alice would watch as Holly selected the largest suit in the pile and tried to guide Alice's stiff legs through the proper holes. By the time the suit was hauled into place, a good twenty minutes would have passed, and Alice, exhausted and breathing hard, would look at the skinny white limbs poking from the folds of her suit, and she would sigh.

Alice was told that HT stood for hydrotherapy, but she liked to think it was for Hot Tubs. All the whirlpool baths were in one basement room, great bubbling aluminum pots surrounded by yellow curtains; steam rose from the tubs and crept through cracks between the curtains.

"And *lift* and *push* and *lift* and *push*," cried voices muffled by running water and howling motors.

Alice was wheeled up to an empty pool and was rolled over on her side. A canvas sheet was pulled beneath her; four wires connected to a cable attached to the ceiling were clamped on the four corners of the canvas, and with a clatter of pulleys Alice was hoisted into the air.

I'm lying in a blue bag on a hammock over a tank of hot churning water, she said to herself, closing her eyes and hanging on to the wires. Once lowered into the tub, she was left undisturbed for an hour and usually fell asleep, her head lolling to one side, her mouth full of water. At nine-thirty she was pulled out and relieved, with considerable difficulty, of the now sodden bathing suit. Alice would shiver until the dread garment had at last released its grip, and then she would shiver under mounds of tiny terrycloth towels until Holly put her clothes on.

Alice squirmed, pretending she didn't have to pee. "Really? How wonderful," she said in response to something Dr. Davis had just said. She wasn't sure exactly what, but she knew it was about his daughter, whom he adored, so she knew it was wonderful.

"That's great. Really great," she said. But by now she wasn't paying attention at all. How embarrassing, how humiliating, she thought. I can't go to the toilet myself. I'll have to get a nurse and explain to Dr. Davis. Dr. Davis, will you excuse me for a minute while a highly trained, highly paid nurse escorts me to the bathroom five feet away so I can urinate? Thank you, Dr. Davis. You're a doctor, so I know you understand.

"Listen, Dr. Davis, I have to pee, so I'll call a nurse . . ."

"I'll get you the bedpan, my darling. Where is it?"

"No, Dr. Davis, I don't use a bedpan now. Tremendous progress. Special raised toilet seat with safety rails . . ."

"Why, angel, dear one, how wonderful! How absolutely marvelous! Come, little one, I'll help you." Dr. Davis gently helped her into the wheelchair, which he rolled next to the toilet in the tiny bathroom. Just looking at the special toilet seat embarrassed her. Looking at it next to Dr. Davis in his suède shoes made her cringe.

"What a marvelous invention!" he cried, putting out his lovely hand and touching the seat elevated by metal stilts. Alice wished desperately that he would leave. She considered calling the whole thing off but by now had to pee urgently.

"Now let me help you, darling," he was saying, as if he were addressing a child. "That's it. We unzip the pants. What pretty panties! Down they come! What a tender moment this is! A close, gentle moment! Now, over onto the potty . . ."

Bla-a-ah! Alice was thinking.

"Thank you, Dr. Davis," she said.

"How pretty you look. . . ."

"Thank you, Dr. Davis."

"So *intime* . . ."

"Dr. Davis, could you get out for just a minute, please?"

"But, darling . . ."

"Out."

"Now, Alice, love, there's nothing to be ashamed of. It's the most natural thing in the world. . . ."

Blah! thought Alice. Blah! I'm trapped in the bathroom with Havelock Ellis.

"So charming . . . unashamed . . ."

"OUT!" she shouted. "O-U-T OUT!" And out he went. Though he brought up the tender moment, sighing at the memory, time and time again.

Between exercises Alice spent almost all her time lying on her bed, exhausted and half asleep. But there were breaks so short that it wasn't worth the effort of rolling back to her room and struggling onto the bed, and she spent these sitting by a window staring at the helicopters approaching and leaving what she imagined must be a heliport nearby. She sat now looking out the window, politely nodding and smiling at Mr. Malieri, who was energetically explaining something. She couldn't be sure what, because no matter what Mr. Malieri said, it came out as "Jesus Christ, Jesus Christ." He was animated, though, and Alice enjoyed his company.

"Are you tired all the time?" she asked. "I am." But, before Mr. Malieri could respond, Lynn, the leader of the Quad Squad, rolled up and said, "Hey, man, why are you sitting here? Come on. We're going to the roof."

"Goodbye, Mr. Malieri," Alice said. "I'm going to the roof now." Mr. Malieri nodded several times.

Alice followed Lynn down the hall. Why is she so far ahead? Alice wondered, red in the face. She can barely use her hands.

"Lynn!" she called, panting. "Wait a minute. Slow down." Her arms ached and she had blisters on the palms of her hands, which everyone assured her would turn to calluses. "In a month you'll be a pro." She never found this reassuring.

"Lynn!" Alice called.

"Look," Lynn said after they'd gotten in the elevator. She

pulled something out of her pocket. "I lifted it from the nurses' station."

Alice said, "What is it?"

"A forceps," said Lynn, looking at Alice as if she had asked what a paper clip was. Alice wished she had stayed with Mr. Malieri.

The roof turned out not to be the roof at all, but a small room, built for no obvious purpose, that looked out on the roof and the river. Helicopters lifted and dropped in their unnatural, vertical way, and Alice's head bobbed up and down as she stared at them.

"Who's gonna roll?" asked a boy who wore thick black boots with heavy buckles. Wispy hairs had gathered in informal groups on his cheeks.

"My brother already rolled it for us," said a girl next to him, her hands folded haphazardly in her lap, as if someone had thrown his gloves there. Besides Alice and Lynn, there were six teenagers parked in a circle.

Oops, Alice thought. The Quad Squad. What am I doing here? I'm not a quadriplegic. I'm not even a paraplegic. I'm not a plegic at all. The Quad Squad is very exclusive. Why have I been invited? She looked around her in panic, wondering what she should do. Roll the joint? But the joint was already rolled. Pass the joint! But what should she say? Allow me? She decided to say nothing and sat watching Lynn, who placed the forceps between her knees and scooped up the joint in the bend between her hand and her wrist. Alice watched her gingerly move the joint toward the forceps perched between her knees. Maybe I should offer to help, Alice thought again. She watched the boy with the big boots try to light a Zippo lighter held with his wrist. His other wrist was brought slapping across the lighter, over and over again.

"Shit," he said, after each try.

I know I should offer to help, Alice thought. I should light the lighter, put the joint in the forceps, light the joint, and pass it around. But she was too embarrassed to say anything. When the forceps finally began to pass around the circle, from one wrist to another, Alice sighed with relief and asked, "Doesn't anyone mind your smoking pot?"

"No one knows," said Lynn. But Alice thought they must know. Perhaps the doctors thought it was therapeutic, or encouraged independence.

When the joint reached her, Alice politely declined, feeling rather foolish.

"What's your problem?" Lynn asked. "You're not a narc, are you?" The Quad Squad eyed Alice suspiciously. Oh, God, Alice thought, looking at the circle of faces. What do I say now? "Bad trip," she said.

"Wow," said the Quad Squad. "Bummer."

It was true that Alice had had a bad trip. A few years before, a friend had invited Alice, Jeffrey, and five or six others to spend the night while her parents were away. They played poker and Janis Joplin records, and the evening was pretty dull. But considerable lying to parents had been required, so no one would admit to boredom. The next morning Alice and Jeff split a capsule of what Jeffrey claimed was mescaline. "The Indians take it," he said.

Alice swallowed her half and waited. She had read Alan Watts on LSD. She had also seen a cautionary film in health class in which a girl stuck her hand into the flames of a gas stove's burner, thinking it was a pretty rose. Alice waited to hallucinate, but she didn't. She shook and whimpered.

After hours of confused terror, Jeffrey drove her home. He informed her that all the cars had red and blue headlights, and she realized that he didn't have his on at all.

"Asshole!" she screamed, clutching her seat belt.

"Have you been crying, dear?" her mother asked when she walked in.

"Oh, laughing, crying . . . you know . . ." she had answered. Her mother smiled and pretended to know.

She must think I'm unstable, Alice thought. Unstable in the extreme. Laughing and crying, indeed. But then, her mother was keen, but a little off kilter.

"Are you smoking pot?" the voice would demand from upstairs. Alice would answer tolerantly, "No, Mommy. It's incense." And it was.

"Phew! That silly incense stinks!" Alice often heard her mother say to her father or brother or the maid. But that was when she was smoking pot. Her mother was consistent. Odors never escaped her. She just never got them right.

"Oh, laughing, crying . . . you know . . ." she had said. And after that night she couldn't bear the thought of getting high on anything, even pot.

"Bad trip," she said to the Quad Squad, conscious of how silly that sounded. But the Quad Squad nodded respectfully, then shrugged its shoulders as best it could and figured it had more to itself. Alice wished she had stayed with Mr. Malieri.

"Can't you knock me out first?" Alice asked as the ropes were looped around her ankles and she was hauled up off the table. "Can't you knock me out before you hang me up?" she said, her face against the table, her feet aloft.

"We might break something," the therapist said.

"I thought that was the point. I thought you were trying to break something. You just told me you were trying to break the adhesions holding the ball and socket together. You just said that."

"Yes, yes, we do. But gradually. Sort of like pulling a piece of licorice. You can't just snap them, Alice."

"But—"

"We need you awake so you can tell us when we're going too far."

"But I always tell you you're going too far," Alice said. Hanging there in terrible pain, Alice daydreamed. I'll think about pleasant things. I'll think about my happy childhood in Westport! She mused on her little friends, her report cards, her childhood books—*Piggy Went to the Laundry* and *The Little Dog Who Would Not Wag His Tail,* both moralistic tales of uncooperative animal youngsters. Piggy, a round pink pig-boy in short pants, refused to clean up his room and was scooped up with the dirty shirts while taking a nap and sent to the laundry. Alice had begged for this story every night, and every night after her mother or father read it to her and she fell asleep, she woke up sobbing, "Piggy, Piggy, Piggy went to the laundry." The laundry had been vast and white and confusing—very much like the hospital. "Poor piggy," she thought these days. "Poor lazy Piggy."

The other, a great big picture book illustrated with soft water colors, had been her father's when he was a little boy, and he loved to read it to her, pointing out his favorite passages, emphasizing the same words his mother had. "But he *would* not *wag* his *tail,*" he would say, wagging his head back and forth, looking up at her as she mouthed the familiar words and shook her head too. The little dog sulked while the pretty little girl in the bonnet gave candy to his brothers and sisters; the little dog was kicked by a barefoot boy with a fishing pole and suspenders; and the little dog was finally shunned by his own mother, until he gave way and wagged his short brown tail.

What a dreadful story, she now thought. To teach simpering and toadying! Dogs don't even eat candy. Why should he have wagged his tail? She sat scowling in her wheelchair, into which she had been lifted after being untied and removed from the table. She parked near some doddering old people, one of whom rocked backward and forward. Why should he have wagged his tail? I don't feel like wagging my tail. The old people looked shabby and pasty, and the dust on the venetian blinds depressed her. The floor was covered with black skid marks instead of heel marks. The wheelchairs were different colors, all dark—brown, blue, green—and names and room numbers were written across the backs, some of which had strips of scruffy masking tape with new names covering old ones.

Alice had no friends yet. It's because I'm in a private room, she thought, glaring at a woman in a short-sleeved shirt who rolled by singing, "Row, Row, Row Your Boat."

There was always the Quad Squad. But the Quad Squad had reconciled itself to its disabilities in a way she pretended she would never have to. She considered herself a temporary cripple, although no doctor had ever told her she was that advanced. But the Quad Squad knew it could never completely recover, and tried to make the best of it. They were all so reckless—loved to race, to steal things. Alice felt these were things she had cleverly outgrown. She preferred the trembling old people who smiled because she paid attention to them. Conversation was limited, but they were so grateful. She wondered if Dr. Davis felt that way about her: She's so grateful.

Oh, God, she thought, blushing and suddenly feeling warm. She rubbed her forefinger against the gray wheel of the wheelchair and wiped the dust off on her pants. She knew Simchas didn't feel that way about her. He wasn't generous enough. But Dr. Davis was generous enough. He was kind and considerate and probably felt she was so grateful.

But he's so old, she reminded herself. And I'm so young. Maybe it all evened out. Maybe he didn't think: She's so grateful. Maybe he thought: She's so young.

But I am, she thought. I *am* grateful.

She glared at the singing woman who was rowing back again with great jolly strokes.

"I've already seen the movie," the woman said, pulling in next to Alice, facing her.

Alice shrugged.

"Have you?" the woman asked.

"Well, what is it?" Alice said. Sullen, she thought. God, are you sullen. The woman said the movie was *Bonnie and Clyde,* and Alice said yes, she'd seen it.

"I liked it," said the woman, tucking in the loose tails of her shirt. "I thought it was great."

Alice took a deep breath. "So did I," she said. "Great." She took another deep breath. And then she smiled.

She half expected little girls in curls and little boys with bare feet to appear, dancing, tossing candy, blinking big water-color eyes. But there was just the lady in her short-sleeved shirt, singing and stroking down the hall.

Good practice, Alice thought. Next time it will be easier. Then she remembered a child she'd seen sitting on a hammock in Katie's backyard while six tiny pet pugs snarfled and yipped below.

"I like dogs," the child sang suspiciously, over and over, swinging his little sneakers and making up the tune. "I like dogs," he sang. "But not very much . . ."

Dr. Davis wore a quilted leather jacket and carried a suède fishing bag with a leather strap.

"Is that your fall bag?" she asked, lisping, waving a limp wrist.

Perfectly seriously, he said, "Yes." He was holding the wheel of a bicycle. "I just got a ten-speed. It's very elegant."

"You rode? You rode down here? It's almost a hundred blocks from your house. Why didn't you take a cab?"

"Oh, Alice. I like to ride. It's not that far. It's good exercise."

"Exercise? Don't ever mention that word in this room again. I loathe exercise. This place is like a never-ending gym class. But I can't even get my mother to write a note excusing me. I *hate* exercise."

"Stop being silly, Alice."

"I hate, *hate* stupid exercises. I hate them, and I hate sports
too. I hate skiing. Your ankles get sore and you're wet and tired
but you have to keep going to get your money's worth because
you bought an all-day ticket. And I hate sailing—everyone
throws up and you can't get off the boat. And I hate swimming
—you get water in your eyes and your mouth . . ."

"Oh, for heaven's sake . . ."

"And in your *ears!*" she said.

"Alice," he said, pulling his bicycle clips off his faun corduroy pants and throwing them across the room. He sat on
the bed and put his arms around her. His leather jacket
creaked.

"Dr. Davis," she sighed, breathy and mimicking.

Dr. Davis giggled. "I missed you."

She had missed him desperately at first. He visited only once
a week now, on Sunday. He didn't drop in the way he had when
she had been in his hospital. She had missed him desperately, she had daydreamed, picturing his dark eyes and soft gray
hair. She had imagined her face pushed against his neck. A man
had once told her women's skin changes after forty, and that's
why older men go for younger women. Dr. Davis's skin was
over-forty skin, lined, a little bit looser and fleshier than the
smooth full skin of a young man—Jeffrey, for instance. It had
come to seem terribly sexy to her, his older skin, exotic at first,
now personal and familiar. She had imagined her face against
the skin of his neck. But, after a while, she had no time to think
of his skin or his neck. She had no time to think of him at all.
She had her schedule.

"I missed you, too," she said.

He kissed her. "My little jumping jack," he said. "My beautiful delicate push-up, my knee-bend, my toe-touch . . ."

"Cut it out," she said as he kissed her knee and toe.

"My darling chin-up," he said, coming back to the head of

the bed and kissing her chin. "My darling," he said seriously. And he sat on the bed again, leaning his head against the pillows, next to her head. He climbed onto the bed. It was nine on a Sunday morning and she was still wearing her nightgown. He pulled the straps down, off her shoulders, thought about it, put them back up again, got off the bed, and pulled the nightgown off her, over her head. She lay naked, her legs straight before her.

"There's a lock on the door," she said. "There's actually a lock on the door."

He locked the door and came back to the bed. "My pale little girl," he said, looking at her, then lying next to her again. She unbuckled his belt, fumbled with the button on his fly and the zipper, struggling with his pants the way Holly struggled with the blue bathing suits.

"Wait, no. Shift that way, no, your shoe is digging into my ankle. Okay, now, but not, Dr. Da—"

"Right, just lift your arm, little one. . . ."

"You're on my hair. . . ."

"Over that way. No, back a little . . . Wait!"

"Wait!"

This is just like normal people's foreplay, she thought happily. Dr. Davis was very seriously maneuvering his little legs caught in their corduroy, trying unsuccessfully to climb between Alice's immobile thighs. His brow had furrowed.

"Okay, now . . . oh, *merde.*" His face was wet and red. "Darling," he puffed, kissing her behind the ear. "My lovely little one," he gasped. His legs thrashed in the pant legs twisted around his knees. Her legs, a vise that gripped nothing, ached when he tried to squeeze between them.

They had never tried this before. And never, she thought mournfully, again. Never again. I'll never fuck again.

"It's hopeless," she said. "My life is over."

Willie stared out the window, noisily eating an ice-cream sandwich. "Do you miss Dad?" he asked. Tall and moody, he looked a little like Dad.

"Do you miss him?" Alice said.

"I miss everyone. *C'est tragique.* Pookie's nice, I guess."

"Pets are loyal. Man's best friend."

"He's a little boring to talk to, though," said her brother.

"Well, who isn't?" Alice said.

"Yeah."

Alice listened to him chew. He smacked his lips after a minute and said, "Sometimes I sleep in your room."

"That's okay."

"It *is?*" he asked. When she lived at home, Alice had not even let him enter her room.

"Well, it *is* bigger, and it's got a phone and everything, and I'm not there."

"Also I sort of kicked a hole in the wall of my room. I think a rat might have moved into it."

Alice looked at her brother.

"I was in a bad mood," he said.

One day Simchas came in, closed the door, and took off his jacket, throwing it across the room with his usual flourish. But there was a leather strap over his shoulder and a leather lump under his arm.

"Is that a gun? Are you mad?" she asked.

"I don't care," he said, slipping the shoulder holster off and stuffing it into his briefcase. "It's dangerous out there. I live on the West Side!"

"Simchas, do you even know how to use that thing? Have you ever fired a gun? Is it loaded? I wish you would get it out of here."

"Of course I know how to use it. I was in the army. Uggh!

Hollering and stirring up dust . . . Of course it's loaded. A man is entitled to defend himself," he said, his voice suddenly deeper.

Dr. Davis drifted in and out of her hospital room like a soft spring day—sweet, wonderful, yet incidental, a whim of the weather. Simchas was concrete, unpleasant, and dependable. His poisonous, self-serving perspective steadied her; it seemed simply common sense. She saw him every day.

"You must have a camera," he said.

"Then buy me one."

He was silent. She could see he was thinking it over, adding up the expenses he incurred by coming to see her, the cab fares, tape cassettes, extension cords, and then adding up the fees (he charged for only three times a week now) and then estimating his profit. She could see he was calculating whether he could buy her a camera and still maintain a respectable profit margin. She could see he decided he could not. He hated to be taken advantage of.

"I'll convince your father to buy you one," he said.

"Very generous of you. Why don't you just raise your fee to cover it instead? Like overhead."

"I help you!" he ranted. "I charge for only three visits! I'm here every day of the week!"

"Blah, blah, blah," she said.

"I got a new flash so I can take decent pictures of you in this room," Simchas announced. "A bounce flash. It bounces off the ceiling so the white walls won't glare. Well, have they given you a date for standing up? They're not very specific, are they? I've shifted two appointments so I can come earlier on Thursdays. And did you ask about acupuncture? Naturally they laughed, but it might help the pain. They always laugh, provincials. Why do you always wear such bland colors? I'm getting you a red blouse. Or pink. Why don't you wear pink?"

She had become the focus of his outraged life. The newspaper never came on time; Americans misused the word "enormity"; if he deducted too many dinners he would be audited; he couldn't get a gun permit; he couldn't get a properly cooked piece of fish. Self-pity worked as a great equalizer, and he imagined Alice a similar victim. They were compatriots, arms linked, facing the same battle of the unfair and the inane. She too imagined they were allied. His petty hissing sounded like tiny, faraway echoes of her great roaring rage. "Can you imagine . . . never in my life . . . the nerve . . . barbarians . . . and then . . . as if that weren't enough . . . you have no idea . . ." Constant, rhythmic, soothing, like the distant lap of waves on a white beach.

Dear Katie,

We must, we must, we must improve our bust! In a few short weeks, you too can have bulging pecs and swollen biceps. Can I ever really have flunked gym? I have become a vision of robust, rounded muscles. From the waist up. My legs have been less cooperative. I keep telling them flexibility is a virtue, and an absolute necessity if they ever hope to wrap themselves around male legs again. But they just ignore me, stubborn old things. They're a kind of biological chastity belt. Still, life is not all frustration. I kind of like it here. The therapists are a little like cheerleaders. There is something so absurd about them smiling, cheering, shouting encouragement while we do things like: Pick up the ball! Say, He-l-l-l-l-o. Lift the left thumb! But they're young and healthy-looking and they're so used to us and our limbless torsos and gibberish that they honestly treat all of us as if we were normal. I like them. I go to a swimming pool every day, although I don't swim. I stand. It's a pretty great feeling. On the first day I did it, I cried. My mother came to watch. She cried too. The water lessens the weight on the hips so they can take the pressure. Of course, I can't go anywhere, but never mind.

If you have a chemical imbalance, does that mean you're physically sick or mentally sick? Can they cure you? Does it mean you can just take the drugs and skip all the boring rap sessions? And now they can't blame your parents!

Love,
Alice

Alice had been lowered into the pool on the same stretcher that immersed her in the whirlpool. She wore the same blue suit. The water was ninety-eight degrees. The first time she felt it—warm, yielding to her back on the stretcher, seeping smoothly over her legs—she thought of the dream of St. Thomas and the Germans and wetting her bed. At least I don't do that anymore, she thought. At least I don't wet my bed. At least I don't use a bedpan. Even if the toilet has a raised seat, at least it's a toilet. And then the therapist came to her side and lifted her off the submerged stretcher. He lowered her down until her feet felt the bottom. And then he let go.

"I'm standing," she said, holding her arms out for balance. The water came up to her chest. "Hey! I'm standing up! I'm standing up!" Big, hot tears rolled down her cheeks into the hot pool.

"You're standing," her mother called from the poolside, jumping up and down, clapping her hands. She snuffled and surreptitiously pulled her sunglasses off her head over her eyes, as if she were at a funeral or a wedding.

Alice looked at the therapist, who stood beaming as a father beams at his child's first steps. Oh, well, she thought. He's entitled. How much pleasure can he get from this job, paddling around a pool with the disabled? And anyway she could look him in the eye. She was tall again.

"Hey, Mom, I'm tall again! Hey, Mom, I walked! Let's move to a swamp! I can walk!" She waved at her mother, then looked at the therapist again. He was young and trim. And I can look him in the eye, just like a normal upright person, she thought, her eyes moving down his torso and stopping at his tight blue bathing suit.

Alice spent much of her free time examining her muscles. She bent her arm like Popeye and gazed, fascinated, at the round, hard bulge.

"You look wonderful," her mother told her. But then, her mother had once told her she looked wonderful after Alice had been digging in the garden on a blazing-hot summer morning. "You're so pink," her mother said appreciatively, and Alice collapsed in the gravel driveway and spent two days in bed from heat prostration.

"Thanks, Mom," she said, thinking of the gray gravel swirling toward her hot face. But she *had* begun to feel wonderful.

"I don't think I've ever seen you look this healthy," her mother said.

Simchas sulked in a chair in the corner as she showed off her muscles.

"I love all this exercise," she said.

He looked suspiciously at her long, hard arms, and said, "So, strongman, why don't you go into the circus? And lift thousand-pound weights? Or pull a cart through Central Park or something?" She could see that in her wholesome enthusiasms she had betrayed him.

"This is such a wonderful place," she said. "The people are so warm, the staff so helpful. I really think I'm making progress, and I owe it all to the Institute. It's so intelligently organized, so civilized. . . ." She watched with delight as he sank lower and lower in his chair, plugging and unplugging his biofeedback machine. "That's what it is," she said, having pressed the most painful spot. "It's so intelligent, so sensible, so *civilized.* A rational, clear-headed operation."

Her mother looked at them. A little suspiciously, Alice thought.

She still slept through hydrotherapy each morning, but by nine-thirty, when she was stationed between the two pulleys attached to weights that she had to pull forward, pull to the sides, and forward again 150 times, she was wide-awake, chatting amiably with old men and women and two teenage boys who parked next to each other, between their pulleys. The boys always brought an enormous radio, which sat on the lap of one or the other and emitted rapid disc-jockey prattle interrupted by heavy plodding rock.

"I like only Elvis," an elderly lady with a purse sighed. "I don't know from these Neil Diamonds. Elvis, he has a voice. Like an angel."

"What's in your pocketbook?" Alice asked. "I've always wondered. Isn't it a little inconvenient to drag it around? You know, when you're just going to lift weights?"

The lady snapped it open. "Nothing. A handkerchief. A stick of gum . . . Oh, no. No, you don't," she cried suddenly as a nurse pushing a medication cart came up to her. "Not this time. Leave a poor old lady alone. I won't take them. I can't take these biotics. I have side effects."

"Mrs. Siegel, please. Be reasonable. They're *anti*biotics, they're your medicine."

"Such an itch in my vagina! And dizzy! I fell asleep at six last night, woke up at seven. It was seven P.M. and I thought it was seven in the morning and it was still dark. I thought, this is it, the world is coming to an end. . . ."

"Mrs. Siegel, you need this medicine. It helps you."

"Dark at seven o'clock. I was so scared. And with such an itch. How do these poor teenagers take these drugs? And pay for them, and look for them, and take them—dirty drugs. Oy, my poor Elvis, so fat and red. Drugs. It's drugs. It's always drugs. He needs these drugs?" The nurse poured the pills into a tiny paper cup and handed it to Mrs. Siegel with a bigger cup of water.

"*Me* they'll kill," she said, swallowing them with a flurry of gagging. "Look what they're doing to Elvis. And *he* has a voice like an angel."

At that moment, Alice saw a boy across the room. He has a *face* like an angel's, she thought. Actually, she realized, it was a face she had seen in a fresco, a Masaccio face. That face had been darker, but there was the same nose, prominent and elegant and not quite straight. And the same lips, puffy and wide, she had seen in the Brancacci Chapel. It was a Renaissance face and beneath it she was almost shocked to see a T-shirt instead of a doublet. "Surfers Have More Fun," the T-shirt said.

She pulled on her pulleys and stared at him. His lips were actually pink, and there was a slight gap between his front teeth. She tried to estimate his height—starting at his sneakers, gazing up his faded blue jeans, and along his pale yellow T-shirt to his beautiful face—but couldn't. His tan arms stood out against the arms of the drab wheelchair. He smiled at everyone. He smiles too much, Alice thought, for a newly crippled surfer. Perhaps he hit his head when whatever happened to him happened to him. He was all pastels: his blue jeans almost white, his yellow shirt, his pink lips. She couldn't see his eyes. But she could see him concentrating, lifting a barbell, biting his lower lip and leaving it slightly wet.

"Who's that?" she asked Moses.

"Who? Robert Redford over there?" But he was lovelier than Robert Redford. She had never seen anyone look so clean without seeming boring at the same time.

"Yeah. That one." He had high cheekbones without sunken cheeks.

"He's a new car accident. Snapped his spine. Nice kid, too." Nice kid, she thought, and for the rest of the day she thought of his moist lower lip and the gap between his teeth and the pastel figure framed in its gray wheelchair.

"Well, well, we're not so cheerful tonight, are we?" Simchas asked with obvious gratification. "No Olympic Gold today? Not even a Bronze?"

She was sitting, staring at the stars over the Coca-Cola bottling plant. She wheeled back from the window.

"Sorry," she said, as she watched her tire press into the soft leather of Simchas's right shoe. It didn't exactly roll over the shoe, but through it, as a bicycle rolls through sand, leaving a groove.

He sputtered and swore, but softly. He could retaliate against her health, but never against her illness or anything connected with it.

She chain-smoked while Simchas, sensing melancholy, came to life. This patient was an arsonist, but got caught. That one was a homosexual who came to be hypnotized so he could remember the license number of a man he blew under the West Side Highway. Alice paid no attention, barely heard. She wanted him to leave so she could roll into the hall and find the pastel boy's room.

"I'll roll you to the elevator," she said when his stories had run out, and when the doors closed on him and his sheepskin coat and sheepskin hat, she turned and went back down the hall, poking her head into each room.

"Fuck you, Betty Boop," shrieked a girl of about her age from the first room.

"Stroke," said the woman in the bed next to her apologetically. "The pill, I guess."

Farther down the hall, an enraged aide emerged from a room in huge strides, arms swinging at her sides. "Don't you ever talk to me that way," she yelled, coming back to the doorway. "And don't tell me what you'll do to me once you get out of here, 'cause, baby, the only way you're leavin' this place is feet first!"

From inside the room came murmurs of indignation and consolation. "Pay no attention to her," said voices aimed at a sobbing black girl lying on her stomach on a stretcher. Alice recognized her and realized the nurse was probably right.

"Dumb!" a patient hollered at the aide, who was stamping away again. "You're as dumb as a dog."

In the next room, which looked out on the Empire State Building, Alice found him.

"Hi, guys," she said, trying to seem casual. The other occupants looked at her curiously. A rich man from New England who had broken his neck fox hunting. A pleasant fat man, almost well. And a frail brown-haired boy from North Carolina who had broken his back diving into a stream at night. She had spoken to all of them except the rich man, who wore ascots and refused to speak to anyone. But she had never visited them. She tried to think of something to say. The rich man, who couldn't move even his head, closed his eyes. The fat man said hi, and turned back to "The Waltons." Joe, the boy with the broken back, smiled. She couldn't even look at the blond boy. The Empire State Building, brightly lit, loomed outside.

"Hey, can I have a cigarette?" Joe asked her. "You'll have to hold it, though."

She lit a cigarette for him and held it up to his mouth, taking it away when he had inhaled a lungful of smoke.

"Thanks," he said, blowing it out in a gust. She offered it to him again, and this time he blew it out in huge, languorous rings. They floated heavily toward the rich man with his eyes closed, sagging out of shape. She followed them with her eyes and then stole a quick glance at the blond boy, who was bare-chested. He watched the smoke rings too.

"Hey, all right!" he said to Joe. All right? Her fresco-turned-to-flesh opened his pink lips and the words "Hey, all right" came out? She suddenly took courage and looked openly at the tan against the white sheets.

"Oh, Alice, this is Christopher," said Joe in his polite North Carolina accent.

"I broke my spine in a car accident," Christopher said, gesturing dismissively at his motionless legs. "Totaled the fucking car, too."

"Where are you from? California?"

"New Jersey."

The next morning, as Holly rolled her past the room, she saw Christopher still in bed, still without a shirt.

"Hey, Doc." The head of the Institute was bent over him examining his legs. "Hey, Doc," he said again, giving the doctor a light punch in the arm, "I'm improving. I can touch my pecker and wiggle my toes!"

The doctor said: "That's fine, but I want you to wiggle your pecker and touch your toes."

Me too, Alice thought.

She pursued him over the next few weeks. He had been in Vietnam—"But I never killed anyone," he said—and she tried to imagine a helmet on his pale curls. He thought he might try aquiculture when he got out. She tried to picture him harvesting herring from a fish farm. He lived in New Jersey with his parents and two younger brothers. She tried to think of him changing his sneakers in a room with model airplanes and track trophies on the shelves. But she could see him only on the plaster wall in Florence, a velvet hat flopping to one side.

At night they sat on either side of Joe's bed and gossiped

about the nurses and therapists. And her only thoughts were how to advance the affair. Flirtation between wheelchairs was awkward. She couldn't casually brush against him, or accidentally touch his hand, or gaily fling herself into his lap.

"And then when I was in Mexico," he was telling Joe, "we were driving past this little town—a dump, you know, with straw huts—and they were running the bulls, so we stopped. And, oh man, it was really gross . . . they stabbed it and then they stuck the knife in and they twisted it and there was all this blood spurting all over and everyone was cheering, and they twisted the knife around. . . ."

She could invite him to her room. But what could she say? Come to my room and I'll press the button and lower the bed and ask a nurse to help us into it. . . .

". . . But they have great diving and snorkeling . . ."

She decided to ask him to come and listen to records. But, when it came to it, she couldn't. She listened to this story of Mexico, where the car accident had taken place, instead.

Christopher was as languidly cheerful as any surfer in any soft-drink commercial, and Alice would watch in amazement as he leaned back in his wheelchair and stretched his arms over his head while remarking on a passing nurse's figure, on the make of a helicopter buzzing by, on the sandy beaches he had left behind.

Too many drugs, Alice decided. They must have made him stupid, very stupid, too stupid to understand how depressed he ought to be, and she marveled as he tooled around in his wheelchair like someone who has just gotten a new car, pulling into his buddies' driveways with a honk of the horn.

Every morning, Alice tried to calculate when to leave her room in order to pass his room as he was heading for therapy.

"Hey, Brody," he would call. "Wait for me."

And she would stare at the muscles on his bare arm as he pushed the wheels forward and say, "Okay."

God, Alice thought. He doesn't even know he's crippled and pathetic. He thinks getting in here is like getting on the swim team.

Christopher seemed to view rehabilitation as a new sport. The wheelchairs and pulleys and silicone pads, the boards and strings and buckles it had taken Alice so long to accept he welcomed immediately, like new developments in sporting equipment—an advanced design of baseball glove or aerodynamically superior skis.

"Christopher," she said, "you're so, so *tan.*"

And she thought of what she had been missing all these years, all the golden jocks in striped socks and gym shorts she ignored as insufficiently intellectual. She could have spent so many sunny afternoons watching sturdy football players practice grunting, she could have gone to the Y and watched the swim team dive, she could have surrounded herself with all that confident male flesh. It's true she would not have found a surfer. There were no surfers in Westport. But there was a tennis team. She could have watched the tennis team, all dressed in white.

Now she watched Christopher, beside her, lifting weights. They lifted their barbells in unison. They held up their arms to compare muscles, and Alice felt the sweat of his arm against hers.

"Not bad, Brody," he said, looking at her biceps. "But no contest," he added, poking his own with his other hand, taking her hand and placing it on his tensed muscle.

"What a beautiful boy," Dr. Davis said as he came in. "Golden curls, rosy lips . . ."

"That's Christopher," Alice said. "Car accident. Broken spine. He's much better, except for his gluteus maximus."

"That delicate complexion—like a child's. Or a poet's. Yes, a poet's. Is he a poet, your Christopher?"

"Surfer."

Dr. Davis frowned slightly.

"Get back, fool!" Alice heard Simchas Fresser yelling in the hall. He scrambled into the room. "A wild youth in a wheelchair almost killed me," he said.

"A beautiful, beautiful boy," Dr. Davis said.

Simchas shot Alice a meaningful look.

"He's very nice," Alice said. "Car accident. Spine. Better except gluteus maximus . . ."

"He's a menace," said Simchas.

"Surfer," Alice said, and she gazed out the window at the Coca-Cola billboard and sighed. Christopher on a surfboard, Christopher getting off the surfboard, Christopher lying down on a towel in the sun, the water glistening on his chest, his bathing suit wet and . . . Pure luck, she thought, to have found a surfer in an institute.

She looked at Dr. Davis and Simchas. Simchas stood awkwardly, scowling down into his black beard, muttering. Dr. Davis sat on the edge of her bed, humming, smiling, surveying Simchas with mild curiosity. And outside she heard Christopher practicing wheelies.

Dr. Davis admired Simchas's tie and Simchas pulled at his beard. Alice smiled benignly at them, wondering who would leave first. If Dr. Davis left, she would be able to tell Simchas how inept the Institute switchboard was, occasioning his sympathy, or she would fill him in on her improving bowling scores and watch his eyes narrow in disgust. If Simchas left, Dr. Davis might launch into a dramatic recital of "Adonais." It would not be the first time. She wondered if he had a present for her and was waiting for Simchas to leave before handing it over.

"Hi, Alice. Oh, sorry. Didn't know you had guests," said Christopher, speeding into the room.

"This is Dr. Fresser, Christopher. And this is Dr. Davis."

"Doctors. Sorry. I'll come back later. Excuse me. Just came to see if you want to shoot a little hoop later."

"Shoot a hoop?" asked Simchas. His hand moved toward his shoulder holster.

"You're a very athletic young man," said Dr. Davis.

"Well, I *was* anyway. Look, I'll see you later, Alice."

"You have *beautiful* muscle tone. Have you ever thought of modeling?"

"Christopher surfs," Alice said. She thought Dr. Davis was laying it on a bit thick.

"You think I could model? You make a lot of bread modeling."

"A friend of mine is a male model. . . ."

"Not surprised," Simchas said into his beard.

"What? No, it's not surprising, is it? I love beauty, you know. And youth. That's why I love Alice. I *do* love Alice, you know," Dr. Davis said, smiling obliviously at Simchas and Christopher.

Oh, God, Alice thought. Not *now.*

"You have beautiful eyes, Christopher," Dr. Davis was saying. He held Christopher's head in his hands.

"He's an eye doctor," Alice said quickly.

"I have patients like you," Simchas boomed suddenly at Dr. Davis.

"I think I'll take a nap now," Alice said.

No one seemed to have heard. Dr. Davis told Alice she had wonderful taste, looked openly from Simchas to Christopher, and then winked at her. Simchas pulled at his beard as if it were a cord marked Emergency, but it had no effect. Christopher caught Alice's eye, pointed to the side of his head, and twirled his finger significantly. Alice smiled weakly. He looked radiant. His jeans hung low on his narrow waist, suggesting the absence of underpants. He really is irresistible, Alice thought. No wonder Dr. Davis stood with his hand on Christopher's shoulder. The curve from Christopher's neck to his shoulder was an especially lovely spot, and Alice watched it longingly, wondering if his hair smelled of shampoo, his face of Neutrogena soap. And there was Dr. Davis's lovely, gentle hand resting so close. *Was* Christopher wearing underwear? It suddenly seemed important to know.

"Alice, you're leering," Simchas said.

She looked up from Christopher's waist to see Simchas, growling and massive, fuming vigorously. Alice thought he looked wonderful.

"Now you're leering at *me*," Simchas said.

Alice quickly looked back at Christopher. But it didn't help. There he still was, in his white T-shirt. And there was Dr. Davis's hand on the top of his curls. She ogled first one, then the other. And there was Simchas, all flashing cuff links, and Christopher's long eyelashes and Dr. Davis's soft gray hair.

"I've got to take a *nap*," she yelled. "Get out. You're driving me nuts."

"Poor little lamb," said Dr. Davis, softly kissing her on the lips.

She gazed at him, trying to calm herself.

"Rude little lamb is more like it," said Simchas, glowering at her. "And stop looking at me like that!"

"Bye, Alice, see you," said Christopher. And she watched him spin his wheelchair around and leave her room.

Left alone, she closed her eyes and daydreamed. Christopher's sneakers dropped to the floor, then Dr. Davis's black bikini underpants, Simchas's silk tie—it was a hopeless muddle. Alice tried to sort it out, she tried to concentrate—but then it didn't matter anymore, and Alice drifted off to sleep, vaguely wondering if now she would go blind and grow hair on her palms on top of everything else.

.   .   .

"When is it?" Alice asked. "When are they showing it?"

"On Wednesday, but I'm telling you, we're not allowed to see it. It's a big secret. They've already asked the people who are going to be allowed to see it, and they told them not to mention it."

"I've *got* to see it. It's not fair," Alice said.

"Yeah, well," Christopher said.

Alice went to the recreational director and asked him why they weren't allowed to see the film.

"It's not pornography," he said. "It's to help people adjust, to help them live normal sex lives."

"Well, what about me? Don't I get to adjust?"

"Alice," said the recreational director. "We don't want to turn this into a side show. And you're just not crippled enough."

But I *am* crippled enough, she wanted to say. I can't fuck. I can't do it. But she was too embarrassed.

On Wednesday, Christopher came to her room. "Well, they're all at the movie."

"It's not fair," Alice said. "I bet it's hilarious," she said a minute later. "Don't be ashamed of your plastic leg. Your prosthesis can become a meaningful addition to your sexual experience."

"Your stump can be a turn-on," said Christopher.

"Park your wheelchairs beside the bed," she continued in a rich narrator's voice. They both wheeled to the bed, giggling. "Remove the arms of the chairs. You may even want to remove the arms of each other's chairs. Some cripples find this sensitive, sharing gesture adds to arousal."

Christopher, wagging his head and squaring his shoulders like a swaggering hood, snapping the fingers of one hand and muttering, "Hey, baby, wanna remove my arm?" pulled the arm of her chair out and flung it on the floor.

She smiled at him, her head slightly, coyly turned away. She flickered her lashes at him. "Oh, Christopher!" she sighed, and slowly, staring up at him from half-closed eyelids, she lifted the arm from his chair, and put it softly on the floor.

"Many couples enjoy lowering the bed together," she continued in her narrator's voice. "Instead of letting the noise of the motor distract or embarrass them, they concentrate on the sensuous vibrations of the controls in their hands."

Alice and Christopher reached for the controls of the bed and pushed the button together. The bed rumbled down.

"Helping each other onto the bed can be a significant stage in the cripples' sexual process. The physical contact necessary can further stimulate the partners," she said, as Christopher's hands closed around her waist and lifted her from the side of the wheelchair to the bed, "and kindle a sense of intimacy," she continued as she hauled Christopher up next to her. They sat staring at their legs. Hers were stiff, his longer and limp. They had stopped laughing. They looked at each other, in the eyes, for a moment, then looked away.

"Undressing your partner," she began again, again in the narrator's voice, because she could think of nothing else to do, "should be a physically exciting activity. If your partner has legs, and has feeling in them, you may want to stroke them as you remove his, or her, pants." They undressed each other, seriously removing shoes and socks, sitting on the edge of the bed. They unbuttoned each other's shirts and Alice could think of no narration. They were both breathing hard. Christopher had not said one word since "Hey, baby, wanna remove my arm?" She wondered if the door was locked, but she didn't care very much. She wondered how they would manage from here.

"Instead of lifting your own legs onto the bed as you usually do," she quickly said, in the deep voice, "lift your partner's." But when she swung up his long legs covered with golden hair, they went across her lap, pinning her to the bed. Christopher put his hands underneath his knees and lifted them up so she could pull herself back, and out. Then she pulled her own legs onto the bed. Christopher pulled her to him, embraced her, kissing her, breathing loudly.

"Should you discover that sexual intercourse in the missionary position is not yet within your range," she said suddenly, "do not be afraid to explore other possibilities. One variation . . ."

Christopher said, "Oh, shut up," kissed her on the forehead, and then swooped up his legs and spun around. She eyed his tan thighs. And then she heard, from the bottom of the bed, in a long, satisfied sigh, "Pussy."

The occupational therapist tilted his head to one side. "What?"

"I tell you I'm *crippled.*"

"But Alice, I know that. That's why you're here, and you're improving every day. I know it seems slow but . . ."

"Oh, shit," Alice said and rolled away.

In a room downstairs, next to the greenhouse, Alice was taught to get into and out of a car. The room and the greenhouse were part of a suite built by a rich patient for his stay at the Institute. There, in the kitchens where his cooks had worked, patients learned how to wash dishes and make muffins from a seated position. Sheets fluttered down over the bed in which he had recuperated, and patients rolled to its four corners to tuck them in. And in the spare bedroom, where his nurse had slept, a yellow Ford Galaxy stood tolerantly while the disabled opened its doors and slid inside. It had tires but no engine.

"Open the door first," Alice was told. "Then roll up and remove the arm of your wheelchair. Right. Now, here's the sliding board. . . ." It was a wooden board that looked like a skateboard without wheels. "And you put one end on the seat of the car, and then the other end on the edge of the seat of the wheelchair—that's right—and then you put your hands on it and sort of slide in. That's it, very good.'' Alice sat in the car and looked out the door. The room was carpeted. Her wheelchair—with a blue silicone cushion to prevent sores—waited for her.

"Do I fold up the wheelchair and pull it in?'' she asked.

"We'll learn that another time. You don't go out by yourself yet, do you?''

There were patients who went out by themselves. The Quad Squad barreled through the streets, crashing down one curb, rearing up over the next, with six-packs of beer nestled in their laps. But Alice could as easily imagine an infant taking itself out in its perambulator as Alice alone on a sidewalk in her wheelchair.

"No,'' she said. "I don't.''

Her first trip outside, with Stephanie, had been down the street to a nearby department store, where she had looked for shoes; the doctors told her she was almost ready to stand up at the parallel bars, and she decided to buy a symbolic pair of shoes. Sitting in the elevator on the way down, the hems of people's jackets in her face, she felt very much like an old lady let out of the nursing home and was sure she looked helpless and pathetic. She had consoled herself with visions of Cole Porter, who never looked helpless and pathetic.

This training in the yellow Galaxy was for a trip to Westport. She was going home for Christmas. Her parents were both going to be there.

Alice tried to remember what being home was like. Mostly, she recalled, you ate at a table with other people while the dog looked up pitifully at your plate and the cat rubbed against your calf.

"What else?" she asked Christopher.

"I don't know. You hang out with friends. Talk on the phone."

"That's what I do here," she said.

Her father's Jaguar was parked in front of the doors. She slid onto the dark-red leather seat. Her father lifted her legs in and set her heels on the carpet.

"Okay? Everything okay? Enough room? Sure you feel all right? Should I move the seat back? I think it's all the way back already, but if you want . . ." He cleared his throat. "Okay." He closed the door.

From the car she watched him on the sidewalk trying to fold the wheelchair. She could have told him he had only to pull up on the seat and it would immediately fold, but he didn't ask and she watched him struggle. He looked up at intervals to smile gallantly and reassuringly. *I'll have your tricycle ready any minute, sweetheart. Why don't you play with the Barbie doll, right over there, under the Christmas tree? Ouch . . . Nothing but Daddy's thumb . . .*

"Daddy," she finally called after opening the door, since the electric windows would not operate without the keys. "Daddy," she called, in some disgust. Her father looked up, and Alice suddenly felt very close to him, for which she felt very guilty almost immediately.

"Dad has a girlfriend," her brother said when she had arrived in Westport. They sat in his room, which still had mouse cages, bottles of stage blood, and model battleships stashed in its shelves and poking from the closet. The enthusiasms of his youth had been dressing up as a green-skinned monster with blood dripping from the sides of its mouth, letting his ninety-six white mice run over him as he lay on the floor, and burning battleships, which he had worked on for weeks, over heavily populated anthills. "A girlfriend with a son. He's got to. He's been gathering all the Uncle Wiggly books and wants to take them to Vancouver. And he keeps asking me where the electric trains are, and am I sure they're in working condition." Willie absent-mindedly spun a mouse exercise wheel that sat on his desk. "He must have a new girlfriend with a kid."

"Maybe he's entering his second childhood."

"Maybe he's a pederast." The toe of a green rubber monster foot that could be slipped over one's shoe stuck out of a closed drawer.

"Have you told Mom?" Alice asked.

"Of course I told Mom. She pays no attention. She says it's nostalgia. You know Mom. She says they're mementos and that he's very immature. I think she thinks it's sweet. You know, for a smart person, Mom is one of the dumbest people I've ever met. I told her to send a detective out there."

"Me too," said Alice. "When are they getting the divorce?"

Her brother sighed. "Sometime in January. I can't believe they're going to court. What are they going to say? I want to go to college and get out of here. Dad has rented someone's gatehouse for when he's here, and whenever he comes home he asks me if I want to see his 'digs'!" Her brother made a terrible face. "His *digs!*" he said. They both shook their heads.

On Main Street the next day, her brother rolled her through the Christmas shoppers in ski parkas.

"Vroom, vroom," he said, whipping her around the citizens, pretending they were slalom poles. "Woosh!"

"Don't break anything," sniffed a salesman in the Crystal Corner.

"Not even *one* glass?" she whined.

Her brother came home that night with a Christmas tree so big he had to cut off the top to stand it up, and it was so wide

Alice could barely wheel past it. She ran over the cat's tail twice, and when she approached, the dog backed into walls in terror.

Alice lay in her old room. She listened to the furnace rumbling. She heard the pipes banging now and then. The dog's toenails clicked across the floor above her.

It was so good to be home, she thought, and wondered where everyone else was. Stephanie Carter was probably asleep. Holly would be putting out milk and cookies for Santa Claus. She wondered if Simchas was at home, asleep with an issue of *Commentary* on his chest. Or was he at a party? Drenched in aftershave, bellowing sweet nothings at some attractive young woman who was sound of gait and wore a colorful blouse? Perhaps Dr. Davis was at the same party, boring attractive young men with lengthy quotations: "Hail to thee, blithe spirit! . . ." Christopher and her friends at the Institute would be lying in their beds, watching television. They would be watching *It's a Wonderful Life.* Alice wished she had a TV in her room so she could watch *It's a Wonderful Life* too. And why couldn't she sleep?

The day before Alice went home, Mrs. Cohen had moved both her thumbs. A breakthrough. Mrs. Cohen was great. Had she gone home for Christmas? Alice had seen a handsome new outpatient learning to use an artificial leg, and she found out that her cute therapist in the pool, who looked so sexy in his wet bathing suit, was engaged.

Alice lay in her bed, looking out the window at the dark, and wondered briefly where the Coca-Cola sign was. That's sick, she thought. I'm home. There are stars outside. But at every noise her first thought was of a night nurse coming to shine a flashlight in her eyes. It was only the dog, or the wind, or the flush of a toilet, and Alice closed her eyes, trying to ignore the flicker of disappointment she felt.

.   .   .

In the morning, she went impatiently into the living room. "Hmmph!" said her grandmother, who stood in a bathrobe, Kleenex shreds poking from its cuffs and pockets. "The goyim got their white Christmas."

Alice looked outside at the lawn, a white, voluptuous curve toward the woods below. Robins picked their way through the snow, which was not deep but was new and very white. The dog galloped crazily by, scattering the indignant birds. He pawed and snapped at the snow, sweeping his head back and forth in a wide arc, then dropped and rolled wildly. His ecstatic legs pointed to a clear blue sky. Branches coated with ice clicked in the wind. Although no one was at school on Christmas, the shrill bell of the nearby elementary school rang. The bell was set to go off every day, and every day it rang at nine, twelve, one, and three-thirty. Even on Saturdays, even on Christmas. Strings rattled against the school's metal flagpole, making hollow musical sounds. Alice put her bare feet on the carpet, which was warm from the sun. She breathed on the cold window and pressed it with her palm, leaving a bleary print. An enormous nostalgia made her suddenly very happy. Her father had insisted on frying kippers, and the house was full of fishy smoke.

"Thanks for the tape recorder, Grandma," her brother said when they began opening their presents.

"Ooh, I look at you and I salivate!" her grandmother answered.

"Mother!" said Alice's mother.

"Thanks, Grandpa," said Alice's brother.

"Mmwah!"

"I don't want anything," her grandmother was saying. "I have everything. I told you not to get me anything. I don't need anything. . . . Oh! a dish for used tea bags! I've always wanted one! Such a waste, throwing out the bag after one cup . . ."

Her grandfather kissed Alice several times and handed her

a big box. It held a long raccoon coat, "So you don't catch cold," he explained. She put it on and rolled up and down the hall shouting, "JAP-mobile" and making siren noises. She was very excited, feeling this was one step closer to Cole Porter.

"OOH", her grandmother's voice echoed through the house, "I LOOK AT YOU AND I SALIVATE!"

"Willie," her mother called, "turn off that goddamn tape recorder!"

Her grandmother held an album of pictures. "Dead," she said, putting her finger on the face of a man in a row of smiling faces at her daughter's wedding. "Dead, dead, dead, dead . . ." she continued in a jaunty singsong, pressing her finger on the rest of the gray faces. "Dead, dead, dead . . ."

Alice sat in her wheelchair in her fur coat and looked around her at her family. Her father began to complain about the coffee, her grandmother suddenly leaped toward the bathroom for a good sneeze, her grandfather kissed her brother, who squirmed, and her mother exclaimed at how pretty and bright the torn wrapping paper looked strewn on the floor. Alice slid onto the couch and hid her wheelchair behind it. There were bagels and lox and creamed herring, and it could have been almost any Christmas at the Brodys'.

"Well," said her father, striding up to the window, "a fine day, a fine day."

Her mother looked at the Christmas stockings. They were long brown socks that belonged to Alice's father, bulging with oranges, silver dollars, and packs of gum, and reminded Alice of the dangling, misshapen feet of poor Mrs. Cohen at the Institute. She watched her mother take two red bows from the floor and stick them to the brown socks.

"There," she said.

Willie lay on the floor reading the paper. She heard her

grandmother puttering in the kitchen. "Hmmph," she snorted at the rattling pots and pans. "To the woods he has to go? To Canada no less? Oy, oy, oy . . ."

Alice considered returning to her wheelchair and keeping her grandmother company, but she would run over Willie's fingers, or get caught in the kitchen door, or her wheels would become tangled with yarn and ribbons like a kitten with a ball of string.

Her father was dressed, wearing a tattersall vest and smoking a pipe, the sahib among the natives in their wrinkled pajamas.

"Ah," he said, looking out the window. "The barn. The sound of a horse munching its oats, the steamy, horsy smell . . . But those days are gone. . . ."

"Isn't it lovely?" Alice's mother agreed. "What a delightful guesthouse it will make."

"And the Harris's field," he continued, after glaring at her. "Once so rustic and free. Just look what's become of the countryside."

"Yes, isn't it marvelous?" Alice's mother said. "Such a nice fence, and in the summer it's full of beautiful flowers, all around the swimming pool. . . ."

"There are so many new people on the road."

"Such interesting ones. And they obey the speed limit."

For a moment, Alice wondered if her mother tortured her father on purpose.

Her parents were practically divorced, and behaved no differently toward each other than they had for the past ten years, unless they were a bit more polite. Alice was in a wheelchair, and still counted her presents and wondered if Willie had somehow gotten more. If personalities were formed in the first five years of life, then perhaps so were Christmases, and no matter what happened, the Brodys would gather on the gold carpet year after year, maimed, toothless, divorced, dead, and shake boxes, saying, "I wonder what this could be."

But her mother had bought unusually modest gifts, and Alice realized it was because she had no money. It took Alice all afternoon to come up with this explanation, it was so startling. Her father, on the other hand, had given lavish presents, and had wished everyone a Merry Winter Solstice Festival, for he disapproved of Jews celebrating Christmas. He normally left all gift buying to Alice's mother and grumbled about pagan rituals, and Alice accepted the Nikon camera he gave her in the spirit of a bribe.

"Simchas gave me the idea," he told her.

Throughout the day, Alice and Willie were inseparable. She craved his company, and he stayed near her, wherever she went. He didn't say much, but seemed to take some comfort from her as well. Roaming around the house with him towering at her side, she felt a little like a pet. A pet sister.

An odd Christmas, she finally decided. And, of course, the last one they would all spend together.

"It's a historic moment," Willie said. "I think we should document it."

Alice photographed their father's drooping head and took a rather blurry shot of Grandma on the run; Willie taped the accompanying sigh and the "Hetch!" Then they got bored and rolled off to take pictures of Spotnose sleeping on the piano.

"She came home white," her brother told her, weeks later, in her room at the Institute. "I know she wasn't going to tell me anything, but she was so upset. She was really white. And she'd been crying. It was horrible. He got on the witness stand and said the house was messy."

They looked at each other.

"I'm not kidding, Alice. And Mom got on the stand and burst out crying. How can a grown man insist on going to court so he can complain about his wife's not dusting? And you know what else? He told her, last summer, when you were really sick, that he was going on a vacation and that she shouldn't call him. What if you'd . . ." He stopped. "You know," he said.

"I bet he's already remarried," she said.

Her brother looked grim. "I don't think he's a very good role model for me."

When the announcement finally came, they were not surprised. Their father sat on a molded fiber-glass chair.

"I—ahem, ahem. I have something to tell you," he said, his neck twisting in its collar. "It's something very important to me and I realize it will come as something of a shock."

Alice saw one corner of her brother's mouth moving slowly upward, and then slowly down again. No giggling, no giggling, Alice, she told herself.

"And I just want you both to realize how much I, ahem, respect your mother. . . ."

Alice tried to think of a sarcastic remark.

". . . But anyway, I feel that I have found myself in British Columbia. . . ." He went on about fulfillment, independence, and responsibility, and then he said he had met someone. At a ski lodge. She had a nine-year-old son. She was thirty-five. She was a schoolteacher. They were getting married in March.

"Is she Jewish?" her brother asked in a Yiddish accent.

When their father said no, they were both stunned. It was true their father hated New York Jews, intellectual Jews, short Jews, and Yiddish. But he had always forced his children to go to Sunday school, even when they cried and bit. He had forced them to participate in all the watery ceremonies of reform Judaism. He had insisted on their attending high holy day services, he had even been the temple's official shofar blower, and he had been outraged when their mother served ham on Friday night.

"And *we* had to go to Sunday school?" Alice asked. "How unfair!"

.   .   .

Alice's father sent her a clipping from *Time* about a ballet dancer who had a hip replacement, and a Jules Feiffer cartoon in which a little girl pulled a gun on her father. Did she use the camera? he wondered. She refused to write back. She used the camera to take black-and-white pictures of her empty shoes.

Alice's mother seemed slightly dazed most of the time, as if she had just woken up. "What?" she would say, no matter what you had just said to her. And then, quickly, "Oh! Yes, of course!" She had gained a little weight, and whenever she came to visit with Louie Scifo, Alice noticed that he ran to the cafeteria and returned with doughnuts and ice cream for her mother. Alice decided he was fattening her up so that, by the time she came to her senses, she would be obese and unable to get another man.

"Here, Brenda, eat this. It's good," he would say. And, with glassy eyes, Alice's mother would push the danish into her mouth.

"Brenda, *mangia!*" And Alice's mother would lift the wooden ice-cream spoon to her lips.

"Mom, maybe you shouldn't eat quite so much," Alice once timidly suggested.

"What?" her mother said. "Oh! Yes, of course!" she answered, biting into the chocolate cake.

And Louie Scifo would say, "She's hungry. Mommy's hungry. Let Mommy eat."

Alice had been forced to recognize that Louie Scifo was becoming a fixed part of her mother's life, and of her own. The hairs on the back of her neck stood up when he entered the room, but her mother looked so helpless that she was afraid to upset her and never said anything.

Alice had never been a Girl Scout, but she imagined it must be something like being a patient at the Institute. It's true they didn't march in parades like the Girl Scouts, but Alice went to hear Benny Goodman at a benefit for the Institute at Carnegie Hall, and when she rolled in with the other patients, only slightly embarrassed that she was the recipient of a benefit instead of a patron, she felt very much like a Girl Scout, or at least a float, filing along Main Street on Memorial Day. And as at Girl Scout meetings there were pot-holder making, drawing, and cooking at the Institute. The halls of the Institute had become her whole world, like high school. When she went out, it felt like a field trip, an educational excursion, for which she needed lunch money, on which she would have to write a report. When she went to the movies with Stephanie and James, it was the steps—twelve of them, in the dark, covered with dark-blue carpeting—not the movie, that impressed her. She forgot who was in the movie and what it was about almost immediately. But she could recall in minute detail the journey up the steps—Stephanie pulling at the footrests, the usher pushing at her back, James standing awkwardly watching, while she, tilting wildly, covered her eyes with her hands, partly from fear and partly from embarrassment.

All that impressed her from her trip to Bloomingdale's was the severe slope of the sidewalk, which she had never noticed. With Cindy hanging helplessly on to the wheelchair, flapping behind her like a flag, Alice careened along Fifty-ninth Street, desperately trying to stay on course, until the chair, still trailing Cindy, wrapped around a tree surrounded by tiny, dry dog turds. When they had extricated themselves, she and Cindy proceeded slowly to the corner, where they waited, trying to look appealing, until a man in a camel's-hair coat with tassels on his shoes helped them down, and up onto the other side of the street. They finally flagged a cab, whose driver put the chair in his trunk after Alice had slid in, and then said, "Not everyone would've stopped, you know. I mean it's a lot of trouble to. Well, we don't *have* to stop, there's no law or anything, so you're lucky I stopped because as I say a lot of your drivers would have just kept on going, and you would have been standing there a long time. . . ."

Cindy pushed a five-dollar bill through the plastic partition and said, "Shut the fuck up."

Which Alice rather liked. "Yeah," she said, although she would never have said it on her own. And it felt like a field trip, like going to the UN or the Shakespeare theater in Stratford. When she got back, she would tell Christopher or one of the therapists or Moses. Then she would tell her mother, who would say, "What? Of course!" And then she would tell Simchas, who would look at her as if to say, "What did you expect? The world is a series of steps and slopes, and all the people merely wheelchairs." When she was with Simchas, she felt that must be true. Going out seemed as difficult for him as it was for her: the oppressive clicking of the taxi meter, the tyranny of waiters who insisted on being pleasant for good tips, the sidewalk brushing against his custom-made shoes until they would have to be resoled.

One Sunday, Simchas came to get her and for the first time they went to his house. He sat next to her in the cab, tapping his feet, drumming his short pink fingers on the seat.

"Nervous?" she asked.

"Bah," he said.

When he paid the driver, he pulled a billfold and a small change purse out of his pocket. She had never seen a man with a change purse. He counted out the coins carefully, the way tourists handling unfamiliar currency do, peering at every coin, reading the denomination, comparing each in size to the others.

The doorman helped set up the wheelchair, which in the slight rain would necessitate a tip. He and Simchas dragged her up the steps and into the elevator. Simchas, pinned to the wall behind her, drummed his fingers on her head.

"Alice," he said, in a soft, sincere voice. "Alice," he said again in the same tone, so unlike him that it startled her. He put both pink hands on her head, like a priest making a blessing. "Since I met you, Alice," he said, a little catch in his throat, "I've . . . I've stopped taking Elavil."

The elevator doors opened and he wheeled her toward his apartment, pulling out a leather key case in which all the keys were neatly tucked. The apartment was white. The walls were white, the carpet was white. The furniture was not white, but it was Bauhaus and might as well have been. Nothing looked comfortable. She was glad she always traveled with her own chair.

"Chez Simchas," he said proudly, pushing her into the middle of the living room as if he were carrying her over the threshold. He walked around to face her, slightly puffed up, his hands on his hips, opening his smiling mouth to speak, when a look of horror spread over his face.

"What's wrong?" she cried, frightened. "Simchas!" Turning behind her to follow his horrified gaze, she saw two black streaks on the carpet. The white carpet, chaste and disapproving, and then the greasy black parallel streaks, tracks of filth that led directly to her wheels. She felt as if she had shit on the floor.

"Oh, Simchas. God, I'm so sorry. Your beautiful white carpet . . . I guess because it was wet out . . ."

Simchas seemed to be hypnotizing himself—his eyes had rolled back into his head and he was breathing deeply—unless he was having some sort of fit.

"Simchas!" she said. "Are you all right? Hey!"

He took a deep breath, opened his eyes, and said, "Would you excuse me for a moment?" She sat in the middle of the room as if in a desert. He returned with a can of rug cleaner, which he pointed at the offending stripes. Thick white foam hit the rug in loud spurts.

"But, Simchas . . ." she kept saying, as he, completely involved, appeared not to hear her. "But, Simchas! Listen, Simchas," she said when the spraying finally stopped. "How do I get off the damn thing?" His nostrils flared and he looked as if he might cry as he realized she would leave new tracks on her way off the rug. Then he looked at her, and visibly composed his distorted features.

"It's all right, Brody," he said finally. "It's all right," he said, forcing his face into a smile that looked like a grimace. But he held it, waving a hand weakly at the rug. "It's all right."

And at that moment she realized he loved her.

He left the room, returning a minute later with shirt cardboards which he laid in two trails from the wheelchair to the parquet of the hall.

"I'm sorry," she said, as he wheeled her over the cardboard trail. "Next time I'll wipe my wheels."

"It's all right, Brody," he said generously. "I know you won't do it again."

The bedroom was full of books and very shiny mahogany furniture. The bed, she noticed, was really two beds, pushed together under the reign of one massive headboard. Each bed was tightly made, with crisp, sparkling white sheets peering out over lemon-yellow blankets. Each bed had two plump pillows. But somehow Alice, who loved beds and loved getting into freshly made ones, didn't want to get into either one of these, the way she never wanted to bite into marzipan, no matter how good it looked, because she knew it tasted like sawdust. These beds tasted like sawdust. She knew it.

"These are my closets," Simchas was saying, opening the doors on suits and ties and shoes neatly hung in bags. "This is my desk . . . this is my answering machine . . ." He flipped the switch to rewind and then to playback.

"Click. Bzzzzzzzzzzzz," said the machine.

"They hung up. Damn," said Simchas.

"Click. Bzzzzzzzzzzzzzz," said the machine again.

". . . must be something wrong with the machine. . . ."

"We haven't heard from you. It's not right . . . Mom," said an accented voice, as if she were signing a letter.

"I don't want to come anymore," said the next voice, a man's. "I saw you sleeping during Friday's session. I hate you. (Pause.) This is Robert Wills."

"Click. Bzzzzzzzzzzzzzz," the machine continued, and then, "This is Susan James, Dr. Fresser, and I can't sleep. I mean, I couldn't sleep last night. Could you hypnotize me over the phone? Thank you. The number is . . ."

"She thinks I won't charge her!" Simchas was yelling. "She thinks I won't charge her over the phone!" He was incredulous. The machine stopped. Alice rolled past the electric bicycle and the electric valet pants presser into the bathroom. There was a shower caddy, cradling neat plastic bottles of shampoo and cream rinse next to different-sized brushes and different-shaped sponges. There was a magnetic soap holder, which stuck into the soap and then onto the wall. There was a filter on the faucet of the sink. There was soap on a rope. There was an impressive array of colognes and aftershave. There was an electric toothbrush and a Water Pik.

The technology of the kitchen was even more impressive. An electric yogurt maker, electric coffee grinder, a Cuisinart, an electric breadbox, and the battery-operated vacuum for the kitchen table.

"Can I have something to eat?" she asked, afraid to touch anything. He gave her sardines.

"Do you give sardines to the maid for lunch?" she asked.

"Tuna," he said.

"Does the maid like you?" she asked.

"Of course the maid likes me. I'm a sweet person. Why wouldn't the maid like me? I'm very neat."

She was sure the maid hated him in spite of his being neat. She took out a cigarette.

"Not in my house, Brody."

She put it away. He sat across from her at the table, reading through old copies of *The New York Times,* taking notes. She looked more carefully. He was reading the week's restaurant reviews and listing the names of the restaurants in a black book.

They went to a Rumanian restaurant. A balding man in a cheap leather jacket stood behind an electric piano and sang, "Feelinks, nothing more than feelinks . . ." When he began singing "I'm uh Rhinestun Cowboy," she began to giggle. The unlikely musician then "muved ulunk" to some traditional Israeli songs.

"I thought this was a Rumanian restaurant," Alice said, but Simchas, to whom the remark was addressed, had leaped up suddenly and was clapping his hands over his head and singing in a resounding voice. Alice's father had taught her to look accusingly at the next table when she dropped a spoon at a restaurant. She glared at the fat man and his ruddy wife at the next table, but there was no way anyone would believe that Simchas had fallen off their table and not hers. She looked at him. His arms were out and he was on tiptoe in what seemed to be some sort of dance.

"Yabababa," he sang. Alice drank her beer.

On the way home, she sat close to him in the cab. She put her hand on his leg. She nuzzled his neck. She began to kiss him.

"You know I don't like to kiss with tongues," he said, squirming. "It's not sanitary."

"Simchas, don't take me back to that place. Take me home with you, Simchas. Come on."

"Won't they worry?"

"I'll call them. They think it's healthy. Come on, Simchas," she said, moving her hand up his leg, "take me home."

She was a little tipsy and each time her hand found his, she was sure it thrilled him. It probably stirred his blood. Just being close to her in the bumpy taxi was probably testing his self-control. He was muttering, "Dinner with colleague; discussed biofeedback in physical rehabilitation; $30.85" into a tiny tape recorder. It was for tax purposes. "Taxi home," he continued.

"Oh, Simchas," she murmured, as she slid gracefully from car to chair, wrapping her fur coat around her.

"Oy," Simchas groaned in response, for in fact one stiff leg remained stubbornly in the cab and the rest of her had collapsed into the chair onto his arm. "Alice, please," he muttered as she put her arms around his waist, thinking he was hugging her. "Alice," he said, pulling at the arm caught between the back of her seat and her heavy, drunken mass. With his other hand he tried to pry her foot loose from beneath the taxi seat, for the cab driver had begun his sinister approach in search of tips from one side, and the doorman crept up on the other. "There!" Simchas cried, jerking her foot and his arm free at the same moment.

"No thanks!" he said triumphantly to the cab driver.

"That's all right!" he sang to the doorman, as he tugged the wheelchair, one step at a time, up the staircase.

"Well, I am not sex machine," Simchas protested. When he was upset he left off articles. She pictured a vending machine. Her quarter was in it and she pushed and pushed the knob. But the Nestlé's Crunch stayed in the slot, safe behind glass.

"I'm not sex machine," he said defensively.

"That's true," she said, trying to comfort him. He glared at her.

Whenever she visited him after that night, he carefully helped her into the bed on the right and tucked her in very tightly. Then he would put on his pajamas. Then he would open a volume of Cynthia Ozick stories. Then he would start to snore.

"Brody," he would say, whenever she tried to move

through the sheets tight as corsets toward his bed, "you are sex fiend." She would sigh and try to turn the other way. Maybe he's a little nervous, she would think. Maybe he needs more time. Maybe when I get better, whenever that will be. Then she would try to turn back to look at him.

"Sex fiend!" he would say, catching her glance.

And she knew it wasn't because she was sick. It wouldn't get better when she was better. It was because she was better.

"I took a *Valium,*" he would add, seeing she was still staring at him.

By the end of March she was walking. When they first aimed her at the parallel bars, she felt joy at the prospect of walking so many steps on dry land, and loathing at the bars themselves, reminiscent of all the public-TV documentaries on heroic cripples. She would be walking, so she knew she was getting better. But developing an intimate knowledge of yet another piece of equipment designed for the disabled made her feel somehow more crippled. However, once she walked the six feet through the bars, swinging her legs in small, stiff semicircles, she was exhilarated. She walked as if her pants were down around her ankles, but a smile kept creeping across her face. She had bought new, very expensive shoes for the occasion. Other patients watched her from tilt tables and mats and cheered. She thought, Now I'll make a more elegant dinner companion. Maybe Dr. Davis will leave his wife.

When she went out, she went out using the walker. She went on a walk with Stephanie on a warm, wet day. The sidewalks were wet, and the walker crunched along, making tiny extra footsteps. They crossed the street so slowly that the light changed.

"We're done for," Alice moaned, looking at the wall of roaring yellow taxis. But they made it to the other side and Alice put the walker up on the curb and then pulled herself up after it, just as she had practiced on the fire stairs of the Institute.

They walked to a small park a half block away and Alice collapsed on a bench. The walker stuck out in front of her at the same angle as her legs.

"I'm leaving my husband," Stephanie said.

"How come?" Alice asked. Her eyes were closed. The sun felt good in the wet air.

"My boyfriend committed suicide. I'm going to Los Angeles."

They sat on the bench, facing the sun, their eyes closed.

"That's terrible, Stephanie," Alice said.

"Well, you don't really need me now."

"I meant about your boyfriend."

"I thought he was a little weird. His bedroom was painted black."

The sun went behind a cloud and Alice suddenly felt cold.

"My name isn't really Stephanie," Stephanie said.

Alice looked at her.

"It's not," Stephanie said. "It's Lizzie. I changed it when I was in the army."

"You were in the army?"

"I hated it. They told me I didn't look like a Lizzie, that I looked like a Stephanie. So I changed it."

"You do look like a Stephanie."

"I know. I won't leave until you can really spare me, you know. I don't really want to go. But I've got to start over."

"Yeah, me too," said Alice.

They walked back and Alice felt terrible, because she knew they would write to each other only once in a while, and then not at all, and she was attached to Stephanie.

And Alice remembered the first time she had met her, how proper she'd been, how formal.

"He hung himself," said Stephanie. Alice had been yearning to ask.

Her doctors told her she was progressing beautifully. Alice decided that if she couldn't get into graduate school when she finished college, she would become a physical therapist. She made a vow. Of course, so had Martin Luther, she sometimes reminded herself. She herself had vowed every Yom Kippur to stop masturbating and picking her nose. And look at me, she thought mournfully.

Jean, the therapist, was hollering, "Quit slackin' off, Brody! We're in training, remember?"

How, Alice wondered, could I forget?

"We have only two weeks to get in shape, so let's go!" hollered Jean through her frosted lips. "I saw the second floor training this morning, and they are gonna be tough to beat, let me tell you. They may not have many legs, but some of them can use their arms pretty good, so let's go! Up, down, up, down . . ."

Alice put her hands behind her head and began doing sit-ups.

"Up, down, up, down . . ."

As she pulled up she saw the other patients in a peripheral whirl. As she fell back, she closed her eyes.

"Up, down, up, down, come on, guys, move it!"

They had been chosen to represent the fourth floor in a volleyball game against the second floor.

"Riva, forget the sit-ups. Just sit. Try to stay upright. Okay. Good. But the rest of you, work!"

They had a special training session every day to get in shape. Alice looked at Riva's shape. It was leaning precariously to one side. Alice stuck out her hand and nudged the middle-aged woman back into place before Jean could see.

"Thanks," came the slow voice.

"Faster, faster," yelled Jean, jumping up and down in her enthusiasm. "Go, go, go!"

Alice hated volleyball. People played it at the beach in TV commercials. Not sitting on gray mats. Alice had always missed the ball when she played it in school, and it made her feel stupid in a way that only missing a ball can.

"Okay," said Jean. "Quittin' time! Tomorrow we set up the net and start practicing. You did great! You're a great bunch," she said, pulling the two skinny, silent stroke victims into their chairs. "I'm proud to work with you," she said as she hauled Riva into her chair. Jean helped Alice stand up, and she stumbled back to her room behind the walker. She was exhausted.

For two weeks they worked out. Riva swayed dangerously while the rest of them sweated and panted and the three who could speak complained. Jean danced enthusiastically before them as they lifted their arms toward the ball. Alice had never seen a ball look so big. It looked as big as a medicine ball and hurtled from the sky at them as from the gods. When they missed, it thwacked the mat and lay still. When it was aimed at the stroke victim named Mrs. Antonini, she would lift her hands, cover her face, and turn her shoulders to fend it off.

"That's not how we *play!*" Jean would cry in exasperation. When it was aimed at the other stroke victim, he would catch it.

"That's not how we *play!*" Jean shouted again.

"Way to go! All right! Good eye!" she would shout in between.

Alice's arms were by now plump and round. She could lift fifty pounds in each arm fifty times. She wore short-sleeved shirts. She began to hit the ball back to Jean instead of swiping at it impotently. She began to enjoy the game, hitting the ball with a loud, hard smack and sending it over Jean's bobbing head.

"Do it! All right, Brody! Way to go!" the therapist would cry, and Alice would self-consciously note how gratified she felt, she, an intelligent person, at hitting a big ball over someone's head.

"No, no, Mr. Sopkin. You're not supposed to catch it. Try to hit it back," said the therapist.

"He can't help it," Christopher said. "It's too fast for him."

"I think he thinks he's supposed to catch it. Look how pleased he is. Mr. Sopkin? Can I have it back? Will you try to hit it back next time? Thank you, Mr. Sopkin."

"This is what you want to become?" Riva would thickly whisper to Alice, nodding at Jean.

"It's not an easy job," Alice would reply with dignity.

Then the ball would whizz between them and Riva would shriek "Yaaaaaaaahhh!" and tip over.

"That is definitely not how we play," Jean would mutter, propping Riva from behind with a rolled-up mat.

And all this time, sitting behind Alice, was her therapist from the pool.

"Nice one, Brody!" he would say when she hit the ball, shifting his position. He sat behind her, his knees against her back, holding her up. She couldn't bend enough to sit up herself. She leaned, as if feminine and fatigued, on his knees bent in his white pants.

On the morning of the game, patients from the second floor came up in a convoy and gathered at one end of the exercise room. There were three referees, with a total of two legs, lined up in an asymmetrical row, looking around in excitement, occasionally nudging each other, exchanging professional tips. The floor was covered by the gray mats, a truncated net stretched across the middle a few feet from the ground. It reached the therapists' waists as they tightened it.

"Yay!" called the fourth-floor patients as Alice and her teammates filed in.

"Booo!" said the second floor.

Riva giggled uncontrollably. Christopher clasped his hands high above his head as if in victory. The stroke victims smiled mildly, their eyes darting from person to person. The wheelchairs rolled onto the mat and their occupants unloaded while the spectators, surrounding them in wheelchairs and stretchers, called, "Go!" Alice stopped her chair at the edge of the mat and was handed her walker. As she stood and guided it to her position at the net, a man on the other team yelled, "No fair, no fair! No fair! She can walk!"

Everyone stared at him.

"Shut up, Arthur," said one of his teammates.

"It's not fair," he muttered.

Alice looked at him as a therapist lowered her, like a leaning tower, to the floor. Arthur had legs, but from their casual arrangement on the floor she suspected they were useless. Still, she thought, Arthur is a beast.

She sat on the far right, close to the net. The man who caught the ball sat next to her, a mild stroke named Mickey next to him. A therapist sat directly behind her, propping her up with his knees, and Riva behind him. The lady who ducked sat in the middle, and Christopher on the end. It was not an impressive assembly, she decided. But then neither, on the whole, was the visiting team.

"The opposition's key player," whispered Jean to her team, "is that pretty girl on the Swedish tilt table." Towering above her teammates, a lovely fair-complexioned girl leaned over a table that had been cranked upright. Pillows surrounded her on the floor although she was strapped in.

"Oh, man," Alice's team was whining. "They'll slaughter us. . . . Is that fair? I don't think it's fair. . . . She's so tall on that thing. . . . Nobody *said* . . ."

Jean, a whistle around her neck, told them to pipe down. "Oh, wow . . . What a rip . . . I don't believe it. . . . They'll *slaughter* us," they continued.

Moses stood at the net and spun the ball on his index finger. "Ahm dee *score*keeper, man! And ah say, play ball!"

The other team served and Riva, miraculously, returned the ball. It lobbed gracefully to Arthur, the man who had objected to Alice walking. He smashed it down over the net.

"Spiking! Spiking!" called all the referees at once.

"That's not spiking," shouted the man, grabbing the ball, which had rolled back to him. "*This* is!" And he lifted up his brawny arm and slugged the helpless ball so hard that Alice couldn't even tell where it had gone, until she heard a loud resonant smack behind her. The lady who generally ducked the ball had picked that moment not to. She had been gazing stupidly at the ceiling. Now she lay dazed on the mat, a round red splotch on her face. Great tears rolled down her cheeks to the mat.

"Booo," called the spectators.

"You asshole," yelled Christopher.

"He did it on purpose," said Mickey, who rarely said anything.

"I did not," Arthur began, but he was interrupted by a terrible sound, a kind of whinny. "Yee-ee-ee," came the cry from the stricken woman. Jean dried her eyes and sat her up.

The game ended quickly. Christopher served the ball to one side of the girl perched on the tilt table and then the other. While Arthur swore, the ball sailed over his head, past the lax, flapping arms of the quadriplegics posted beside the pretty girl, just beneath her fingertips and onto the pillows with a soft plop.

"There," he said without a smile when it was over. "It's not nice to hit old ladies," he said to Arthur. Alice thought he looked almost heroic, pulling himself into his wheelchair and rolling straight-backed from the room.

"Mr. Sopkin, please give us the ball," Alice heard, as she left. "The game is over, Mr. Sopkin."

Alice walked behind her wheelchair, pushing it, leaning on it for support.

"See?" said Arthur to a nurse who had come up to get him, and he pointed an accusing finger at Alice.

Soon after the volleyball game Christopher asked Alice to meet him in the greenhouse. She went with her walker and sat on a wooden crate to wait. The greenhouse had the largest collection of begonias she had ever seen. Plants from patients' rooms, probably. They had become huge, spilling over their pots.

A shimmering green parrot flew suddenly from one end of the greenhouse to the other. "Ted!" it screeched. "Ted! Ted!"

"You scared me, you stupid bird," Alice said. She was terrified of birds. Robins used to fly inside the barn and flutter frantically against the walls trying to get out. She looked up at the parrot against the glass panels of the roof and wished she weren't afraid. For here was a potential pet.

"Wendy says!" cried the bird, blinking.

Alice looked at its bill—two knife-edged sea shells clicking ominously together. Its long, scaly bird toes wrapped around a bar suspended from the ceiling. Just like my trapeze, Alice thought.

"Wendy says!"

"Says what?" Alice asked the bird politely, hoping it wouldn't charge. It seemed to her as large as an eagle, and as fierce. "Who is Wendy? Who's Ted? Why are you telling me this? Do you want to sit on my shoulder?" She shuddered. It was no good. She was sure it would grab her in its claws and drag her through the foliage. "Look, forget it, okay? You're much too noble to be a pet. Hail to thee, blithe spirit, and all that? Born free, et cetera?"

The parrot clamped its toes on its bar more firmly and began calling for Ted. Alice wrapped her fingers around the walker and waited for Christopher.

When he came, he was beaming. He slapped her shoulder, slapped her knee, cuffed her on the side of her head, slapped her five, saying, "All *right,* all *right,*" as if someone had just hit a game-winning grand-slam home run.

"Guess what? Guess what? Alice, guess what?" He gave her a light punch in the stomach. The bird was flying in circles above them, screeching about the authoritative and vociferous Wendy. "I'm going home!" Christopher said. "I use a walker this week, man, and then I go home to New Jersey, and then I'll be an outpatient at the rehab center there, and then I'll be better!"

He was so happy she felt she could do no less than slap his shoulders and knees in return, but when she cuffed his beautiful head, she realized just how much she would miss his shoulders and knees and soft blond hair.

"I'll miss you," she said.

"Ted!"

"Hey, me too. But we can write, phone . . ."

"Ted! Ted!"

". . . and I'll come into the city. And you'll come see me, won't you? At the *beach,* Alice. The beach!"

Alice tried to imagine herself visiting Christopher at the beach. She wasn't entirely convinced that New Jersey had a beach. And, while she had thought since meeting Christopher how odd it was that they should have gotten together at a rehabilitation institute, it seemed now as though that were the only possible common ground. She loathed the beach. It had been fine when she was a grubby child smearing herself with

Fudgsicles; but it had gotten so hot at the beach, the water had grown so cold, and the sun so bright. You couldn't read. You couldn't sleep. It was boring at the beach. And she burned easily.

"Wendy says!" the parrot croaked from its trapeze.

"Look," Alice said, "I don't give a shit if she does! Just shut up!"

"Ted!" said the bird.

"You're a *monster*," she yelled back.

"Alice, don't say that. I'm crazy about you, but I've got to go home. . . ."

"What? Of course you have to go home." She suddenly remembered a line she had been handed once. "What we had was wonderful," she said. "A sort of, um, existential moment."

Christopher blinked at her.

The parrot blinked at her.

"A *fling*," she added.

"Right!" said Christopher, brightening up.

Alice loved to see him smile. Even if she did not look forward to spending even one afternoon with him on a beach, he had a lovely smile. And he had not been smiling much recently. Although he had set up a sun lamp in his room, his tan had faded, and he had been brooding about it. And it's true, Alice thought, that Christopher without a tan would be somewhat unnatural. It might sap his strength. He might waste away, like a cooped-up wild animal.

She smiled and congratulated him and tried to convince herself that it was for the best. She told herself she was being noble, like Joy Adamson freeing her lions to frisk across the plain and kill pretty gazelles. For an instant, she considered frisking over to Christopher and killing him among the houseplants. He was, after all, when all was said and done, deserting her. But he was so pleased, wriggling in his wheelchair, wrapping an arm around her neck, punching her chin, that she couldn't help laughing. She thought of him, standing, his jeans hanging low on his bare waist, his feet deep in the warm sand, his hands on his hips. She sighed.

"Christopher, you'll be so . . . so *tan,*" she said.

"No, that one's ugly," she said, and the salesman pursed his lips. "It's too *thick,*" she explained.

Her mother and Stephanie stood leaning against the counter. "That one is lovely," one would say, and the other would nod enthusiastic agreement. "Lovely, lovely."

Alice would say, "I hate it," and the salesman would bring another.

"No, no, oak is for old men and furniture. Nope, too tacky. Ugly handle, bumpy handle, not comfortable," she said with each offering, until even she was bored and decided on a pair of ebony canes with bone handles, one shaped like a duck, the other like a dog.

Of the transitions from gadget to gadget that represented recovery, none was as exciting as the move from metal crutches to canes. Even the progress from wheelchair to parallel bars paled next to acquisition of the two ebony canes with bone handles. These canes, Alice thought, the morning after she bought them, patting the duck fondly, were not designed solely for cripples. This is a breakthrough, she concluded.

Stephanie went to L.A., Holly got married to a Filipino dermatologist, and Alice was left on her own. The Institute thought this was a wonderful development, and harbored hopes that Alice would bloom into a truly independent invalid. Alice sensed she was at a turning point, a watershed in rehabilitation, and did not want to disappoint anyone, but she missed her nurses. She sometimes woke up and muttered something to the absent Holly, as a wife reaches for a husband who's already gone to work. She sat moodily after her day of exercises, longing for Stephanie, unwilling to go out in search of someone else to talk to.

The routines of dressing and undressing, which had gone so smoothly under the nurses' supervision that she had never paid much attention to them, were now arduous and prolonged, like boot camp. Reaching her underwear was not a problem—it was kept in a drawer near the bed. But, because her legs did not bend, she had to get both legs in at once, and then wiggle them until the underpants came up to her knees, where she could reach them and pull them up the rest of the way. To put on her socks, she had been given a contraption that was admittedly clever but made her want to cry whenever she looked at it, although it was covered in cheerfully flowered fabric that looked like guest-room wallpaper. Like a shoehorn, but much larger and softer, like a Claes Oldenburg shoehorn, it hung from a long elastic loop. Each morning Alice would separate a ball of socks and slip the sock horn into one. There were clips that attached to the top of the sock. When she had fastened them, she would send the sock-covered, flowered, shovel-shaped part sailing toward her feet. She felt as if she were casting nets, dragging the river for feet. She would pull the thing back and try again, tossing it toward her feet, holding on to the elastic loop. When it finally landed near a foot, that foot would be maneuvered toward it, into it, into the sock, and Alice would pull on the elastic, pulling the sock horn up past her heel, which pulled the sock onto the foot. When she gave a sharp tug, the sock horn would unclip and come flying toward her. The sock would stay dutifully on the foot. The procedure had to be repeated for the other foot, and while Alice admired the technology of the thing, she often became frustrated and impatient and threw it on the floor. She then had to pick it up, which took time—to get out of bed, hobble over, bend over, hobble back —and exhausted her.

"I think I can, I think I can, I think I can," she would

grumble, throwing her pants toward her feet and trying to wriggle into them.

"I think I can, I think I can, I think I can," she would sigh without enthusiasm as she followed her canes to the bathroom and listlessly brushed her teeth. With a wistful look at her bed, she would walk in her odd, stiff way through the door. She was very independent, she knew. But it all seemed like a waste of effort—the struggling to get dressed, to wash, to get a pencil when she wanted to write a letter. It wore her out, hurt her real work, she thought, things like weight lifting and volleyball.

"But this is what the therapy is *for,*" the doctors told her.

No, she protested. The therapy was to help her adjust to normal life.

"That is normal life," they explained.

In order to convince her, to remind her what she had been missing all these months, they ordered a day, a full day, outside of the Institute. "Spend a day with your mother," the doctors said. "And spend the night."

So Alice went to spend the night at the apartment her grandparents had sublet for her mother.

"Isn't this fun?" her mother cried, handing her a tremendous bowl of soup. "Look at all the pretty lights outside. Red and green! And *white!* Look at all the little cars!"

Alice looked at her soup, from which big, bare bones and pimply yellow chicken skin occasionally peeped.

"Peasant soup!" her mother explained.

"A sleep-over!" her mother cried, as she tucked Alice in. Then she began to cry and held Alice in her arms. Alice cried too. "I'm sorry," her mother said. "But I thought of you when you were a little girl. And now you're all grown up." She wiped her eyes. "And you've been through so much."

"There, there," Alice said, and then began to cry harder.

"There, there," said her mother, again in tears.

"You've been through a lot too," said Alice, her self-pity momentarily diluted with gratitude and sympathy toward her mother. The gratitude and sympathy toward her mother led her quickly to resentment of her father. "You should have married someone else," she said.

Her mother said, "That's a terrible thing to say. And then I wouldn't have you and Willie."

"Yes you would."

"No I wouldn't."

"Oh, so what? So we'd be better."

"Alice," her mother said.

It began to rain and the drops fell noisily on the air conditioner outside.

"It's so cozy," her mother said. "I love the patter of the rain on the roof."

"We're only on the fifth floor."

"Yes, dear." Her mother kissed her, turned off the light, and went into the bedroom, where she began almost immediately to snore.

Alice stared into the darkness. She had seen little Louie Scifo suits in the closet, and the smell of his cologne wafted through the apartment like poison gas. The thought of Louie Scifo made her angry at her father.

"I have a lovely day planned. Look!" said her mother the next morning, pulling a piece of paper from the pocket of her robe. "No, that's a parking ticket. Is this it? Where are my glasses?"

"This one says 'Oranges, Ajax, paper towels . . .' "

"Here they are," her mother said, pulling her glasses from one pocket. "Here it is!" she said, pulling a sheet of paper from another. "Our schedule."

The schedule said:

A TYPICAL DAY

1. A Nice Breakfast
2. A Lovely Walk [This entry was crossed out]
2. An Errand
3. Shopping
4. Lunch at Rumpelmayer's
5. A Visit to a Nice Friend
6. Tea at the Plaza
7. A Nap

Alice read the schedule and decided real life might not be so bad after all.

"An adventure!" her mother sang out.

The Nice Breakfast was served on a tiny table, squeezed between the kitchen window and the stove, described by her mother as "snug." Her mother poured coffee over a tea bag, but otherwise the meal went smoothly, and her mother ended it by sprinkling croissant crumbs on the window sill for what she called "the rock doves."

"They're dirty old pigeons, Mom."

But her mother had recently joined the Audubon Society and was not to be dissuaded.

The Errand that followed was to enroll Alice's mother at the nearby Amerigo Vespucci Society, for Italian lessons.

"Why are you taking Italian?" Alice asked suspiciously. She saw her mother tilling fields in Sicily, calling, "An adventure!" "Planning a visit to the old country, Mom?"

Her mother thought this was uproariously funny, and after laughing heartily, said, well, actually, she and Louie *were* planning a little trip to Sicily, which was supposed to be magnificent, full of Roman ruins and Norman ruins and Moorish ruins. . . .

It was only a few short blocks to the Amerigo Vespucci Society, but their path was strewn with obstacles in the form of fragrant and cheerfully lit bakeries. Alice's mother seemed to live in a neighborhood of bakeries, and she pressed her face to every window, sniffed at each open door, and dawdled and sighed with such abandon that even Alice, clumping along on her canes, became impatient with the pace.

"Come *on,* Mom," she said.

But her mother wandered into a children's bookstore and two more pastry shops before they reached the red brick building that housed the Amerigo Vespucci Society.

"Yes?" said the tall, narrow Italian woman, elegantly made up, who answered the door. The word squirmed listlessly up her gullet. "What can I do for you?"

"I came to enroll for Italian lessons," said Alice's mother.

"M-m-yes," said the lady. She stared at Alice, openly appraising her. Alice looked at the woman's clothes—very chic. "You are . . ." The lady paused, as if seeking the right word. "Beautiful!" she said at last in her odd Italian accent, rolling the word with great satisfaction over her tongue. She put her hand out and stroked the line of Alice's jaw with it.

"Oh, thanks," Alice muttered.

"Bee-yuh-tee-ful-l-l," the lady repeated.

"My daughter already knows Italian," Alice's mother said proudly.

"Your daughter?" said the Italian lady. "I thought she was your . . ." and she paused dramatically, running a finger across Alice's lips, " . . . your friend."

"Mommy!" Alice cried when they got outside. "She thought we were dykes! She thought I was your girlfriend!"

"My God," Alice's mother said. She began to laugh.

"Look at us! Dykes!" Alice pointed at her own khaki pants,

leather jacket, and sneakers; at her mother's trench coat, pants, and sensible walking shoes. They had been walking arm in arm.

"It's disgusting," her mother said, and then began laughing again.

The typical day continued. Alice's mother consulted her schedule, saw Shopping was next, and suggested buying a hat. She was, however, distracted from this "nice project" by a shop devoted to pale, delicate linens from Milan. Alice, surrounded by the most beautiful sheets she had ever pressed to her cheek, thought she liked real life better and better.

"I think you're adjusting to the outside world beautifully," her mother said, as they picked out a set of pastel striped sheets and four pillowcases covered with baskets of violets.

They took a Checker cab—Alice couldn't fit into the smaller ones—to Fifty-ninth Street and Fifth Avenue and leaned on a wall separating them from Central Park.

"Look, dear, a bird. What is it? I can't tell without my glasses."

"A sparrow, I guess."

"Isn't that nice," her mother said, and they crossed the street and entered Rumpelmayer's, a restaurant specializing in ice cream and toys that appeared to be patronized almost exclusively by little girls in black patent-leather shoes and elderly ladies in spectator pumps. Alice's mother had ice cream for lunch.

Next on the schedule was the Visit to a Nice Friend. Alice refused to visit any of her own friends, and so they decided to pay a call on Joannie Schrecker, a young woman Alice's mother had met in a class. She had just had a child and Alice's mother wanted to take the new arrival a gift. She wondered whether that might turn the visit into another errand, thereby pushing them off schedule, but Alice assured her it would not, and they proceeded to Joannie Schrecker's apartment.

As a puzzled Joannie Schrecker thanked Alice's mother for

the lovely letter opener she had just unwrapped, and Alice's mother realized she had sent Uncle Herbert a tiny smocked dress for his birthday, Alice decided real life was really quite amusing.

"And this must be the baby's father," she heard her mother say, picking up a framed photograph from the piano.

"Mom," Alice said.

"What a handsome man!"

"Mom!" Alice said.

"I think the little creature looks like him."

"Mommy!" Alice said in despair. It was a photograph of Gertrude Stein.

"Why, isn't that a coincidence!" her mother said. "Alice? I mean, just this morning . . ."

"Mom!"

Alice was delighted with their visit to the nice friend.

"Now isn't real life fun?" her mother asked as they left the Schreckers'. And Alice had to agree it was.

They then went to tea at the Plaza, where they ate strawberries, listened to the violins, and sighed wistfully for the grand days, the old New York of Edith Wharton.

"Of course, in those days, we would have been pushing pushcarts, wouldn't we, dear?" her mother said. "Of course, that must have been very . . ." She paused. Alice wondered how she would get out of this one. That must have been very . . . romantic? Fun? Cheerful? Cozy? ". . . profitable!" her mother said, smiling at the thought of all those industrious merchants.

On the way back to her mother's apartment, Alice looked out the window as the taxi lurched and bounced and her mother pointed out that they could be on a stagecoach in the Wild West. The sky was blue, and they drove through a Central Park dense with white flowering trees.

"Isn't New York beautiful?" her mother said, looking around her. "Why, we could be in . . . in Westport!"

Alice only nodded. She was planning her nap on the pastel striped sheets and the pillowcases covered by baskets of violets.

Real life was not so bad. But when, Alice wondered, would she be well? The adhesions adhered and no one talked about breaking them anymore. They discussed strengthening Alice's muscles, increasing her endurance, but each time her range of motion was tested, it stayed the same; she could not bend or spread her legs, and no one seemed to expect anything different.

"When?" Alice began asking her doctors. She felt as if she were waiting for the last day of school. As if her entire illness had been a series of terrible semesters at an unsavory boarding school. As if she could transfer.

"When?" she asked, pulling on their sleeves. But they couldn't tell.

"We have decided," said her doctor one day, "that you need surgery."

"But what about the adhesions?" Alice asked.

"They won't break. The surgery would remove your hips, *but*—" as Alice's face contorted in preparation for tears—"we'll replace them."

"With what?" Alice asked suspiciously.

"Devices!" said the doctor.

Alice's face buckled. She began to sob.

"Alice, Alice," said the doctor. "These are good devices. Prostheses! Made out of metal and plastic. They're very strong. They last a long time. You'll be able to tie your shoes."

Alice looked at him narrowly. "Tie my shoes?"

"Mm-hmm."

"And put on my socks without that . . . thing?"

"Yes, if it's successful, which I think it will be."

"Swear?"

"Well, naturally I can't guarantee it will work. . . ."

"You *don't* swear?"

"Well, no. But I really think the procedure will help. Really."

"Tie my shoes?"

"Almost perfect mobility, full range of motion."

"Well, okay," Alice said. "I'll think about it."

"At least these devices will be hidden," Alice told her mother, although even that consolation was marred by fleeting thoughts of Mr. Machine, a plastic toy that creaked awkwardly through the TV ads of her childhood.

The thought of removing a part of her body, even such a useless and diseased part, terrified her. Removal of the diseased part of the femur would create a gap of only a few inches, and only until the prosthesis was put in minutes later. But that gap widened and grew in her mind, opened into a sort of existential chasm. I'll never be quite the same, she thought, as if she were going to lose not her hips but her virginity.

"It's a wonderful operation," a kindly lady wrapped in folds of pink skin as soft as baby blankets told her. "Everyone in Miami has had it."

"My husband had it!" added another woman. "Rest his soul."

"My sister had it! . . . My wife had it! . . . My brother . . . My brother's wife!" they all called out happily.

"And I had both hips done!" a small creature cried. The woman was confined forever to her electric wheelchair, which she operated with the one stiff finger she could still move. Alice stared at the woman, opened her mouth, but was unable to speak. She stared as a rabbit caught in a speeding car's headlights stares and stares.

"But, dear!" cried the woman, motioning with the stiff finger toward her hips. "It worked!"

Alice nodded numbly.

"It *did* work," the woman said. "It's the plastic knees and ankles and wrists and elbows and *fingers* that don't work. My hips are fine."

"Ahh," everyone sighed.

When Alice had walked in small rigid steps back to her room, she sat crooked in the chair from which a tiny sliver of the river was visible. Tugboats nuzzled low, straining barges, and a seaplane landed.

If the operation was a failure, she would still be able to walk. She would walk like the woman down the hall who had no hips and waddled between two canes. She looked no more ridiculous, had no more pain, and was neither more nor less efficient than Alice. Actually, Alice thought, she has one advantage over me. She can be folded up to fit into taxis. So what the hell? Alice thought, wondering at the same time what a seaplane was doing on the East River.

"This operation is for very old people," said the first specialist they consulted. You oughta know, Alice thought, looking at him. He was grim and gray, with bad brownish teeth. A jar of yellow liquid stood on his desk. The label said, "Princess Radziwill."

"We have been doing this procedure for only fifteen years," he said. "We know it lasts for fifteen years. After that?" He sighed dramatically, and lifted his hands, palms up. "We just don't know."

"What do you mean, we don't know? What don't we know?" Alice asked. "Does it rot or something? Or cause cancer?"

"Oh, no, no, no," the doctor said. "The glue. It's the glue. How long does it last? After five years, we worried about the next five. After ten years, we wondered if it would last for fifteen. Now we know the device lasts for fifteen years. But after that?" He shrugged.

"Fifteen years is better than none," Alice suggested.

"We recommend it only for older patients," the doctor said.

Because they die before their fifteen years are up, Alice thought.

The doctor said: "I feel you are too young for this operation."

Alice said: "I feel I am too young for this disease."

Her mother suggested they leave. "Alice, he's not your father. You mustn't be so rude."

Alice curled her lip.

"This operation will stir up any dormant infection you might still have," said the next specialist. "Why not try this instead?" he asked suddenly, whipping a shiny piece of metal out of his desk drawer. "It caps the femur, rather than replacing the whole hip! Of course, you won't get full range of motion. In fact you'll get only about thirty percent of what you'd get with a total hip, but . . ."

"Doctor," said Alice, "if digging around to put in a total hip would stir up infection, wouldn't digging around to put that on do the same thing?"

"Oh!" The doctor looked quizzically at the metal in his hand. "I guess it would."

Next! Alice wanted to say, but her mother was casting warning glances in her direction.

Alice curled her lip.

"Why fool around?" said specialist number three. "You can walk, can't you?"

Alice recalled the report she had seen sitting on specialist number two's desk.

Caucasian female, 5'7", 118 lbs. With assistance of two
canes, patient can ambulate for 1/2 block without discomfort. Cannot tie shoes or clip toenails.

"Why take the risk?" the doctor repeated.

"I can ambulate," Alice finished for him, curling her lip
eloquently.

Her father came back from Vancouver for her operation,
and brought Patricia Brody née Hum along. He asked Alice if
she wanted to meet her.

"No," Alice said, although she was curious. Willie called
her Patricia Hum, Step-Wife, and described her as endlessly
polite.

"What an *interesting* religion you have," she had told Willie.

"Do you enjoy the youthful independence of living outside
the nuclear family unit?" she asked. (Or so Willie claimed; Alice
wasn't sure she believed him.) "No? I see. Well, of course,
family activities and a daily household routine are also important to a young man's maturation process," she had allegedly
continued.

"They drink a lot of tea," Willie told Alice. "They 'hot the
pot' and then Dad says, 'You be Mum,' and then Patricia Hum,
Step-Wife, pours. You know, tea doesn't really have any taste,
does it?"

Alice agreed that tea was tasteless, and she sympathized with
Willie for having to spend an afternoon with the happy couple,
who were staying at her father's sister's house in Westport. "She
sounds really awful," Alice said.

"Well, no," Willie replied. "She's sort of like from outer
space or something, like she learned the language and concepts
of Earth from a phrase book. She's . . . she's . . . *determined,*"
he said finally.

.   .   .

"She would love to meet you," her father told her.

"I think I'll take a nap now, Dad. I'm sort of tired," Alice said. As she watched her father leave the room, she wondered if she had hurt his feelings. She hoped so. This parading of step-wives past crippled daughters in hospital beds was highly insensitive, she felt. And Patricia Hum would probably ask her if her illness had been a learning experience.

"He brought her to the house!" Alice's grandmother exclaimed. "He wanted his riding boots!"

"They were in the guest-room closet covered with mud," Willie said. "And I packed up everything from his dresser— pencil stubs, shirt cardboard, broken combs—and put it all in cardboard boxes in the sauna."

"He brought that woman to the house!" Alice's grandmother cried again, putting her hand daintily to her throat, to demonstrate dismay. "And with my delicate constitution. Well! You can imagine what a shock it was to open the door and see him and . . . her! And for that he left my Brendala? Well! It's unbelievable. Unheard of in the civilized world. He left a *Rolls-Royce,*" she said, breathing reverently on the two words, "for a Model-T Ford! She'll take him to the laundry, that farmer woman. Mark my words. And Grandma is not talking through her nose!"

"Cleaners, Grandma. Hat," said Alice.

"They came to the door," her brother said, "and Grandma answered it and Patricia Hum stuck out her hand to shake Grandma's when Dad introduced them, and there was a pause, and then Grandma took her hand, and then—Grandma shrieked! And Patricia Hum went white. And Dad went white. And . . ."

"It was that goddamn dog, sticking his cold, wet nose up my dress. . . ."

"It was great!" her brother said.

". . . such a goddamn long nose. And so wet? Maybe he had a cold. . . . Imagine, bringing that farmer woman to your mother's house . . ."

"But what did they say when you screamed?" Alice asked.

Her grandmother, pink and excited, said, "I told them it was the dog with his snout, and that woman said something about something, I don't know. . . ."

"She said," Willie said, " 'What a lovely household pet.' "

Alice spent the week before her operation in Westport. She sat on the terrace, her feet out before her, a Panama hat on her head. She read Perry Mason mysteries, read so many so fast that she sometimes thought a character from one book had murdered a character from another. It was warm and the air was fresh with wet smells—new grass, tiny buds on the maple tree, forsythia. She dozed off, the hat pulled over her eyes, and listened to the flies buzzing against the windowpanes, trying to get into the living room. Why? she wondered. Inside, flies buzzed against the glass trying to get out. She heard the hollow notes of a mourning dove, then the titter of a robin and, late in the afternoon, a rumbling frog. On Monday she heard the children descending on their school, and she heard the bell in the morning, then at lunch—when the dog would appear with milk and bits of sandwich dribbling from his mouth—then at recess, then at three-thirty. "Yay!" the children would shout. Then: "Give me that! I am not! I'm telling!"

A big bee would collide with the living-room window, make a petite thud, and then sputter away like a cranky old man.

Planes left thin white lines behind them when the sky was blue, and the moon came out, pale and transparent, before the sun set. This is nice, Alice thought, listening to the rope banging gently against the flagpole at the school.

This is nice, she thought, when two mallards waddled by on their way to the swampy pond at the bottom of the hill.

Even this is nice, she thought, when the dog's wet, cold nose pressed into her palm and woke her from a soft nap.

The cat ate a family of baby cardinals and brought her their little carcasses. She cried. She walked across the terrace barefoot and stepped on a grape that seemed to say "Eeep!" and turned out to be a tiny toad. But nature is cruel, she reminded herself. Darwin said so.

When they drove back to the hospital, she left her window open until they were caught in traffic next to a huge trailer truck.

"Oooo! Cow flop!" cried her mother. "Foul cow flop!" The windows were rolled up.

They drove past the Institute driveway and through the entrance to the hospital parking lot.

"Too bad I couldn't keep my old room," Alice said.

"I hope you have a decent roommate," her mother said. "Maybe it will be someone fun!"

Alice had suggested a semi-private room, hoping her parents would insist she take a private room. But they didn't.

She sat on a couch while her brother dragged in her bag and her mother checked her in.

"Cruisin'!" yelled a mother at her child. "You are *cruisin'*," she repeated, as the boy jumped up and down on the couch across from Alice.

Someone coughed.

"I'm an old woman," whined an old woman. "Why do they make me wait?" She looked accusingly at Alice.

Alice's brother went to buy food at the cafeteria.

Someone came with a wheelchair.

"But I don't need it!" Alice said. "I can ambulate," she said proudly.

"Hospital rules," said the orderly, and he wheeled her upstairs.

"Funny smell," Alice said, as they proceeded down the hall. "Sort of sweet," she added, as it got stronger. The orderly stopped at the doorway of a small dark room. The blinds were down. The bed by the window was surrounded by yellow curtains. "Woooo," groaned someone behind the curtain.

"There, there, Mother," said a voice, "You've still got your other leg."

"Mommy, I don't like this room," Alice said.

"It smells funny," said her mother. "Maybe it's flowers. Or fruit."

"Mommy, I don't think it's flowers," said Alice.

"Or fruit," said her brother, who was holding his nose.

"Poor Mother," said a middle-aged woman, looking out from the yellow curtain. "Diabetes . . . gangrene . . . she just lost one leg . . . the other doesn't look much better . . . sorry if her moaning disturbs you."

"Oh, no," Alice and her mother and brother all said at once. As soon as the woman disappeared behind the curtain again, they quietly left.

Dear Katie,

I can't sleep. Tomorrow is my operation.

I was supposed to go into a semi-private room, but my roommate was deteriorating at an alarming rate, and the fragrance of gangrenous flesh mingling with her moans was too depressing. Even my doctors thought so.

So here I am in another private room.

I hate Simchas. He hasn't visited or called today. He sucks. They gave me a sleeping pill but I'm so mad at him and so scared that I can't sleep. If he's here when I wake up after the surgery and he brings me flowers and the flowers do not come from a stand in the subway, I'll forgive him. You would hate him.

How come you didn't flush the pills down the toilet? I mean, I don't know why you don't want to take them in the first place, but if you're going to go through the trouble of hiding them under your tongue and pretending to swallow them, don't you think you could have come up with a better way of disposing of them than piling them on the window sill? Well, better luck next time.

Do you realize I am handicapped and there are special seats on the bus for people like me? If this operation fails, I'll have to forfeit my series of lessons at Dorfman's Danceland. I'll never ice skate again.

Love,
Alice

A woman had shuffled into her room pushing a cart and wearing rubber gloves, but this time Alice knew she was not the cleaning lady. She was the barber.

As the razor skimmed quickly over her legs, Alice said, pointing at the pubic hair, which had grown back, "I suppose you'll have to do that again?"

The woman, heavy-set and slit-eyed, pulled her hands away. "Whatever for?" she said, stepping back and gaping at Alice. "They're operating on your *legs.*"

"Yeah, great, but you see last time they shaved that and I just thought . . ."

"Takes all kinds," the woman muttered, gathering up her things and throwing Alice one last, disgusted, sidelong glance.

Then Alice waited for Simchas to come. He would say, "Brody, I hope they use Black and Decker power tools, and not some inferior brand." Then he would say, "Brody, I got you some jogging shoes." Then he would ask her why she didn't wear a brighter-colored nightgown. Then he would express amazement that she had never read some Jewish author. Then he would say Dickens was anti-Semitic. He would pick and nag and tell flat jokes; she would groan in mock dismay, and then it would be midnight and she would fall asleep. But Simchas didn't come.

Alice lay in bed thinking how ugly he was. What terrible shoes he had—black with buckles!

She growled, turning over and over, dragging the inflexible legs tangled in the long nightgown. Maybe he'll take the wrong pill tonight and die, she thought. And she finally fell asleep, frowning.

She woke up early the next morning and waited. A yellow tulip stood in the vase Simchas had given her on the window sill. The sun shone on it directly, and its petals looked waxy and bright. If the rat doesn't bring me flowers I'll never speak to him again. What can't you get from the flower stands in the subway? Hyacinth! Hyacinth or it's all over, she decided.

"Awake already?" said a nurse. She rolled Alice over and jabbed her with a needle.

"This will make you a little drowsy," she said.

And Alice waited. The Van Gogh replica on the wall made her dizzy and slightly nauseated. She switched on the radio and turned the dial, but it went from static to more static. She gave up and breathed slowly and deeply. I won't die, she told herself. And, if I do, I won't know it. I won't be more crippled, and maybe I'll be less crippled. It won't hurt. *I'm going to die!* Shut up. *They'll cut off a leg, I'll get gangrene.* Shut up.

"Hello," she said to the intern who came to insert an IV line. But he didn't seem to hear.

"Hello," she said to the orderly who came to wheel her to O.R.

But he just sang, "Rock the boat, don't rock the boat, baby."

"Hello," she said to a bundled-up patient on a stretcher parked next to her. Either he's dead, or I'm addressing his feet, she decided when he didn't answer. Maybe he has no feet and I'm talking to his stumps. Maybe he's dead *and* I'm talking to his stumps.

"Hello," she said to the woman in the stretcher on the other side. The woman coughed and spit into a basin.

"Heads up, guys," shouted an intern rolling a stretcher. "I've got his hand."

"Whose hand?"

"The guy's hand. It fell sixteen fucking stories, but we found it."

"What guy?" interns and orderlies were asking each other. "What hand? Whose hand?"

"Well, what do I do with it? What room is he in?"

"Who? Do with what?"

"The hand."

Oh, dear, Alice thought. Someone's hand is on that stretcher. Couldn't they have brought it in quietly? In a bag?

The dead man with stumps beside her groaned. So you're not dead, Alice thought. But do you have stumps?

"Put it in the refrigerator," someone said.

"What?"

"The hand. You said you've got a hand."

"Yeah, but . . ."

A new voice. "Has anyone out here seen a hand? We're waiting for a hand from the West Side."

"Well, it's about time. Where do you want it?"

Alice thought maybe the man next to her with the stumps was Simchas. Maybe he had been hit by a bus and that was why he hadn't called.

"Well, hello there," her doctor said heartily, leaning over her stretcher.

She tried to answer, but her lips felt thick and wouldn't move. Her doctor looked very hairy today. His arms were furry and tan, and an abundance of curls fluffed over the V-neck of his operating greens. He looked so big. And then all she could think of was *"Dies Irae,"* which they had learned in Latin class. *Dies Irae, dies illa,* and then some words she forgot, and then *cum favilla.* What was a *favilla* anyway? What were the rest of the words? *Dies irae . . .*

"And a-waa-a-a-y we go," the doctor sang, wheeling her into an operating room.

The anesthesiologist has dandruff, Alice thought, as he leaned over her, peering at the IV. I don't think an anesthesiologist should have dandruff. It's not right.

He injected something into the tube, and said, *"Dies Irae."*

"What?" she tried to say.

"Feels okay?" he asked again.

She nodded.

The anesthesiologist rolled her on her side. "Just a needle in your back," he said.

She couldn't feel anything.

A light glared from above. She could see her reflection in the aluminum shade: an expanse of crumpled blue sheets, at one end a little white face, at the other white legs. People in green bustled around her. They all had shower caps on their shoes. And then, in the reflection of the aluminum shade, she saw a saw.

"A saw!" she thought she cried. But it couldn't have been very loud. No one paid any attention. Then she saw a hacksaw. "A hacksaw!" she cried, this time louder.

"Doctor," said the young man in green carrying the tool, "the kid is saying something, I think. She's pulling on my shirt."

"A saw and a hacksaw!" Alice called out to the doctor. "And a drill!" she shrieked, seeing a big electric drill being plugged in near her feet.

"What's that, Alice?" asked the doctor leaning over her. "A saw? Of course there's a saw. How can we get the hips out without a saw? . . . Doris, quit it."

"Wha-a-at?" whined Doris, a nurse holding a tray.

"Quit tapping."

"I'm not tapping."

"You are too. You're tapping. Isn't she tapping, Peters?" he asked the intern carrying the saw.

"Gee, I guess so, doctor."

"See? Now quit it."

"I'm not tapping. I'm *arranging,*" she said, rattling things on the tray.

The doctor sighed. "Peters, you cut," he said.

"Gee, sure, doc," said Peters.

Alice watched in the aluminum reflection. Peters took the scalpel from the nurse.

"Doris, are you chewing gum?" the doctor asked. "Could you quit snapping your gum? You know I hate it."

Yeah, Doris, Alice tried to say. Quit snapping your gum. You know he hates it.

"It makes me nervous," the doctor added.

Doris! Alice tried to scream. It makes him nervous!

"Gawd, I don't believe you," Doris whined. "I mean you're really *mature,* aren't you?"

Peters took the scalpel, looked at it earnestly, and pressed it against Alice's thigh.

"Oh, Christ! All over my glasses! I can't see. Where's a towel?"

"Gee, doc, I'm really sorry. I didn't mean to."

"Doris, spit out the gum?"

Alice looked up at the aluminum shade, but it was spattered with blood and she couldn't see anything anymore. A drill roared. Saws rasped.

"Doris, you're whistling!"

"So sue me."

"No, Peters, actually that's *not* right. It's upside down."

"Gee, doc . . ."

"Doris . . ."

"Well, don't make a federal case out of it."

"How's this, doc?"

"Where's the thread? What makes you think this is enough?"

"So pardon me for breathing."

"What do I do with this stuff, doc?"

"Hey! That's a pretty neat job, if I must say so myself. What do you think? Peters? Doris? Not bad, eh?"

"It looks swell."

"Big deal."

"Alice, you're a new woman."

Alice opened her eyes.

"Why are you crying, dear?" asked a nurse.

But Alice didn't know. The nurse offered her a basin and she dutifully threw up.

"You're in the recovery room."

"What hap—"

"You're fine. It was successful!" said the nurse. "Your hand will be as good as new."

"Whah?" Alice said, her mouth slack and heavy.

"They found the hand, right there on the sidewalk, next to a fire hydrant, and it's all sewed on tight."

Alice laboriously lifted her hands and looked at them.

"My! What a neat job they did!" said the nurse in admiration. "You can hardly see the stitches."

Alice brought her hands to her face and looked for stitches.

"Congratulations," said the anesthesiologist, coming up to her stretcher. "Feel any pain?" he asked.

She held out her hands for him to see and looked at him pathetically.

"Why are you crying? Don't cry," he said. "Everything is

okey dokey. Nice new hip. Lovely new hip. Clean scar. Yes, you have very nice hands. Shall I hold your hands? Feel better? Cold? Nurse, can we have another blanket over here? It's from the anesthetic—it's wearing off. That's why you're crying. Don't be afraid. That's a good girl. Now let go of my hands. Miss Brody, please let go of my hands. Just for a moment. I'll come back, I promise. You're fine, really. That's a good girl . . ."

When Alice next opened her eyes, her mother was there. They were back in her room.

"Mommy," Alice said. She was hoarse and blinked at the light. "Did they do anything to my hands?"

"No, sweetheart. Why would they do that? But your hip is a great success. I spoke to the doctor. He's very pleased."

"That's good," said Alice. "That's very good. I guess the nurse thought I was someone else. You mean it's okay? Really?"

"Yes, love. Go back to sleep."

When she woke up again, it was almost dark and Simchas was there too.

"The Bionic Teenager," he said. "I brought you some flowers." They were carnations.

"Get them in the subway?"

"Well, actually yes. I've heard flowers sold in the subway are taken from used funeral wreaths, but these seemed fresh enough."

"They're red."

"Yes, cheerful, don't you think?"

"Italian funeral," she said. Louie Scifo? she thought hopefully. But Louie Scifo, she knew, would never die.

"Italian funerals are very beautiful, you know," her mother said.

Alice stared at Simchas's cuff links, her favorite gold knots, and was glad he had come, red carnations and all. He had, after all, been good to her. He *helped* her, as he would say. And he loved her. In his fashion. She had been crippled, a bedridden invalid with pimples, and he had loved her. He had fed her sardines and helped her put her shoes on.

"Simchas," she murmured, reaching for his hand.

Alice's mother, sitting by the window, said suddenly, softly, "Oh, my God."

Alice looked at her and Simchas looked at her, and then Alice and Simchas pulled their hands away from each other.

"Oh, God," said Alice's mother.

I've committed incest, Alice thought. I was right about them all along. She began to sweat.

"Brenda," said Simchas, "you don't understand."

"You skunk," said Alice's mother.

Alice began to cry. "Skunk," she said to Simchas. "Go away."

Simchas left. "I *helped* you," he said at the door, absent-mindedly taking the carnations with him.

Alice stared at her hand. Disgusting, she thought, over and over. Disgusting, disgusting. And then she saw the room was dark. "Mommy," Alice began, but she could not continue. It was too humiliating.

"Your mother went out for a minute." It was her father's voice. She couldn't see him in the dark. Had she been asleep? Then perhaps it was a dream. It must have been—from the anesthesia.

"Daddy?"

He turned on a light.

"Daddy," she said, "am I really better?"

Her father sniffled and dabbed at his eyes with a crumpled handkerchief. Then he smiled. "You're all better," he said, and then hugged her, almost crushing her. He hadn't hugged her in years. She could smell his mustache wax and his aftershave. She didn't know its name, but she had never smelled aftershave on a man without wondering why it didn't smell as good as her daddy's had when as a little girl she used to hug him. But why did he use mustache wax? He didn't make the whiskers twirl in preposterous loops like some men, but he was absurd enough to wax them carefully until they stood out with military starch. She looked at her father with his bristling mustache and thought he was perhaps the silliest man she had ever met. Her mother was silly, too, of course. Her mother could find romance in a tangerine. Her fantasies overwhelmed her, but they were innocent, portable fantasies, personal ones that accompanied her wherever she went, like a cloud of perfume. For Alice's mother, there was no struggle to create a world where sunlight dappled the pavement, where the fruit was always ripe, sofas always comfy. If she bit into an apple, it became ripe; if she sat on a couch, the cushions softened. Even on dark, rainy days, her mother would look out the window, spread her arms, and say, "Oh! What a day. Listen to the wind! We could be on the moors!"

But for her father there was so much planning involved. Alice sometimes felt that all of them—she, her brother, the collie, the horse, the gardener—were props; that her father was a huge, lumbering child arranging furniture in his doll house.

"Would you like something, Alice? A spot of tea?" he asked. "A biscuit?"

"No thanks. Maybe some water." Alice watched him fill a paper cup with water. She and her brother had watched him pour his coffee every morning, each holding a tiny white pellet of saccharin, waiting to drop it into the dark, steaming coffee. "Oh, my toe! Ouch, my knees!" they would say, pretending the saccharin was drowning in the scalding liquid.

"Remember when we dropped saccharin in your coffee and yelled, 'Oh, my toe'?"

Her father laughed. "I don't drink coffee anymore. I find I prefer 'a nice cuppa.'"

Alice looked at her father in his blue blazer and silk ascot and thought how difficult it must have been for him to watch her turn from a happy girl earnestly coaxing her spirited pony over a stone wall into a sullen teenager locking herself in her room to listen to loud rock and roll. A chair in the doll house that suddenly violated the décor. She had always been surprised at how easily she could anger him. She would walk right by him without saying a word, go into her room, and lock the door. And he would invariably slam his fist against a wall and shout, "How dare you? Open that goddamn door, damn it. Open that door!" She would lie on her bed thinking, He's persecuting me. Why won't he leave me alone? He hates me.

"I hate you," she would shout.

"How *dare* you?" he would holler, banging on her door.

But then, Alice thought, undercooked bacon had the same effect on him. Any variation in the details he had carefully arranged—a sulking daughter, soft spaghetti, a shivering wife on the ski slope—was as treacherous as any other.

Her father began to comb his mustache. He wore white bucks with red rubber soles. He called his pants "bags." Very dapper, Alice thought. And then of course I was sick as well as sullen. He must have found that a kind of obscenity.

"Would you like a serviette?" he asked suddenly, seeing Alice had spilled water on her pillowcase.

Alice stared at him. At any moment he might say, "Harumph, well, then, you've had rather a nasty time in hospital, eh what?" When she next saw him he would probably carry a walking stick. Maybe he'd wear plus fours.

As Alice stared at her father's ascot, the doctor came in. "Alice, you are as good as new," he said. "Watch this!" And he gently picked up her leg by the ankle. Alice watched as if the leg were far away, or on a TV screen, or on somebody in the next room. The leg bent at the knee and the hip. She watched the knee moving back toward her. The doctor led the leg this way and that and Alice watched. It seemed almost impossible to her that it could be her leg that bent outward one moment, inward the next. She remembered going to a concert with her father when she was very, very young. It was her first concert —the high-school band. They began to play loud, banging marching music, and she asked her father, "Where is the music coming from?"

"From the instruments," he said.

"Don't make fun of me," she cried, stamping her foot. She sat awed in the high-school gym, looking for the record player and little red record, unable to believe the sound could come from so many different instruments. Now she stared, awed, at her skinny white leg sailing through the air, guided by the doctor's hand.

"You're okay, Alice," said the doctor.

"Thank you, doctor," Alice said, still staring at her leg, which the doctor dropped gently back on the bed. He pinched her cheek and left.

"Congratulations!" said her father, wiping his eyes with the crumpled handkerchief.

"I can hardly believe it."

"You're sure you don't want a spot of tea?"

"No thanks, Daddy. Daddy?"

"Yes?"

"I'm glad you're here." The words just slipped out. Damn, she thought. He's such a rat. Why did I say that? But her eyes filled with tears as he hugged her again, and the scent of his aftershave again made her think of him on those mornings when they marched across the blue carpet of his bedroom while brass bands blared on the radio and her mother peacefully slept.

I must be delirious, Alice thought. The anesthesia has made me delirious.

Alice's hip surgery was a success. Six weeks later her other hip was replaced, and eager to try the prostheses out, she seduced a friendly aide, who brought along a bottle of Ripple. Satisfied that the devices had restored her to health, Alice went home. It was a year almost to the day from when she had gotten sick, and Alice gave her doctor a tie. Simchas Fresser went into a deep depression and they had to stop seeing each other.

I'm free! she told herself each morning. Today I'm going to get up bright and early. I'll take a walk, go to the Cloisters, read *Middlemarch*, go to Bendel's. But the pillow was so soft against her cheek. And her foot would slide happily between the smooth, crisp sheets. The quilt, as if of its own accord, had billowed between her eyes and the light from the window. I'm too weak to walk. The Cloisters is so far away. *Middlemarch* is so long. Bendel's is so crowded.

"Alice!" shrieked her mother, whose hair was standing up. "Alice!"

"What? What's wrong?" Alice cried, sitting up in bed, her heart beating fast. "What happened? Are you okay?"

"I'm going to gas the dog and I don't want any *back talk!*" her mother screamed.

Mom, Alice thought, your eyes are actually rolling in your head. "Um, okay, Mom."

"Get up this minute!"

"Okay, Mom," Alice said meekly.

"This room is a pigsty! You could catch a disease in here. Why haven't you made your bed?"

"But, Mom, I'm still in it," Alice said.

"Get up!"

Alice sighed. Living with her mother had its ups and downs.

"I'm sending the dog to your father. Do you hear me, Alice? I'm putting a nasty note around his neck and putting him on the train with a one-way ticket."

Alice began making her bed.

"Why do you sleep so late?" her mother asked. "Are you depressed?"

"No, Mom," Alice answered mechanically.

The dog pranced in, wagging his long plumed tail innocently. He looked at Alice's mother, wagged his tail harder, and plopped down on the floor in front of her with a grunt. He lifted his leg.

"Alice!" her mother cried in despair.

"*I'll* do it," Alice said.

"Never mind. I'll do it. He's used to me, aren't you, Pookie?" The dog yawned and thumped his tail against the floor. Alice's mother left and came back carrying a tiny tube of cream and rubber gloves. The dog thumped his tail on the floor even faster.

"I can't believe I'm rubbing cream on this dog's balls," Alice's mother murmured from the floor. "But *'dog iz zick,'* " she said, imitating the Russian dog dermatologist they had taken Pookie to. " *'Dog'z zgrotum zick.'* "

"I never really realized what a scrotum was before," Alice said, fluffing her pillows.

Pookie had resisted treatment at first, but now, whenever he saw Alice's mother, he wagged his tail, lay down, and lifted his leg expectantly.

Alice had been at her mother's apartment for three months. (The house in Westport had been sold, the profits split between her parents.) She began to sleep on top of the bedspread so she could sit up and present a properly made bed as soon as her mother came into the room.

.   .   .

One evening Alice sat in her room staring at the page of colored butterfly plates in the dictionary.

"Ciao, Alice!" her mother called as she came into the room, Louie Scifo scuttling beside her. "We're off now, dear!"

"Have a great time, Mom," Alice said. "I've heard Atlantic City is wonderful," she added, turning politely to Louie Scifo.

"The de Scifos have always found it so," Louie Scifo answered gravely.

"Ciao! Ciao!" cried her mother as they squeezed out the front door with their bags. "Take care of yourself, Alice! I'll be back tomorrow!"

"Okay," Alice said. "Ciao, Mom."

She went back to her room and sat down at her desk. "Dear Daddy," she wrote on a piece of stationery with her mother's name on it. "The kilt looks really swell on you. I guess Patricia took the picture. When do you wear the kilt? I hope you don't wear it to my graduation. Love, Alice." Then she looked out the window.

There were nuns living across the street ("Just like Italy!" her mother said), and Alice watched their dignified comings and goings with admiration.

Maybe I *won't* be a physical therapist if I don't get into graduate school. Maybe I'll be a nice, quiet nun, she thought. A narrow bed with crisp, clean linen. Simple, good food spooned from a plain bowl. I could sit at a long wooden table, the light from the bay windows at my back, poring over Tacitus and Catullus and Horace and Virgil.

She sat up very late, imagining herself in the convent. She would need a new name. Sister Dido perhaps. Sister Beatrice? Sister Lesbia!

"Sister Lesbia! It's six o'clock! You've missed matins."

"Just ten more minutes," said Sister Lesbia from her bed, a high, narrow white bed, high as a tree house, white as a new sneaker. Her cell had venetian blinds.

"Matins!" cried the squawk box above her head. Her room filled with nuns bearing hypodermics. "Matins! Matins!"

"You're sick," said Sister Darty, lumbering toward the bed. "Sick."

"You're escaping," said Brother Witherspoons. Alice saw only his habit. A white habit. He had no feet, no head, no hands. "You're escaping reality," he said.

"Matins, matins, matins," cried the crowd of nuns, squirting her face with their hypodermics.

Alice sat up in her bed. "Pookie, quit it," she said to the dog, who was stretching his nose toward her to continue licking her face.

It really was six o'clock. The nuns across the street were already up, bustling about. I've got to get out of bed, she thought. She leaned against her pillows and lit a cigarette. Got to get out of bed. I'm sick and I'm escaping reality.

Pookie suddenly dropped to the floor and lifted his leg.

But why should I get up? I have nothing to do. My friends are away, my mother's away, my father's away, my brother's away. I have no nurses to talk to. I'll go back to sleep.

Pookie waved his leg in the air. He thumped his tail on the floor.

I've got to get out of bed. She lit another cigarette. Maybe I could just read. In bed. But I'm so hungry. And the food is in the kitchen. The coffee is in the kitchen.

Pookie was rolling on his back, waving both legs in the air.

"I don't want to rub your scrotum," she said. Balls, said the queen. If I had them, I'd be king. And if _I_ had them, Alice thought, I'd probably just want them rubbed with cream.

Since she'd been home, she had faithfully watched the soap opera that took place in a hospital and had done little else. She spoke on the phone to elderly relatives about arthritis in general and the weather in relation to arthritis; she read the articles about health and illness in the newspapers; she watched the muscles in her arms grow weaker while those in her legs grew slightly stronger. She couldn't bear her friends, who had never been sick and so lacked character and moral strength. She climbed out of bed late every afternoon, ate lunch lying on the couch in front of the TV set, then climbed back into bed to read another mystery. She was furious when the Institute refused to recommend her for a special parking permit for the disabled.

I must get up. Alice said it to herself and then realized she really did have to get up—she had an eight-thirty appointment at the Institute for a checkup. She hadn't been there in two months and hopped out of bed as pleasantly excited as if she were going to a birthday party. I'll see all my friends, she thought.

In the elevator, Alice saw no one she knew and was disappointed. A stranger with no legs sat in a wheelchair beside her. One pant leg was tucked beneath him, the other hung down like a flag. Alice looked away quickly.

On the fourth floor, the linoleum scarred with black skid marks looked so far away. The ceiling was so much lower than she remembered it. And what an ugly color the place was. Pale green. Hospital green. It's good to be back, Alice told herself. I wonder where all my friends are. She was walking rapidly down the hall, not even glancing into the rooms on either side. A nurse wheeled an empty wheelchair past her. Its sagging green seat and turned-up footrests were shabby and familiar. That's my wheelchair. Alice clenched her fists.

"You look great, Alice," said her doctor. "I won't have to see you for another six months."

As Alice returned down the hall she wondered what she would do for those six months. She saw open doors from the corner of her eye, but moved past them without a glance inside.

She thought she smelled things: limbs and bedpans and alcohol. There was no window in the long hall, but on either end the windows were pale and shining. The hall stretched between them, narrow and close as a tunnel. Alice headed straight for the elevator.

"There's Alice!" said a little old woman whose name Alice could not remember. She and three others wheeled out of an exercise room. "Alice! Alice! You look great, it's so good to see you, how are things on the outside?" they all asked.

Alice felt a little warm and wiped the sweat from her forehead. "Fine, fine," she said, but she felt funny, shaky. No breakfast, maybe. "Wonderful to see you. How are things on the inside?" She looked down at the crowd that had gathered in their wheelchairs. These were her friends. She couldn't remember her friends' names. Each time she looked at one of her friends, she found herself looking immediately away, at the elevator door. It was about ten feet from where she stood surrounded by her friends. She sweated and answered questions politely, staring first at the elevator, then at the floor. Some of her friends would never get better. Red and ashamed, she looked at her shoes. Elegant sandals. I don't like my friends, she realized. I don't like them anymore. I can't think of anything to say to my friends. I'm as uncomfortable as my own stupid visitors were. I'm pathetic. I'm a traitor. She looked desperately at the elevator door.

"You really do look wonderful," said the little old lady. She smiled and patted Alice on the hand.

"Mrs. Cohen!" Alice said, suddenly remembering her name. She squeezed Mrs. Cohen's hand and bolted for the elevator, whose doors had just opened.

Alice woke up early the next morning, so early that it was not quite light out. She lay in bed and waited for someone to

visit. Oh, how pathetic, she thought. I'm lying in bed and waiting for someone to visit. She looked at her bedside table: three
empty glasses, an empty cup and saucer, the crumpled foil of a
Ring Ding Jr. Oh, how pathetic, she thought. It looks just like
a hospital bedside table. She thought fondly of her hospital
bedside table for a moment, then sat up. Nostalgia for the
hospital. Pathetic. She picked up the dirty glasses and headed
for the kitchen. This was it. She would take vitamins. She would
exercise. No more hospital behavior. But that's what I did in the
hospital, she thought. I took vitamins and exercised. A glass
dropped and she watched it bounce on the carpet.

"Shit."

"Alice, is that you?" her mother called from the kitchen.
"What on earth are you doing up at this hour?"

"Cleaning my room," Alice said, leaving the glass where it
had rolled and entering the kitchen.

Her mother looked worried.

"Then I'm going to walk the dog. Then I'll clean the cat box
and mop the floor. Then I'm going to drive to Westport and
mow someone's lawn. I'm never going to bed again as long as
I live. Never. It's a trap. You starve to death there and the
telephone doesn't reach." She began to wash a glass.

"Alice . . ."

"Don't try to talk me out of it. My mind is made up."

Alice washed one glass and left the other in the sink dirty.
She sat down and poured herself a cup of coffee. "Mom," she
asked, "why are you up?"

Her mother's eyes lit up. "The migration!" she said, almost
clapping her hands in excitement. "The sea-bird migration!"

"Ah. The birds asked you to come along?"

"I'm going to the shore with my bird-watching class. I'm so
excited. And I think you should come. Oxygen, Alice. What
you need is oxygen. You'll come and *breathe!*"

"Birds carry disease," Alice said. But she thought of all the days she had spent lounging on her bed contemplating the hum of the air conditioner. Perhaps she did need oxygen. She might be coming down with something. Cabin fever or something.

Oh, God, now I'm turning into a hypochondriac. The situation is getting desperate. But I will not give in, she thought, squaring her shoulders. Looking at birds beats mopping floors, surely. And she would be miles from her bed. She would go. She would see the sun come up. The birds would be much too busy migrating to flutter threateningly around her head. They would soar, far, far above her.

Alice slept in the car. When she woke up in a parking lot overlooking a green marsh, the sun was out.

"We're late," her mother said, and they set out on a wide dirt path in search of the bird-watching class.

Alice walked beside her mother, who kept stopping to point. "Look! A bird!"

"Mom, we'll never find your class if you don't hurry up."

"It's brown!"

Alice waited as her mother, trying to train her binoculars on the bird, became sidetracked by a pretty cloud formation.

"Look!"

"Yes, Mom," Alice said, and her mother forged cheerfully ahead.

Other people with binoculars passed them and said, "Seen anything?"

"Oh, yes!" Alice's mother answered.

"Great! What?"

"Why, *I* don't know," Alice's mother said, smiling.

Alice walked along and watched the narrow white clouds stream slowly by. She was out of bed. She was walking. What had been a miracle a few months ago was now expected of her. How soon they forget, she thought.

"Are you okay, Alice?" her mother asked. "Not too tired?"

"Of course I'm okay. I'm not a cripple anymore, you know,"

she said. "I'm perfectly healthy and you will never, never catch me in bed again."

Except with him, she added silently, suddenly seeing a tall, young man with a beard. He towered over the little group of people around him. He was mountaineer size, and Alice felt he could lift her easily in the palm of his hand. She wished he would. He was huge. He was magnificent. He stared across the water through his binoculars.

"Here we are!" Alice's mother called. The tall man waved hello. "That's the teacher," said Alice's mother.

Alice sighed a bitter sigh. A teacher of bird watching. She looked at his sunburned forehead furrowed in concentration. What could she possibly talk to him about? She hated birds. There were flocks of them, wheeling across the sky. He loved birds. Birds were probably his life. The little spotted birds that ran along the beach, trying to balance their long, narrow bills, were of great interest to him. He probably wrote monographs on them. His house was probably surrounded by bird feeders, drawing the fidgety creatures from far and wide. His name was probably Ted, and the only words he spoke would be "Wendy says." But he was so tall. She stood next to him. He cast a large, cool shadow. But it was hopeless. He would find her effete and uninteresting. She had no idea how to flirt with a man devoted to birds. She wasn't even sure she wanted to. But what a shame. His beard was a kind of auburn color.

"Hello," he said.

Alice stopped breathing. He had long eyelashes and wrinkles near his eyes. She tried to think of a response. She failed.

"Have you seen the godwit?"

Alice's heart sank. She shook her head.

"I'll find it before this day is out."

Alice nodded. He was so determined. So strong-willed.

"You came with Brenda?"

Alice nodded. She forced a smile this time.

"My daughter, Alice," her mother said. "This is Nick."

Oh, Alice thought. Nick. What a beautiful name. Nick. Nick. She knew she had to say something soon. Something clever and striking.

"Hello," she said.

"So, are you a birder like your mom?" asked Nick.

"Oh, no," said Alice. "Not really. I mean, no."

"Oh," said Nick.

"Yeah," Alice replied.

"Just along for the ride?"

"Yeah," said Alice. "Right."

Nick started to turn away. His binoculars were in his hands.

Oh, Christ, Alice thought. Speak, Alice, speak. She opened her mouth, hoping that might start things going. "So, you teach ornithology," she blurted out. "Do you teach at a, at a, like a university or something?" Brilliant, she thought. She looked at the ground.

"No, no," said Nick. "This is just a hobby."

Alice looked up hopefully. "What do you do?" she asked.

"I'm a doctor."

"A *doctor?*" Alice said. Her eyes opened wide. She moved closer to him, her heart beating fast. There was hope. There was hope after all. She looked up into his eyes, smiled slightly, and said, "I used to be a patient."

A NOTE ON THE TYPE

The text of this book was set via computer-driven cathode-ray tube in Garamond, a modern rendering of the type first cut by Claude Garamond (c. 1490–1561). Garamond was a pupil of Geoffroy Tory and is believed to have based his letters on the Venetian models, although he introduced a number of important differences, and it is to him we owe the letter that we know as old-style. He gave to his letters a certain elegance and a feeling of movement that won for their creator an immediate reputation and the patronage of Francis I of France.

Composed, printed, and bound by
The Haddon Craftsmen, Inc.,
Scranton, Pennsylvania

Typography by Joe Marc Freedman